I0629590

RILEY DOESN'T WANT TO FIGHT EVIL

SEA OF INK PRESS

RiLeY DoeSN'T WANT TO
FIGHT EVIL

Cover Design: Litepla
Editing: A. P. Mobley at Sea of Ink Press
Interior book Design:Enchanted Ink Publishing

The text type was set in EB Garamond

ISBN: 979-8-9874347-3-4 (Paperback)

Thank you for your support of the author's rights.

WWW.SEAOFINKPRESS.WORDPRESS.COM

SEA OF INK PRESS

RiLeY DoeSN'T WANT TO
FIGHT EVIL

Written by D. R. Mills

SEA OF INK PRESS

HELLO I AM... Riley

PROLOGUE
GRAVEYARD SHIFT

IT WAS AN UNEVENTFUL TUESDAY NIGHT AT GROCERY Hut, the store empty and silent. Not that I was complaining. Ordinarily, it would make the night drag on for what seemed like years, but this time was different.

This time, I had several carts full of product that were beginning to take up space in the back room rather than on the shelves, and I was one of the last staff members working until close.

Who needs meditation when you've got an empty store and a list of chores?

My current project was a new brand of wet cat food called Roman's SeaBlends. Apparently, it was some special vegan recipe for cats. Six boxes of the stuff were nearing the end of their four-month shelf life, and I had saved them for last on my final cart of the night.

They were marked down to about a quarter of their usual price, and I was meticulously stacking them along the bottom of our markdown shelf. Soon I was a full shelf happier, but I was still heavy on one and a half boxes.

Who had ordered *so* much of this cat food? We didn't even have the space for it. No wonder we'd had it sitting in the back room since we'd received it.

Begrudgingly, I picked up the half-empty box and heaved it onto the stock cart next to me. At least the stuff on the cart was more organized, and there was less of it than there had been earlier. I needed to celebrate the little victories.

My name is Riley Thomas, and I'm probably the only employee at Grocery Hut who doesn't completely hate my job. Yes, it's retail. Yes, the customers are terrible. Yes, I have a lot of lazy and sometimes entirely MIA coworkers who are younger than twenty-one. But it's not all bad. It's only mostly bad.

Here's the thing: I love that Grocery Hut is *normal*. It's not extreme or extravagant. It's not somebody's dream workplace either. It's just a grocery store. A dingy, questionable, just-barely-skirting-by-the-health-code-guidelines grocery store.

And that's perfect for me.

As I began pushing the stock cart toward the back of the store, the overhead bell rang throughout the building. Someone had come in through the sliding doors up front.

I glanced down aisle six, which gave me a perfect view of the entrance, and my stomach dropped when I saw the man hurrying inside. He was short and much older than me, somewhere in his late fifties if I had to guess. He clutched a shoulder bag at his side and wore a clean jean jacket and a black shirt, but his pants and shoes were soiled, as if he'd been sprinting through muddy backyards before getting here. *Oh, great*, I thought. *He's here to shop.*

My reaction might seem mean to certain people. *"Is there a problem with somebody purchasing goods at your place of business?"* they'd probably ask. And I'd say no, not necessarily.

But if they're asking me questions like that, they clearly haven't worked enough retail.

Folks with my job know that if the store is empty, it sucks when someone decides to come in and shop. Bonus points if they arrive sometime within the hour before closing.

Despite the fact that this man had unknowingly committed an atrocity, I offered him a wave and a smile. "Welcome to Grocery Hut!"

He only looked at me for a second, the doors closing behind him, before he continued into the store and vanished from my sight.

Maybe he'd have seemed out of place to others, but to me he seemed pretty average, especially compared to the clientele the store usually receives around ten o' clock at night.

Listen, folks around here are weird. Odd is such a common flavor of person in this town, it's practically vanilla ice cream. Simply put, I was so accustomed to strangeness that I didn't see this man's red flags.

I continued down the aisles to the doors leading into the back room and pushed them open with the cart. The back room was rather large and open; you'd never guess from the outside that there's so much space. On this particular night, other stock carts of various colors rested in neat rows along the concrete floor.

Standing against a stack of boxes that held gallon jugs of drinking water was my coworker, Tasha. She had her phone in hand, her short black hair swept to the side and covering her left eye. Thick black lipstick painted her mouth, and beneath her purple Grocery Hut vest she wore a graphic tee for some death metal band I didn't recognize. She'd also donned shorts, fishnet tights, and black boots.

Tasha tapped a foot rhythmically against the wall as she scrolled on her phone. I approached her, and she glanced up. "Did you get the rest of that cart finished?" she asked.

"Absolutely." I slid the cart into place next to the others. "We still have a bunch of the stuff, but I bet with the markdown price it'll all be gone by the end of the week."

Tasha rolled her eyes. "Super." She pocketed her phone and stood up straight. "I heard the bell a moment ago. Do you mind covering the front while I smoke real quick?"

"Didn't you take a smoke break a half hour ago?"

She grabbed her coat. "Yeah. I need another one." Her tone grew sharper with every word, and I got the message. Don't press the issue, or else.

I raised my hands defensively. "Sure thing."

She smiled wide with her straight teeth. "Thanks, Riley." Before I could respond, she was out the back door.

I returned to the front, stuffing my hands into my pockets as I walked toward our one functional register. We had six of them, but four had burnt out years ago, and the owners still hadn't bothered repairing them. The fifth register just had a bum laser gun and a keypad with some missing buttons. Its new scanner was scheduled to arrive by Friday.

I guess it's cheaper to replace a scanning gun rather than a register.

I made my way to aisle eleven. Just as I was about to round the corner, the man I'd seen enter the store earlier exited the same aisle. He nearly ran into me as he speed-walked, halting just before we made contact.

"Whoa," I said, and he sighed, seemingly relieved yet also annoyed at my presence. "Sorry," I added.

"Don't be." His voice was tired and gruff, and he spoke quickly, as if paranoid. "My fault." He glanced over his shoulder down the aisle, and I took a closer look at him.

He appeared as though he hadn't been sleeping well. His eyes were bloodshot, heavy bags beneath them, and grease coated his hair, his graying beard disheveled. Beads of sweat formed on his forehead as he stared down the empty aisle.

I didn't consider those things red flags, though. What struck me as suspicious was that he no longer had his bag.

I opened my mouth to ask him about it, but he swung around to face me, cutting me off. "Tell me something," he whispered. He paused to look down at my vest before continuing. "Riley. Tell me where the kitchen knives are."

Surprisingly, that didn't strike me as alarming either. Everybody uses kitchen knives, right? Who was I to decide whether he needed them at this hour?

"Aisle thirteen." I pointed to my left. "There's a sale on them right now, actually. Full set for fifty bucks."

The man glanced toward aisle thirteen, then seized me by the shoulders. "Okay, listen very carefully. Find somewhere safe to hide and call the police."

My face heated in irritation at the man's brazenness. "Actually, I can't leave the front end unattended for too long while customers are in the store."

5

"Trust me," he went on, his grip on me tightening, "this place is the least of your worries right now." He shook me, as if to reaffirm his words. "Stay quiet. Now go." He released me, pivoted, and ducked, then peered cautiously down the aisles as he crept toward thirteen. Finally, he vanished around the corner.

I decided to humor him. Well, sort of. I *would* be calling the police, but only to let them know some crazy asshole was in my store shopping for kitchen knives.

Interestingly enough, it wouldn't have been the first time I'd made that exact call. I would have owed Keith a hundred bucks if I'd have made it a second time.

I walked down aisle eleven as I'd initially planned, the register in sight on the other end of the store.

I heard shuffling, then the squealing and crinkling of plastic a couple of aisles over. The man must have found the kitchen knives he wanted. Thank God they were sealed in that annoying plastic packaging. You know what I'm talking about—the thick stuff you need a knife just to open. It's funny how things work out that way, isn't it? I need a knife to open a set of knives.

I neared the front of the aisle and noticed a bottle of white hand lotion had been tipped over. It sat unevenly among the rest of the shampoos, conditioners, and other various creams we carry.

I tried to straighten the lotion, but it wouldn't stay in place. Pushing aside some other bottles, I discovered what was causing the issue.

The kitchen-knife guy's shoulder bag had been haphazardly shoved onto the shelf behind product.

I spent a few minutes fixing the mess and reorganizing the shelf before taking the bag and continuing on my way. *I'll hold it at the register for him*, I thought.

Now, I'm sure my lack of urgency regarding the situation seems odd, especially considering I planned to call the police on kitchen-knife guy. But truth be told, I wasn't in that much of a hurry to contact them. This kind of thing happens regularly enough that it's a—well, it's a *regular* part of the job. In short, I'm used to it. Desensitized, if you will.

After I arrived behind the register, I set the bag on the rack near my legs, grabbed the store phone attached to the wall next to the register, and started dialing the police station number.

I'd only dialed about half of the number before I realized someone was standing behind me.

A tall, muscular man ripped the phone from my grasp. He snapped the cord with one sharp tug, snatched me by the vest, and hauled me up off the ground. Surgical scars decorated his expressionless face, his eyes as pale and glazed as a dead man's. He wore a spotless pressed suit with a black tie, his white hair slicked back to complete the look.

Before I could scream, he tossed me to the floor. Pain shot through my side. I let out a grunt.

The click-clack of shoes on tile sounded from the right, and a pair of fancy Oxfords stepped into view. A young man—somewhere in his mid-twenties, I'm guessing—knelt down next to me. He had swept-back platinum-blond hair, and he sported a dark pinstripe suit and a black band on his right ring finger. A mole protruded from his chin, two coarse hairs sprouting from its center. It reminded me of sausage chunks on pizza—lumpy and brown.

The man grinned at me. "Hey there." He reached for my name tag, pinched it between his fingers, and examined it. "Riley. I was hoping you could help me find something." He spoke in plain English, but he had a slight accent I couldn't place, and even as he talked, I couldn't completely focus on him. My eyes kept finding his blemish.

"Happy to serve," I replied in my best customer-service voice. The best I could muster, anyway.

He rested his hands on his knees, his smile growing wider. "Excellent. I'm looking for an old codger, about yea high." He motioned at the space above his head. "He might have come in here a few minutes ago."

I've never been hypnotized, so I don't know how it works, but the hold this guy's mole had on me must have been magical. Even if I were blind, I wouldn't have managed to avert my gaze.

Transfixed, I didn't reply, and the man lost patience with me. "Hey," he barked, snapping his fingers in front of my face. "I know what you're staring at. Knock it off."

I tore my eyes away from him. "I wasn't staring."

"Yes, you were." He pointed at me. "You're doing it again!"

And he was right. Involuntarily, my attention had snapped back to the mole, locking onto it as if I were preparing to assassinate it.

"For crying out loud." He covered my eyes with a hand. "The old man. Where is he?"

"Aisle thirteen," I gestured in that direction.

"Excellent." Mole-man pulled his hand away from my eyes and stood up. He turned to the giant, dead-looking guy who was with him. "Pete, get grandpa over here."

With no emotion whatsoever, Pete trudged off toward the kitchen goods, and despite his large stature, he was nearly silent as he moved.

I had tons of questions running through my mind at this point, but the one I was most curious about was how the *hell* these guys hadn't tripped the bell sensor when they'd entered the store.

Mole-man faced me. "You've been a great help, Riley. Five-star serv . . ." He trailed off and let out a long sigh. "You're doing it again."

"Oh," I said, realizing that I was staring. I covered my eyes with my hands. "Sorry."

"Make it four-star service," mole-man muttered.

There was a loud crash. I chanced uncovering my eyes to see what had caused it. Initially, I couldn't identify anything out of the ordinary, but then pained yells, a wet snap, and a scream sounded in the air.

More cries, and Pete appeared, a butcher knife lodged in his heart. He dragged the old man by a leg as he ambled toward the front of the store. The old man cradled his right arm to his chest, the limb bent at an unnatural angle. White bone jutted out from the mangled arm's sleeve. Red seeped into the fabric.

Mole-man tsk-tsked, crossing his arms. "Really, Adam? You thought you could hide from me in some rinky-dink grocery store?"

The old man—or Adam, I guess—groaned in pain. "Fuck you," he managed through spittle and gritted teeth.

Mole-man stepped toward Pete and Adam as they approached. "What about the book? Where is it?" He gestured at Adam. "You tried to hide it, didn't you?"

It was then that I remembered the man's bag—you know, the one that had been haphazardly shoved behind product in aisle eleven. It was also then that I started to recognize the familiar beats of this story. Honestly, it shouldn't have taken me so long to realize what was going on.

Every now and then—usually once a year—I'm confronted with situations ripped straight from fantastical or paranormal movies and books. I'm talking circumstances that are essentially the equivalent of a pilot episode for some fucked-up, fictional television show on the supernatural.

The thing is—the situations I'm thrust into never quite "stick." I'm not interested in embarking on an epic journey or in saving the world, so I never play along.

I'm not that guy. I'm just Riley Thomas, Grocery Hut employee.

But somebody upstairs must think I'm hero-material . . . because the weirdos keep coming.

Like I said before, these unusual events normally take place annually, but at the time of this story, they'd started happening more and more. In fact, meeting Adam, Pete, and mole-man was my third "incident" in a *month*.

It was getting ridiculous.

Is there a manager I can complain about it to?

"You're never going to get your hands on that book, Rivers," Adam said.

Mole-man—er, *Rivers*—stroked his chin in thought. He brushed the tip of his thumb over his blemish a few times, clueing me in to the fact that I was staring at it again.

Seriously, was that thing enchanted? Or was something wrong with me?

"I know you had it when you came in here," Rivers replied. "You think I won't turn this dump upside down to find it?"

That broke my trance. Turn this "dump" *upside down*?

A vision of Grocery Hut—destroyed, demolished, totally trashed—played in my mind. If Rivers did that to the store, all my hard work from the past four hours would be rendered useless. I'd have to commit to some major overtime just to get this place back in order.

I had to do something. I couldn't let that happen.

"Is the book in a bag?" I blurted out.

There's usually a little voice in my head that tells me when I've got a bad idea on my hands. He must have been on vacation when I mentioned the bag, because what transpired next was nothing short of disastrous.

Rivers and Adam fell silent. They slowly turned toward me, glaring at me as though they were rabid dogs, and I held the mother of all dog biscuits.

Oh well, I thought. *It's too late now. Might as well double down.* I climbed to my feet, brushed myself off, walked back to the register, and grabbed Adam's bag.

"No!" Adam screamed, scrambling to stand. Pete slammed him face-first onto the floor.

Rivers wouldn't take his eyes off me. Actually, he wouldn't take them off the bag in my hands. "Yes," he said, an unsettling grin turning up his lips. "That's it."

He lunged toward me and snatched up the bag, then spun around, opened it, and yanked out a tome that appeared to be bound in ancient leather. There were no words or pictures on its cover, and the whole book had a handmade quality about it.

Rivers let the bag fall to his feet and raised the book above his head as if recreating the iconic *Lion King* shot. "Finally," he began, "the Book of Merlect." He lowered it and threw it open. "I've been searching for two hundred years, and now it's mine."

Adam squirmed on the ground. Pete placed a boot on Adam's back and pressed him down.

Rivers flipped through page after page. "With these spells, I'll have an army of the dead at my disposal. Complete and total world domination will be mine." He slammed the book shut. "The power of death in the palm of my hand. Gates to the underworld. Access to and command over the legions of souls trapped in the veil. A guarantee that I won't burn in Hell forever. It's all *mine*." He faced me once more. As he continued, his tone was mocking. "Thank you for your wonderful customer service."

I looked over at Adam. The old man shook his head in disappointment at me.

I threw my hands in the air. "Hey, how was I supposed to know? You weren't exactly informative. You were cryptic and mysterious."

Adam's expression twisted with disgust. "He's going to kill everyone, you fucking idiot!"

Rivers nodded. "I *am* going to do that, yeah." He stared down at the book. "You know what they say, Adam. No time like the present. Why wait until the reckoning?"

Pete was on me in a flash. For such a big guy, he sure did move fast. He forced me to my knees and held me in place.

Adam tried rolling over, but Rivers kicked him in the skull, knocking him unconscious.

Rivers adjusted his suit jacket. "Shall we begin?" He opened the book to a page I couldn't see.

Then he started to read.

The words were in a foreign language, and it didn't sound modern either. Maybe it was Latin? I kind of doubt that, but Latin would have made sense, considering everything going on. Rivers's accent paired well with whatever tongue it was, and I figured he was fluent in it, at least.

Thunder boomed outside, and I looked out one of the nearest windows. Storm clouds gathered rapidly in the night sky. Lightning flashed, electricity exploding in the center of the parking lot, and more thunder rumbled.

Rivers kept on reading. As he did, gusts of wind swirled around him, through the store. The gales picked up all sorts of loose items and tossed them around the building—products from the shelves, scanning guns for the registers, even my half-finished bottle of iced coffee behind the customer-service counter.

Heavier objects—shopping carts, cases of water, and the endcap shelving from the nearest aisles—lurched into the air next. They floated around Grocery Hut as if they'd been transported to space. Basically, if it wasn't human or rooted to the floor, the supernatural hurricane sucked it up. Soon the lights flickered on and off, then went out completely.

Just then, the voice in my head decided to return. He offered proverbial pats on the back, as well as a gentle, *Maybe that wasn't a great idea, Riley. Maybe you should have thought it through. Maybe doubling down* wasn't *the play.*

I have to admit, he made a fair point. But then again, where had *he* been when I'd first come up with the bad idea?

More wind gusted through the store from who knows where, emerald flashing in my peripheral. I looked around to see deep-green light spilling like syrupy goo down the aisles and between the shelves and registers.

There was a sound like Velcro tearing, and the air in front of me ripped open like a portal in space-time, revealing a green galaxy glittering on the other side. Seriously, it was identical to the stuff you see in video games and on TV.

Rivers started laughing, and of course he didn't have a regular laugh. He had a full-on mustache-twirling evil-villain type laugh. At the same time, the portal of swirling emerald opened wider and wider—an expanding wound in reality.

Another crack of thunder shook the store. The walls creaked and groaned. I feared the building might collapse.

Rivers raised his arms. The book was floating now, hovering in front of him so he could easily read from it. He glanced over at me. "Are you ready to meet Merlect, Riley?"

"Merlect?" I asked.

"The God of the Dead." Rivers said it matter-of-factly. "That's the deity's true name." He stepped toward me, smiling smugly. "Because I've summoned him, he's going to do my bidding. And since you were such a great help—and I'm such a nice guy—I'll make sure you're rewarded."

I gestured at the aisles around me. "Can you fix the store, so I'm not stuck here until tomorrow morning?"

Rivers tilted his head and scratched the back of his neck. "I was thinking you'd get to die more quickly and less painfully than everyone else, or something like that."

I bit the inside of my cheek. "I guess that's more in-line with what's going on here, huh?"

"Indeed," Rivers replied. "I have to ask you a question, though."

I nodded. "Of course."

"You know, before I have Merlect peel the flesh from your bones."

"As one does."

"Why did you just hand over the book to me? Are you some kind of moron? What happened there?"

"Honestly . . ." I sighed. "I figured if I gave it to you guys, you'd leave, and I could get back to work."

Rivers gave me a sassy side-eye. "You don't want to be a hero?"

"It's not just that I don't *want* to be a hero," I said. "It's also that I'm *not* a hero. I can't be, period. I'm just Riley Thomas. If I'd have taken the book for myself—you know, to keep it from you—I'd be running for my life for the foreseeable future, which sounds exhausting. I don't have that kind of time or energy. Moreover, if I'd have done that, I'm sure it'd eventually lead me down a path where, at the end, you and I would be locked in an epic battle to determine the fate of the world, and that is *not* my thing."

Rivers seemed taken aback by my response. His expression grew somber, and he knelt down next to me. "Not a fan of the expectations and stress, huh?"

"Not really."

"Me neither, to be honest." Surprisingly, Rivers sounded empathetic. "I've been alive for a *really* long time, and in that time, I've learned one thing of great importance. Death seems like the bad side of the coin, but it's not. Living is, and death is the only real escape from . . ." He paused and steepled his hands, covering his mole with a thumb. "You were doing it again."

The spell broke. I covered my eyes. "Sorry."

"Right in the middle of my backstory, too."

"I'm sorry," I repeated.

"I was trying to connect with you." Rivers huffed. "Do you know how long it's been since I actually tried to talk to somebody?"

"Look, man. Really, I'm sorry. I can't help it."

There was shuffling, and suddenly Pete released me.

"Hey!" Rivers shouted.

I uncovered my eyes. Adam was awake and on his feet. He had a second knife, probably from the same set as earlier. Adam stabbed Rivers in the back. Rivers cried out in pain. Adam yanked the blade free, and Rivers stumbled to the side.

Adam rammed into Rivers. The force sent Rivers to his knees. Adam raised his weapon, then slit Rivers's neck from ear to ear. Blood sprayed all over my clean tile floor, a wet gurgling sound escaping Rivers's throat.

Pete swept past me toward Adam. He seized Adam by the collar and pitched the man into the nearby pharmacy stand. Bottles of vitamins and pain medications scattered across the ground.

"Riley, get the book!" Adam yelled, trying to stand. "Run!"

Pete grabbed Adam again. I tore my gaze from the struggle and faced the book in question. It fell to the ground and slammed shut.

Rivers clawed at his wound. The bleeding had slowed, and his choking had lessened. That's when I noticed something peculiar: Rivers's gaping throat appeared to be sealing itself shut. He glowered at me, attempting to climb to his feet, but instead he gagged and collapsed.

Behind Rivers was the portal of green, swelling and swirling. But now it wasn't *just* a galaxy; now it looked as if it were a pool of stars and slime big enough for a small car to sink into. Something moved behind it, making it pulse like a skipping heart.

As I stared hard at the vortex, I knew what I had to do.

I took a step back.

Rivers choked out something, but I couldn't understand him. He managed to rise and stumble forward. All the while, his throat finished healing itself. "You're down to three stars, you little shit."

The portal pulsed once more. Something was coming.

I took another step back.

Rivers knit his brow in fury. "You'll both suffer several eternities for this. I control the God of Death now, and I'll make you wish you *were* dead!"

Pete tossed Adam toward the portal. Adam crashed onto the floor, his body mangled and broken.

He wheezed, the sound somehow piercing through the booms of thunder all around. His chest fell still, and he stared lifelessly at the ceiling.

Then shit *really* hit the fan.

Hundreds of long, skeletal protuberances shot out of the vortex. They wriggled like the tentacles of an octopus, but they were made of bones, and each appendage ended in skeleton hands, which ended in more skeleton hands, which ended in *more* skeleton hands, and so on. The "tentacles" hurt to even look at, not because bright light shone from them or anything, but because I could barely comprehend them.

One of the bony appendages snatched the book from the floor and jerked it through the portal. It vanished into the goo, no trace of it left behind. "Oh *fuck*," Rivers said, and I'll admit, the fear in that single curse word made me uneasy.

Three tentacles wrapped around Pete and dragged him away next. A fourth protuberance plucked up Adam, and he disappeared in an instant.

Rivers sprinted in my direction.

I took yet another step back.

Just before Rivers reached me, a fifth tentacle seized him by the wrist. He screamed, the appendage yanking him into the vortex.

A slew of otherworldly voices chanted and sang and moaned on the other side of the portal, its stars and slime spinning faster and faster, its wind scooping up everything within reach—more product, some shelves, a few shopping carts, even the blood on the floor. The gale didn't pick me up, so I think I (thankfully) stood outside of its range, or maybe whatever was behind the portal wasn't interested in me.

After what felt like forever, the tentacles retreated into the portal. There was a blinding flash, a loud snap, and then the vortex sort of just . . . exploded? I'm not sure how else to describe it. I closed my eyes and shielded my face with my arms as its green goo showered the store.

Pretty soon the gusts inside dissipated, the storm outside dying. Thumps and clunks and thuds echoed throughout the building as the stuff that had been floating in the air crashed to the floor. I heard the lights flicker, then finally buzz back on.

And that was that.

It took me a bit to work up the courage to open my eyes and lower my arms. When I did, I was welcomed by an absolute mess of destroyed shelves and damaged product, all coated in paranormal fluid.

Other than that, the store was back to normal.

Nine times out of ten, the weird situations I'm thrust into resolve themselves without my involvement, similarly to this one. And while this one's outcome wasn't ideal, it wasn't totally awful either.

I walked around the store and surveyed the damage. It appeared that everything closest to the portal had received the most harm, and the stuff farthest away had remained untouched. That was good. That meant I wouldn't be there *all* night—so long as I had help setting Grocery Hut back in order.

As if on cue, Tasha wandered out of aisle eight. Still wearing her coat, she gaped at the disaster around us. "What the hell happened in here?"

I shrugged. "Nighttime crazies." If I'd told her the truth, she wouldn't have believed me.

"I am *not* staying late to clean all this up," she retorted.

I nodded in defeat. Somehow, I'd known that would be how this story ended.

CHAPTER 1
PROMPTED AND PROTAG'D

THE NEXT FEW DAYS BREEZED BY WITHOUT INCI-
dent, and I worked the large number of shifts I was
scheduled, although the only reason I had to come
in so often was because several of my coworkers kept
calling in sick or not showing up. In fact, the only employee
who seemed to be reliable other than me—and (debatably)
Keith—was Tasha. Regardless of how much she hated working at Grocery Hut, she got to work on time, usually com-
pleted her tasks, and was pretty fast on the register.

Today was Friday, and Fridays are busy at the store—I'm
talking hordes of people in line to check out. Tasha had been
assigned to the register, and since our new scanner gun had
been broken en route, there wasn't much I could do to help
her. She was on her own for the time being.

I stood behind the customer-service counter, watching
Tasha as she worked. Taking a sip of my iced coffee, I glanced
up at the clock. *Still four more hours to go*, I thought.

"Hey, bro," Keith said, his voice deep and casual. He walked up to the counter and went around to stand next to me.

For as long as I'd known him, he'd had messy black hair and had been a bit on the pudgy side. Today he'd donned a backward baseball cap with "commit tax fraud" printed on it in sporty-looking font. Besides wearing a purple vest and a name tag like the rest of us, he also had on ripped jeans, white sneakers, and a T-shirt that read "may the forks be with you," two crossed lightsabers with forks for blades beneath the words.

He ran his fingers through the side of his short beard before hopping up to sit on the counter. "You look tired."

I shook the half-empty glass bottle of coffee at him. "I haven't had a day off since last Thursday, and I'm pretty sure this iced mocha is the only reason I'm not passed out in the break room right now."

"Ah, you work too hard," Keith said with a grin. "This is just retail. It's not worth killing yourself over."

"Definitely not. My bills, however, will not be paying themselves." I downed the rest of my drink. "Besides, it's not like I have anything better to do."

Keith reached into his vest pocket and produced a roll of Wonka-brand Bottle Caps. He devoured a bunch of the candies every day, and I struggled to think of a time I hadn't seen him with any on hand.

He popped a couple into his mouth. "What you need is a hobby."

I turned away and tossed the empty bottle into a nearby trash can. "I have hobbies," I said, a bit more defensively than I'd meant to.

Keith laughed once. "Dude, sitting at home and watching *Jeopardy!* or reading a book doesn't exactly qualify."

"*Jeopardy!* makes me a menace during trivia night," I replied. "And reading is . . ." I trailed off. Reading was something I'd used to love, but then my life became way too similar to the stories I'd once enjoyed. I shrugged, letting out a sigh. "I'll give you that one."

Keith motioned with his finger as if giving himself a point in a game. He gestured at me next, but he blew a raspberry rather than giving me a point. "Face it, bro. You're boring. As your friend, it is my duty—nay, my *honor*—to help you become cooler."

"I'm not boring, and even if I was, there's nothing wrong with that."

"Maybe not. But is 'boring' what you want to be if you're still trying to ask out Ari—"

Hissing out a shush, I covered Keith's mouth with my hands before he could finish saying her name, then looked around to make sure no one had overheard our conversation. "*Dude*," I whispered, "why would you say that out loud?"

Keith chuckled as he pushed me away. "*Dude*, you've only been talking about it for the past two months. You know she's not going to hang around here forever, right?"

I stepped back and leaned on the counter. "I'm working up to it."

Keith peered around the corner. "Well, you better work up to it quick."

Predictably, this was Keith's way of letting me know that my crush was fast-approaching. Also predictably, I didn't take the hint until it was too late. Before I had the chance to mentally prepare for her arrival, Ariel Quinn appeared from around the corner and walked up to us.

She wore a baggy purple hoodie marked with the Grocery Hut logo and a matching cap, an apron hanging over her left arm. She pulled her deep-red waves free of her hairnet, and butterflies exploded in my stomach as she shook her head, her hair falling over her shoulders. Smiling, she blinked a few times, her green irises shining like emeralds, and leaned on the counter across from me. "Whew! You boys working hard today?"

Keith patted me on the back. "Please. Riley here doesn't know how to do anything else." He cupped his mouth and whispered what he said next, as if shielding me from his words. "Seriously, he doesn't do anything besides work. It's really sad."

"Dude." I rolled my eyes. "For real?"

Ariel faced me, her smile widening. "With how often I see you here, I'm not surprised. Don't worry, I work all the time too. Especially as of late."

"What can I say?" I forced out a chuckle. "I like my job." I thought I sounded confident, but the little voice crack halfway through "like" didn't convince anyone, apparently.

Ariel giggled, and Keith laughed along with her. She brushed some hair out of her eyes. "Whatever you say, Riley." Biting her lip, she stepped away from the counter and glanced around. "Have you guys seen Henry? I need him to check the bakery so I can go home."

Keith jerked his head at the wall behind us. "Last I knew, he was in the back office."

"Great." Ariel flashed us one last smile. "See you boys tomorrow."

23

"Y-yeah—uhh—see ya," I called as she vanished around the corner. I slumped against the counter. "Keith," I whispered.

"Yo," he replied.

"Please help me be cooler."

"Already on it."

I looked over at him and realized he was now wearing sunglasses. "Where did you get those?"

He crossed his arms. "The cool-guy store." Pulling off the shades, he smiled wide. "Nah, just kiddin'. I snagged 'em off the glasses rack in Pharmacy on my way over here." He handed them to me.

"Okay," I said, taking them in my hands, "but you *paid* for these, right?"

"Yeah." He popped another piece of candy into his mouth, then glanced back and forth and returned the roll to his pocket. "Sure. Anyway, look—you just wear these and say the first thing that comes to mind. Oh, and you *have* to either cross your arms or put your hands in your pockets."

I looked down at the sunglasses, then up at Keith. "What?"

"They're shades, dude. There's more to them than just *wearing* them. Everybody knows that."

I pinched the bridge of my nose with my free hand. "Let me get this straight. You think the secret to being cool is sunglasses, crossed arms, and saying the first thing that comes to mind?"

He took the sunglasses from me, put them back on, and crossed his arms. With a stoic expression and a calm voice, he said, "Yes."

I had to admit, he was pretty cool.

He handed them to me once more. "Now you try."

I put them on and crossed my arms. "How do I look?"

Keith slammed a fist against the counter. "Like you're gonna beat me up and take my lunch money!" He jumped off the counter to the floor, and I noticed that Tasha and a couple of the customers in her line were watching us now. I gave them an awkward smile and a wave.

"Okay, Riley," Keith continued. "What's cooler than cool?"

"I—"

"Nuh-uh!" Keith wagged a finger at me. "Arms."

I resumed my position. "To answer your question, I would assume that 'frozen' is next in line—you know, after 'cold' or 'cool.'"

Things were uncomfortably silent for several seconds before Keith cleared his throat. "Was that, uh . . . was that the *very* first thing that came to mind?"

Things were uncomfortably silent for several more seconds before I answered. "Yes."

"This might be harder than I thought." Keith hummed, cupping his chin in contemplation.

I took off the sunglasses and slumped against the counter again. "I'm doomed."

"Hey man, don't be like that." Keith patted me on the back. "It's never too late. If shades don't work, the next step is finding you a dragon to slay."

"Har har. Don't tempt fate, or else we'll probably get one stomping down aisle five for our troubles."

"That would be cool, actually."

"No," I snapped. "No, it wouldn't. It would be a mess that I'd end up having to stay late to clean."

Keith gave me a playful jab with his elbow. "Is that why you stayed late on Tuesday?"

"Well, it wasn't because of a dragon. But yes, basically."

Keith's grin fell. "Wait, really?"

"Remember when I got Molly in the mail? She came with that letter inviting me back to some old town on the coast where my 'rich Aunt Mary' left me a small fortune."

"Hey, haunted doll aside, that sounds like one hell of an adventure. And a fortune to boot?"

"I'm not willing to endure the many evenings of ghost-hunting required to *get* said fortune, Keith."

"What does that have to do with Tuesday night?"

"An immortal dude and . . ." I realized that I hadn't really known who Adam was. ". . . some other guy? Anyway, the two of them had a spell book, and the immortal guy tried to summon the God of Death, but then they both got sucked into a portal and died."

"Metal as fuck," Keith said with a nod.

"They trashed the store with their little ritual, and I had to stay late to clean up." I rubbed my eyes. "And that was just Tuesday. A couple of days before that, there was the merchant who tried to sell me a basket of cursed artifacts, and before *that*, there was the monster-hunter who needed my help tracking some supposed 'She-Devil.'" Relaying the increasingly common scenarios thrown my way reminded me *why* I liked "boring." *This* was why I'd stopped reading books.

Why would I read Lord of the Rings when, at any point, Gandalf could show up at my door and ask me to take the One Ring to Mordor myself? I couldn't risk making that a reality.

"Boring" was fine. In fact, "boring" was great. "Boring" didn't get me thrust into hectic life-and-death situations.

Well . . . not usually, anyway.

"Dude," Keith said in a deathly serious tone. "You're getting Protag'd."

I slowly faced my best friend. "What?"

"Protag'd," Keith repeated. "You know. Golden Ticket moment, letter from Hogwarts, Ben Kenobi teaching you the Force. The call to action."

"Yeah, I know what a call to action is."

"Getting *Protag'd*." Keith said it as if he'd just solved all the secrets of the universe.

"I'm not calling it that."

"Fine. May I suggest Code: Tom Cruise?"

"I'm not calling it that either."

"Well, what *would* you call it, then?"

I pinched the bridge of my nose. "An inconvenience. I'm not interested in slaying dragons or fighting death gods, Keith. I'm an adult with a full-time job. For crying out loud, I've got car payments to make!"

Keith steepled his hands and motioned at me with them. "Let me see if I understand this. You're consistently given the option to go off on insanely dangerous and exciting adventures, automatically becoming one of the coolest people *ever*, and you instead decide to remain a boringly normal individual with a standard nine-to-five retail job?"

I took his words as if they were an objective summarization and not a criticism. That was more or less my predicament, yeah.

I picked up the sunglasses, put them back on, and crossed my arms. "Yes."

For a while, Keith didn't react. He seemed to be processing his thoughts. "Why?" he finally asked.

I lowered the shades and raised a brow at him. "Game of Thrones is cool, but that doesn't mean I want to *be* Jon Snow."

Keith pursed his lips. "You make a good point."

"I'm glad you get what I'm saying." I returned the sunglasses to the counter.

After a few seconds of silence, Keith muttered, "*I'd* still like to be Jon Snow."

I opened my mouth to reply, but then I noticed Ariel walking out the front entrance on the other side of the store. I also saw Henry approaching the customer-service counter where Keith and I were standing.

"Gentlemen," Henry greeted us. He looked at Keith. "Keith, I need you to sweep under the front aisles of the pharmacy. They're disgusting."

Keith saluted Henry. "I'm *so* on that." He vaulted over the counter, but his foot got caught, and he face-planted into the floor with a loud thud. Before Henry could ask if he was okay, he hopped to his feet and hurried off as though nothing had happened.

Henry mumbled something under his breath. I swear I heard, "Why haven't I fired that guy yet?" Then he sighed and turned his attention to me. "Riley, care to follow me to my office for a chat?"

Instantly, my palms grew sweaty. Never has there been another string of words to put the fear of *any* god into you.

I swallowed hard. "Yeah, sure."

He turned and walked around the corner, and I slid out from behind the counter to follow him to the back office.

Henry had been the general manager since before I'd started. He wasn't the strictest, but he ran a tight enough ship to keep the store's sales effective. He had buzzed hair the color of sand, and his thick, oval-shaped glasses made his eyes appear large and round. Today he wore a simple dress shirt and a bright-purple tie paired with brown slacks and clean shoes. The only thing he had on that maintained the dress code was a name tag.

I followed him past the pharmacy and into the employee break room. It wasn't small, but it wasn't big either. A TV on the far-left wall played daytime television, and unfortunately, it wasn't good daytime television. We also had no way of changing the channel since somebody—whether currently or previously employed, I wasn't sure—had stolen the remote.

To my right sat a couch, a table with a couple of chairs, and a fridge. A counter stuck out of the wall beside the fridge, equipped with a coffee pot that no one used. Not if they valued their health, anyway.

Straight ahead loomed an open doorway that led into the back office. But from where I stood, the room might as well have been the gallows.

It was smaller than the break room, with pale-gray walls and no personal touches in sight—not even a bookshelf or a filing cabinet. All it had was a desk, a computer, and a pair of matching chairs.

I followed Henry inside. He took a seat at his desk and began typing away. I grabbed the chair across from him.

After what felt like whole minutes, he stopped and looked at me. "So, remind me. Why exactly were you here so late the other night?"

"Oh." I clasped my sweat-soaked hands and rested them in my lap, trying to remain calm. "Uh, there was a group of people who came in right before closing, and they trashed some of the aisles. I stayed to clean up."

Henry hummed in affirmation and returned to typing. "That's what I thought. What did these hooligans look like?"

Crap, he wanted descriptions? What was I supposed to tell him?

I blew out a breath and shook my head. "There were three of them, but they were just regular guys, I guess. One of them was really tall, one of them was older, and one of them was dressed like he just came from prom."

Henry stopped typing and gave me a sharp glance.

Did he know I was hiding something?

"Riley," he said sternly, "I don't even have to check the cameras to know *exactly* who you saw that night."

"Y-you don't?"

"That's right." He clenched his fists, his pale face turning scarlet with rage. "It was those goddamned teenagers! I swear, I have to kick them out every other day!"

Correction: he did *not* know I was hiding something.

Henry shook his fists as if about to bring them down against the desk, but he paused and took deep breaths instead, allowing his hands to relax. "Those little rat bastards skip school, come in at all hours of the day, and agitate the customers. I've had it with them."

It suddenly dawned on me that I'd met the three kids he was talking about. In fact, I'd had a few run-ins with them, but they weren't the criminals Henry made them out to be.

No, they were *much* worse.

They entered public spaces all around town and tormented people while recording themselves for social media, and their pranks weren't harmless either. A lot of the time, they assaulted people and ran away, but while in the store, I'd seen them throw fruits and vegetables across aisles, not caring whether the produce hit anybody. I'd also caught them trashing items like milk and shampoo in the name of online clout.

I hadn't encountered them in a month or so, but apparently, Henry dealt with them regularly. Or maybe he held a mean grudge.

Either way, I nodded at him, playing along. "Oh, yeah. Those three little"—I made a fist and shook it rather unconvincingly at the floor—"uh, teenagers."

Henry closed his eyes and rubbed his cheek. "Oh, they make my blood boil." He took more deep breaths, then returned to typing. "Well, that's enough to complete this police report and have them dealt with. Thank you."

I stood up, eager to leave this dungeon and get back to work. "Glad I could help!" I swung around to leave.

"One more thing, Riley," Henry said.

I stopped in my tracks and pivoted to face him again. "Yeah?"

"I'm going to have to send you home for the rest of the day. You know how the owner feels about overtime."

My stomach dropped. To be honest, my heart probably stopped too. I'd died right there, in the single most depressing room any human being had ever constructed. "But I'm only halfway into my shift," I argued. "It's just Tasha and Keith out there today."

Henry nodded. "Yes, unfortunately, but we only have the one register, so it's not like I can put you up front anyway. Four hours of overtime needs to be cut, and it's the end of the week. It's got to be today or not at all."

My shoulders slumped. Leaving early wouldn't impact my paycheck, but it meant I had to go home.

Which meant I had to be alone . . . with my *thoughts*.

I shuddered. "Are you sure I can't do two hours today and two hours tomorrow?"

"Tomorrow is the start of the next pay cycle." Henry's voice grew more authoritative. "Like I said—today or not at all. Sorry."

Forget my shoulders, my whole body sagged now. There was no way out of this. With a sigh, I begrudgingly accepted my fate. "All right. Are you sure you guys will be okay for the rest of the night? Just the three of you?"

Henry waved as if shooing me away. "Go home, Riley. Get some sleep. Lord knows you need it."

I scratched the back of my neck. Maybe having a quick dinner and going to bed early wouldn't kill me. "Okay." I exited the office and returned to the break room.

On the wall next to the TV was a rack that held the employee punch cards, a big shelf with a built-in clockface attached to the rack. Unlike places with up-to-date equipment, Grocery Hut retained the time-card system of the '70s and '80s.

I grabbed my card and inserted it into the slot below the clockface. Once my time stamp had printed, I returned my card to its spot, grabbed my hoodie off the coatrack, pulled the garment over my head, and waved goodbye to Henry.

As I returned to the store, I spotted Keith sweeping the shelves outside the break room. He'd already gathered a mound of stray pills and fragmented plastic bottles from the pharmacy. When he saw me approaching, he stopped. "Dude, you okay? Henry didn't let you go, did he?"

"Nah." I stuffed my hands into my hoodie pocket. "I'm going home early to cut the overtime from Tuesday night."

"Ahh." Keith returned his attention to the floor. "That must be where all this stuff came from." He stuck the broom under the shelves and swept out more broken plastic and loose capsules.

"Yeah, I probably missed those when I was cleaning up."

Keith kept working, and suddenly the tiles grew slick with . . . goo? He stopped and lifted the broom to examine its bristles. A green substance, thick and sticky, oozed off them and plopped onto the floor.

I quickly realized where the substance had come from. "Oh no."

"The hell is that?" Keith asked.

"Part of the death-god portal."

Keith grinned. "Sick."

"I guess so."

He gazed at the goo as though in deep thought. "Okay, here's the plan. I'll deal with this, and within the hour, I'll be at your place with video games, pizza, and a movie. It's time for a boys' night."

"How is that a plan? You don't get off for another three hours."

Keith leaned in close. "Not if I were to quote, unquote, *slip* and *fall* on this gunk."

I stared at him. Then down at the sludge.

And then I turned around and left.

I didn't have the energy to continue this conversation. It would be a miracle if I even made it home.

The whole way out to my vehicle, I couldn't stop thinking about the fact that a bit of the green muck had been left behind from the death-god portal. Was it a bad omen that I'd missed some?

Oh well, I thought. *It's probably nothing to worry about.*

CHAPTER 2
BOYS' NIGHT (BATTERIES NOT INCLUDED)

RIVING HOME WAS ABOUT AS DULL AS YOU'D expect. Traffic was crazy, and thanks to my shitty little four-door Nissan, I felt as if I were trapped in the slowest, most boring amusement-park ride ever.

Finally, I neared the end of my hour-long journey home (which should have only lasted twelve minutes, mind you) and turned onto a street of what's probably the lowest-income suburb this side of the Midwest.

At the end of the dreary road lined with abandoned or low-maintenance homes was my place—a square two-bedroom house, its original yellow hue now so discolored it was pale green. A gutter on the left side of the house hung free, threatening to fall off entirely. The front porch was missing one of its three steps, and the sidewalk had seen better days too. But best of all, the mailbox had been secured to the sidewalk with at least four rolls of heavy-duty duct tape and had a tilt not even God could fix.

I pulled my Nissan into the one-vehicle driveway and killed the engine, then grabbed my backpack out of the passenger seat, threw it over my shoulder, and climbed out of the car. I didn't keep much in the bag—usually just some spare clothes and non-perishable snacks in case of an emergency at work.

As I made my way up the cracked path to my front door, a man to my left greeted me, and I stopped. "Howdy, neighbor," he said. "Home from work early today, huh?"

I fumbled with my keys and looked up to see Carlos standing at the edge of his driveway. Slightly older than me—maybe thirty or so—Carlos had disheveled brown hair and a pencil-like mustache. He wore a dirt-stained white shirt that said "ask me about my petunias" and a pair of equally filthy blue jeans, gardening gloves sticking out of the back pockets. His brown skin had darkened from hours in the sun, and he held a mug of steaming coffee in one hand. He smiled at me and sipped his drink.

I gave him an awkward wave. "Yeah, I got out late a few nights ago, so I'm cutting early today."

"Bastards." He shook his head, his smile unwavering. "They never let you have shit in corporate America, do they?"

I returned my attention to my keys and picked the house one out of the bunch. "Uh, no." I shrugged. "I guess not."

"You see the garden?" He gestured with his mug toward the flower bed that divided our yard space. It stretched almost the entire width of his lawn, organized by sections of different blossoms. I noticed red cardinals, pink peonies, and even some white roses.

I nodded. "Looks great." Just then, I spotted a batch of

bright-purple blossoms at the end of the flower bed that hadn't been there this morning. I couldn't tell what species they were either; I'd never seen anything quite like them before. "Where did the ones at the end come from?"

Carlos sipped a bit more of his coffee, his uncanny grin still plastered on his lips, and turned toward the purple flowers as if he were a robot, his torso moving on a rusted swivel. "Black Cat's Bloom. Planted them a little while ago. Rare imports from somewhere in Wyoming." Slowly, he faced me again. "Beautiful, aren't they?"

"Absolutely," I agreed, wanting to end this interaction. "You sure do have a green thumb."

Carlos bowed. "Thank you, sir. Appreciate it. And since I've got you, I thought I'd ask: do you mind if I expand the bed a bit into your yard? That soil is a lot richer than the stuff on my end."

"Yeah, it's probably because of the bodies," I said casually.

His smile vanished, the mug shaking slightly as his hand began to tremble. "B-bodies?"

I unlocked my front door. "Yeah, bodies. Some spree killer lived here before I did. Detectives dug up the yard and pulled, like, seven corpses out of the ground. Kind of fucked up, but I imagine that does wonders for the soil, right?"

Carlos let out a nervous—and yet somewhat relieved— laugh, his grin returning. "Oh right, right. Of course. Corpses would do wonders for the soil, indeed. O-or so I'm told, anyway." He took a skittish swig of his coffee. "Speaking of serial killers, did you hear about the one prowling around town?"

I was halfway through the door, but Carlos's words trapped me in a conversation with him once again. "Serial killer?"

Carlos gestured to me as if what he said next was common knowledge. "The missing people all over town, you know?"

This jogged my memory. I guess it *was* common knowledge.

For the last several weeks, people around town had been going missing without a trace. Some in broad daylight, some in the middle of the night. Some from their homes, some from their cars, some from their workplaces. None had been found or even seen again. It was as if they'd been plucked out of our reality altogether. "They're chalking that up to a serial killer now, huh?"

"Word on the street says so," Carlos said. "Nothing official, but then again, you don't have this many missing people on your hands without it being something bad, right?" He motioned as though elbowing me, letting out a chuckle.

I responded with a nervous laugh. "Yeah, I guess not."

Carlos stopped chuckling and put his free hand in his pocket. "Well, anyway, you have a great night. And stay safe, Riley." He raised the mug to his lips, still curled in a smile. "Would be a real shame if somebody as kind as you went missing next."

My heart was suddenly beating twice as fast as it had been a moment ago. More than anything, I wanted to enter my house without another holdup. "Yeah, ha ha, okay! I'm heading in now, talk to you later."

Then I was inside and shutting the door behind me. I locked the deadbolt and leaned against the wood, letting out a long exhale as I tried to scrub his uncanny-valley grin out of my brain.

It was only when I opened my eyes again that I realized the horror of the living room before me.

Everything in the average-sized room was red—the walls, the floor, even the furniture, the phrases "I'm back" and "miss me?" written in scarlet marker over and over again. And in the center of the room, seated upon the vandalized couch, was little Molly the doll.

Old and dirty, the jester doll's silver-and-green outfit stuck out like a sore thumb in the sea of red. Her left eye socket was empty and dark, and her one remaining eye glowed a soft blue, a crack zigzagging up from the pupil. She didn't have any hair peeking out of her coxcomb cap, but the floppy parts of the hat fell down her back, one side of it green, the other side of it black with silver polka dots.

Her crafted smile seemed to grow wider as I stepped forward, and I noticed she clutched a red marker in her porcelain hands.

Permanent. Marker.

"Seriously?" I shouted, stomping over to the doll. I snatched the marker from her hand and shook it at her. "You scribbled all over my house? Have you ever heard of *paper*?" I sighed and put my face in my hands for a second, then dropped them and waved the marker at Molly again. Her good eye stared up at me now. "Where did you even *get* this?" I stopped scolding her to inspect the writing utensil. "I don't own any markers."

Predictably, Molly didn't answer me. She might have been a haunted doll, but she was still a *doll*. Toys couldn't talk. That was ridiculous.

What she did do, however, was vanish. When I returned my attention to her, I found her seat empty. I swung around to look at the open doorway that led into my medium-sized kitchen.

Molly sat on the counter next to my coffee pot, her left arm situated behind the appliance. I clasped my hands, pleading with her. "Molly, please. Be reasonable."

That little monster stared me dead in the eye as my coffee pot tumbled to the floor. The glass shattered into innumerable pieces and scattered across the tile.

I fell to my knees. Shards stabbed through my pants, into my legs. This was it. It was over. How could I survive without coffee? It was practically the lifeblood of America, and now, if I wanted my fix, I had to spend my barely existent funds at places like the Ass Top or Grocery Hut for it.

I looked back up at the counter, but Molly was gone. Leaving me to pick up the pieces.

I set to work, grabbing a trash bag and a broom. The "anger" part of the grieving process must have kicked in, because I suddenly grew furious. What was this shithead even doing here, anyway? I'd sold her to some guy three states over. This was now the fourth time I'd tried to get rid of her, only for her to return.

First, I'd thrown her down a sewer. She'd come back a couple of months later. Then, I'd left her on a curb and *watched a garbage truck crush her*. Two weeks later, she'd arrived in my kitchen. Desperate, I'd taken her into the woods, stuffed her in a barrel, burned it, and buried the ashes. That time, she'd been waiting for me on my doorstep when I got home.

Two long months had gone by after that, and finally, somebody answered my SellBay ad and purchased the haunted doll. I'd shipped her out and that was that. Until tonight, I guess.

At this point, it had been about a year since I'd first received her in the mail. As I'd already told Keith, she'd come attached with a note that said I was supposed to visit my "rich uncle" who had recently passed away at home in a town called "Deathmore," which was allegedly located somewhere in Maine. Apparently, Molly was only a small piece of the incredible fortune he'd left me, but I had no interest in traveling to the estate. It sounded as if going there meant I'd be at risk of running into ghosts, unearthing nasty family secrets, and facing whatever demonic force was tied to Molly.

You probably already know what I'm going to say: I don't have time to deal with all that. I don't even have the vacation days to deal with it, let alone the *want*.

Things had been calm at first with Molly around. But the longer I'd gone without responding to the letter, the more intense the ghostly activity in my house had become. It seemed Molly was attempting to spur me into action since I had, in a sense, been dragging my heels on the whole "fortune" thing.

I'd figured the best solution would be to simply rid myself of Molly rather than skipping town, but I'd quickly realized just how difficult that was going to be. Obviously.

I finished cleaning the remains of my innocent coffee maker, set the broom against the counter, and leaned on a wall. In the living room, the TV switched on, and I looked over to see Molly sitting on the couch, watching the local news.

Great, I thought. *Now she's making herself at home.* I snatched a bucket from the pantry and a sponge from the sink, then filled the bucket with warm, soapy water and set to work wiping down the red marker as best I could.

As I worked, I listened to the newscasters talk about more missing people in town. They had *also* vanished without a trace, just as the folks Carlos brought up earlier had. Knowing my luck, it was probably another Protag'd moment circling me before finally deciding to strike.

I paused and closed my eyes. *Not a "Protag'd" moment. Just a "moment" moment. Dammit, Keith.*

Other than reporters droning on in the background, the next forty-five minutes were pretty much silent. Molly lifelessly watched the news, and I tirelessly cleaned her mess. It took three buckets of water, but I managed to smear the red on the walls until the words were gone. However, the color was another matter. Unless I decided to repaint, I'd have to live with pink walls. My pictures and furniture would have to be cleaned another time as well. I was way too tired to do all of it tonight. Seriously, I was beyond exhausted.

As though in response to my thoughts, Molly had turned her head toward me. "Don't look at me like that," I said, defeated. I tossed the sponge into the bucket and stood up. "We've had this conversation a thousand times. I'm *not* going to Deathmore. My aunt can keep her fortune."

Molly replied by staring blankly at me. I bent down to pick up the bucket, and when I glanced over at her again, she'd returned her attention to the TV. Only now, her tiny arms were crossed tightly over her chest, as if she was angry or frustrated.

I returned to the kitchen, dumped the water down the sink, and set the sponge aside. My stomach started to growl, and I figured that food was as good a next step as any.

I opened the freezer and grabbed a pack of frozen waffles. They were a week past the sell-by date, but they were all I had. I ripped the three of them free of their plastic packaging, dropped them on a plate, and placed them in the microwave.

As the appliance hummed, I turned around and walked down the short hallway to my bedroom. It was about the same size as the other rooms in the house, but my bed and the desk holding my computer took up a lot of space.

I booted up the computer and changed out of my work clothes into a black T-shirt and sweatpants. After I retrieved my waffles and checked on Molly, I returned to the device.

Taking a few bites of my spongy quick breads, I logged into my SellBay account to see what had gone wrong with the doll. I'd been using the website for years, mostly due to its resemblance to simple "don't ask, don't tell" sites like Craigslist or eBay.

On occasion, some of my . . . *inconveniences* came to me in the form of enchanted and/or haunted objects. I'd received a mystical talking sword that was convinced I was a modern-day king, the *actual* Helm of Darkness (you know, the invisibility-helmet that belongs to Hades, the King of the Underworld in Greek "mythology"), a Magic 8 Ball that could predict the future . . . yada yada yada, I'm sure you get the idea. Anyway, since I wasn't interested in going on any of the adventures these items presented me with, I'd often listed the objects on SellBay to earn a bit of extra cash on the side. Between the site's occasional payouts and my regular job at Grocery Hut, I could barely afford my ramshackle place. It wasn't much, but . . . well, yeah. It wasn't much.

It didn't take long to track down the archived order log for my sale of Molly. I'd titled the listing "Legit Haunted Jester Doll! Message if interested," added some pictures of Molly, and reused the title for the description (mainly because I'd assumed that the title was self-explanatory).

But as I looked things over, I found something surprising: there were forty new messages from the buyer, MadBlock219, since I'd last checked on the purchase. After Molly had reached the buyer, I'd given them ample time to let me know if anything was wrong with the order, and after weeks of radio silence, I'd figured it was safe to archive it.

Apparently, I'd been wrong.

Due to archiving the order, I hadn't been notified about any of these messages. If I'd never manually looked for them, as I was doing now, I don't think I would have noticed them at all.

Resting my elbows on my desk, I pressed my palms against my eyes and took a deep breath. Then I dropped my hands, took another bite of my waffles, and clicked on the oldest message from Molly's buyer.

From: MadBlock219

Hey dude! Hope all is well on your end. I got the jester doll in perfect shape as listed! It's a great piece. Everything's cool, I just had a couple questions about it. Was hoping you could fill me in on its history a little more! Thanks!

I let out a sigh of relief. That wasn't so bad.

Then again, there were thirty-nine more messages to go through.

I clicked on the next one.

> **From: MadBlock219**
> Hey dude! Hope everything is cool. Just sending this followup cause it's been a week and I haven't heard back yet. Really wondering more about this thing's history. Any help is appreciated!

I began going into denial. Maybe nothing bad had happened. Maybe MadBlock219 just *really* wanted to learn more about Molly's past.

Unfortunately, even if I *had* seen these earlier, I wouldn't have been able to help. I didn't know anything about her either.

Before the denial could fully set in, I clicked on message number three.

> **From: MadBlock219**
> Hey dude! Really need you to answer me back ASAP. Some weird stuff's been going on in my house. I've bought haunted stuff before, but nothing like this has ever happened until I bought this jester doll off you. I NEED to know where this thing came from. PLEASE get back to me.

All right, not as bad as it could have been, but definitely a lot more desperate than before. Message four up next.

> **From: MadBlock219**
>
> SHE SPEAKS TO ME I CANT STOP I CANT
> SLEEP SHE DOESNT STOP EVERY NIGHT
> I HEAR THE SCREAMS OF THE DAMNED
> THE SCREAMS OH GOD I CANT STOP
> HEARING THEIR SCREAMS

Okay.

> **From: MadBlock219**
>
> Hey dude! Just wanted to let you know
> that everything is fine. I'm fine. We're fine.
> She's fine. I don't think I'll message you
> again. She yearns to return. The screams
> don't. Fucking. Stop. Thanks!

The next several messages were just two-page walls of all caps talking about the screams and "she who has risen from the pits of Hell." I couldn't make much sense of that, but when I got to message thirty-two, I finally found a break in the pattern. And by "break in the pattern," I mean the messages were no longer walls of capitalized words.

> **From: MadBlock219**
>
> How could you just send me away? :(

The sudden use of an emoticon caught me by surprise. The buyer hadn't used any prior. I spent a good ten minutes trying to figure out how it fit into the MadBlock219 extended lore before I realized that by this point in the timeline, Molly had probably taken over the keyboard.

Every message following that one sounded the same. They generally consisted of a single question and a frowning face, mostly stuff like:

> *Do you hate me?* 😕

or

> *Aren't we friends?* 😕

This persisted until message thirty-nine.

> **From: MadBlock219**
> I'm coming home Riley 😊

That was only about a month old. I suppose it solved how Molly had ended up back here. Well, sort of. It hinted at her return, at least.

I clicked on message forty, the final one.

> **From: MadBlock219**
> Fuck you.

That could have easily been either Molly or Mad-Block219, and even now, I'm not sure which one of them sent it. It was dated just twenty-four hours after message thirty-nine. Which didn't clear things up in the slightest.

My doorbell rang, the sound reverberating through the house, and suddenly I remembered that Keith had planned for us to hang out. I leapt out of my chair and switched off my computer, then left my waffles behind as I hurried to answer the door. I unlocked and opened the door to find Keith with a backpack, a case of beer, and two boxes of pizza. The top cardboard box had the logo of Keith's favorite place printed on it: Spi-Cee's Pizza, a local restaurant.

Keith held up the food and drink. "Hey, bro! You ready to get absolutely pizza-faced?" He chuckled. "Get it? It's like shit-faced, but with pizza."

I opened my mouth to reply, but before I could tell him that yes, I *was* ready to get absolutely pizza-faced, I recalled that Molly was back. "Oh fuck," I blurted out.

Keith's smile faltered. "Okay, I know, it wasn't that funny."

I pushed the door all the way open. "No, it's not that." I turned around and entered the living room, hands raised pleadingly. Molly had her head turned toward me already, her cracked blue eye staring daggers into my soul. "Molly, listen. Keith and I were going to hang out tonight. Grant me a ceasefire for a couple of hours, that's all I'm asking."

Naturally, she didn't answer. Keith closed the door behind me and approached her. "Oh shit!" he exclaimed. "Molly, what the fuck is up, dude?" He plopped down onto the couch next to her, not a care in the world.

He set his stuff on the coffee table, and I couldn't help but close my eyes and pinch the bridge of my nose. Soon the news clicked off, and when I looked at them again, Molly was positioned toward the screen once more. Her arms were no longer crossed, and the television showed a blank input— the one I usually switched to for when Keith brought over his gaming console. He dug that very console out of his backpack as he continued sitting next to Molly.

I threw my hands in the air. Did he not see the way she'd totally vandalized my place? "Dude!" I cried.

Keith shrugged. "What? Molly's cool. We've chilled with her around before."

"Are you seriously not worried that she's here *now*?"

"Is she mad that you tried to get rid of her again?" He raised his eyebrows at the doll.

I gestured at the middle of the TV screen where the words "miss me?" were written. I then pointed at the couch and the coffee table, both of which had suffered the same tragic fate as the television.

Keith looked everything over for a solid moment or two before he went, "Huh." Then he grabbed a game case from his bag and grinned at me. "I brought *Super Champion Brothers Four*!"

He was hopeless. Shoulders sagging, I sat down on the floor in front of the couch and snagged a slice of pepperoni pizza while he hooked up his console. "Count me in," I said, and took a bite of the pizza.

After Keith finished setting stuff up, he looked around the living room, confusion spreading across his face. He was acting as if he'd never been in my house before. "Dude, have your walls always been pink?"

CHAPTER 3
WHISPERED WARNINGS

T HANK YOU FOR SHOPPING AT GROCERY HUT. Have a great day!" I handed the receipt to the lady at the checkout, and she wheeled her cart toward the exit. With my line of customers tamed for the moment, I snatched up my fourth coffee of the morning and downed a huge gulp.

My boys' night with Keith had lasted until nearly four in the morning. Now here I was, bright and early to work at eight. This level of tiredness went beyond needing sleep— my body was actively trying to pass on from this life. When boys' night had ended, and I'd crawled into bed, sleep had come fast and easy, but it was too short, and I'd already been exhausted beforehand.

Today was going to be rough.

Somebody cleared their throat behind me. I nearly leapt out of my vest, spinning around with an undignified squeal.

Tasha stood behind me, arms crossed. "You're pounding down that coffee pretty hard, dude."

I caught my breath and gave the almost-empty bottle a shake. "Yeah. I think I'm beyond the wonders of caffeine at this point."

She nodded, squeezing into my space behind the register. "Well, vamoose. I'll take the register for a while."

I got out of her way and finished my coffee. "Are you sure?"

"Yeah," she said with a hint of sarcasm. "Go take a nap in the break room or something."

"Bad idea." I leaned on the register behind me. "If I fall asleep now, I might not wake up for a few days. Better to keep moving until I'm home."

Tasha shrugged. "All right, then. You can deal with the men's restroom if you want. I've had some customers complain about the sink drain being clogged."

I waggled a finger at her. "*That* I can do."

She smiled a bit and shook some hair out of her face. "If I don't see you in ten minutes, I'm sending Keith back there with an air horn."

I turned around and began walking away. "Better make it a shovel. If I fall asleep, that might be it for me."

I headed down aisle nine toward the back end of the store. The bathrooms were just ahead, the door to the employee stockroom to the right of them. The stockroom was about as big as the back room, which was on the other side of Grocery Hut's back end and contained the store's inventory, but the stockroom held supplies for employees to use rather than for customers to buy. Mops, cleaning chemicals, paper towel rolls, spare toilet paper, fun things like that. Once inside the stockroom, I walked past shelves of boxes until I found a half-used bottle of drain cleaner.

Guaranteed to "kill" drain clogs in twenty seconds or less, or so it was advertised on the jug. I made my way out of the stockroom and headed toward the men's restroom. Just as I was about to enter, the door to the women's room swung open, and I caught a flash of familiar red in my peripheral. Ariel stepped out, and when she saw me, her lips turned up in a beautiful smile.

I froze. If she were a car, then I would have been a clueless deer about to be turned into fine mist.

Ariel eyed the bottle in my hand and raised a brow. "You've got the fun job this morning, huh?"

I'm not sure if it was Ariel's presence, or the lack of sleep, or maybe a mix of the two, but I couldn't manage to get a straight word out of my mouth. What I meant to say was, "Oh, it's for the sink, actually." What came out instead was something in caveman language.

I paused, processing my sudden de-evolution, and Ariel giggled. "Would you like to try again in English?"

I took a breath, cleared my throat, and held up the jug. "It's for the sink," I said plainly. "But thank you for your concern at the horrors I may or may not face when I make it inside."

Ariel laughed again. "No problem."

Things went quiet for a second, and panic set back in. I cleared my throat once more. "So, how's the bakery?"

"Oh, it's absolutely *swell*." Ariel rolled her eyes. "Let me tell you, spreading dough and baking cakes is the greatest."

"I thought you liked baking?"

"Maybe as a pastime," she said with a shrug. "Doing it for a living kind of sucks the fun out of it."

"Oh . . . Well, what would you rather be doing? What's your dream job?"

Ariel's smile grew wider, her gaze drifting wistfully. "*Artist*. I love to paint. If I could do it all day, I would."

I wasn't sure how to respond. The sincerity in her voice had silenced me, and all I could do was remember a time when I'd been as passionate about something as Ariel was about art. Back when I'd had hobbies and aspirations . . . back before my life had become a horror show of rotating story prompts. There were things I hadn't done or even thought about doing in years.

Ariel broke the quiet. "Someday, for sure. But today, I have bagels to take out of the walk-in oven." She pivoted, about to march off.

"Maybe I can see your paintings sometime," I blurted out. The "bad idea" voice sounded in my head, screaming at me for ejecting such words without first consulting him.

Ariel stopped to look over her shoulder at me. "Yeah?"

"Yeah."

She pursed her lips playfully. "I'll think about it," she said, and her smile returned. She let the statement hang long enough for me to realize that she'd meant it in a positive way, then waved and left for the bakery.

The butterflies subsided, my pulse returning to normal. As far as conversations with Ariel Quinn went, that had probably been my best one. Sometimes when you have a crush, all you can think about is holding their hand, spending time with them, or cartoonishly floating after them with hearts in your eyes.

Perhaps there is no "love at first sight." There's "crush at first sight," and love is what happens when you make a connection with someone.

The door to the men's room opened behind me, and a guy stepped out. With my trance broken, the duty at hand returned to my attention.

Before entering the bathroom, I had the urge to look at the man who'd just passed me. He was of average height and build, with a short beard and brown hair, and he wore a gray business suit with a red tie and carried a briefcase. He cast me a curious glance, then continued through the store.

Something about the man struck me as odd, and I couldn't put my finger on it until I'd entered the restroom. *Isn't the sink supposed to be clogged?*

He hadn't said anything to me about the sink. Had he even washed his hands?

Unbelievable.

The bathroom was small, with only two urinals and an accessible stall. At the front, close to the door, was the sink, with no "out of order" sign in front of it. I supposed Tasha *had* said she'd only been notified about the issue today.

I approached the sink and set the jug on the counter. As I began to unscrew the lid, my thoughts drifted back to Ariel. To her red hair, her green eyes, her artistic endeavors. What did she paint? What did the pieces look like? Were they environmental illustrations? Self-portraits?

My mind kept wandering, and I thought back to what she'd said.

"She has risen."

Absolutely beautiful.

. . . Wait, that wasn't right.

I looked around. Nobody else was in the bathroom. Was I hearing things?

"*Risen, and free,*" the voice of a young girl whispered, and this time I was positive that it was real. I had *heard* it.

"Hello?" I said. "Is somebody in here? You know this is the men's restroom, right?"

"*You let this happen, Riley.*"

"Let what happen?"

"*We are damned. Each and every soul will be claimed.*"

It dawned on me that the voice was coming from in front of me. From the *sink*.

I leaned over the sink and gazed down the drain. "That doesn't sound good."

"*She has risen,*" another voice whispered, this one a little boy's. "*She is coming for us all.*"

"Am I to assume that you're some of the 'already damned' souls?"

"*We are the innocent ones,*" a new girl replied. "*We could have been saved.*"

"*We are the damned,*" a second boy added.

"Well," I started, "are you the innocent, or are you the damned?"

"*She has risen,*" the four of them said in unison.

I sighed. Talking to a bunch of—I don't know, ghost children? —in the sink drain of the Grocery Hut bathroom just felt silly. *I* felt silly. "Okay?" I responded awkwardly.

"*She can't be stopped,*" a third girl insisted.

Then *another* new girl chimed in. "*She will claim all. None will be spared. When the reckoning begins, all will be damned, just as we are.*"

I finished unscrewing the drain-cleaner cap. "So, the reckoning hasn't started, but you guys are already damned?"

A pause, and then the second boy said, "*Uh, yeah?*"

"Then there were damned souls before she started the reckoning?"

"*What? No.*" The original girl spoke now. "*Once the reckoning begins, all will—*"

"Yeah, all will be damned, just as you are," I finished for her in irritation. "This is starting to sound like some contrived plot element to make me uneasy more than anything else. How can you all already be damned if being damned doesn't happen until the reckoning?"

"*She. Has. Risen,*" the children said sternly, as if attempting to stay on topic and warning me to do the same. But I didn't have the time to deal with whoever had "risen." And I was way too tired to put up with another one of . . . you know. Yeah, *that*. I'm *not* calling it that.

"All right," I said, and began pouring the contents of the jug down the sink.

"*The reckoning will begin on— UGH! Hey!*" The first boy was cut off as the cleaning solution oozed through the drain. All the children started talking at once, but they sounded as though they were being waterboarded, so I couldn't understand them. Their cries grew quieter and quieter, until finally their voices faded away altogether.

I stopped pouring the cleaning solution and listened.
Silence.

I turned on the faucet and let the water run. It went down the drain without issue. No flooding, no voices.

Cool. That solves the issue.

I replaced the lid on the bottle and exited the restroom, my thoughts returning to my conversation with Ariel, as well as my approaching lunch break.

The next couple of hours went smoothly. With how exhausted I was, I was thankful that the day hadn't been entirely insane, and all through the morning customers arrived in a slow crawl, making the day breeze by. I might not have had a ton of work to keep my eyes off the clock, but the fact that I was fighting to stay awake was a full-time job in itself.

I stocked and reorganized two aisles, dusted the tops of the milk racks in the cooler, and covered Tasha's break on the register before I went on my lunch. I took my packed meal from the break room fridge and headed out back, as usual.

There wasn't much of a view behind the store, but it was peaceful, the warm midday sun beaming. Next to the back doors sat an old picnic table large enough for four people, and down the hill from the store grounds, vehicles roared across the highway—although after all the time I'd spent working here, the sounds were basically just white noise to me. On my left lay a ramp we used to unload trucks into the back room, and on the other side of the ramp rested a storage container in which we kept extra stock. The store's large blue dumpster was back here too, pushed up against the storage container. It would be another two days before the garbage truck picked up the waste.

I slid into the picnic bench with my back against the wall and plopped my lunch box onto the table. I unclipped and opened the box, revealing my homemade BLT, a lunch-pack sized sleeve of Oreos, a bottle of apple juice, and a mini bag of potato chips.

After I devoured my food, I'd go to my car for a short nap until it was time to return to work. That was the plan, anyway.

I took a bite of my sandwich, pulling out a full strip of bacon in the process. I had nothing in me besides coffee, so having something solid in my mouth was enough to settle my upset stomach.

I set the sandwich aside and opened the bottle of juice. As I sipped on the drink, my thoughts danced around Ariel and our conversation from earlier. But surprisingly, my mind didn't stay on Ariel. Instead, I began thinking about what my life was like before—before the insanity, before Grocery Hut.

Back then, I recalled being normal like everyone else. I'd still had high hopes for my future. I'd still read three books a week. I'd still done photography.

I'd still had my family.

It was hard to believe that it had already been seven years.

I picked up my sandwich and lifted it to take another bite, when a loud bang sounded from the dumpster. At the noise, I nearly leapt out of my seat. It was as if someone were striking the inside of the container with a tire iron, and that someone was a professional baseball player swinging for the fences. With my sandwich halfway into my open mouth, I locked my gaze on the dumpster.

Another bang. It shook the whole container. A flash of green, and garbage began to float out of the open top. Then metal screeched as something split the dumpster clean in half, revealing an emerald rift in space-time.

I lowered my sandwich from my mouth with a sigh. "Really? Right now? Of all times?"

I couldn't believe it. I was on my lunch, and another death-god portal swirled before me, only this one quivered as if it was having trouble staying open. It also seemed much smaller than the last one, and it didn't appear to be growing. Had the leftover gunk I'd tossed into the garbage banded together to open yet another gateway?

A figure tumbled out of the portal, born from it like a baby mammal in a nature documentary. Coated with a thick layer of slime, the figure fell to the ground. In the same instant, the portal broke down, spilling into the space between the two halves of the cracked-open dumpster with a disgusting wet splat.

I stared at the figure for several moments, and soon I recognized him. Completely naked, Rivers had returned from beyond.

Rivers scrambled to his feet, his breaths quick and unsteady. He slipped in the slime but managed to keep himself upright. Shielding his eyes from the sun, he started looking around, and I realized through the nearly transparent gunk that there wasn't a scratch on him. I guess that shouldn't have surprised me, considering that before, I'd watched his wounded throat seal itself shut.

Finally, his eyes settled on mine. At first, he must not have recognized me, or maybe his sight was adjusting, because he peered curiously at me for a solid minute before his expression contorted into a scornful grimace. He pointed a goo-covered finger at me. "*You.*"

Some gunk dripped off his face, revealing his mole in all its glory, and my gaze trained on the blemish. I reminded myself to look elsewhere, but then there came the issue of Rivers being nude. After spotting a few body parts that I had no interest in seeing, I covered my eyes. "So, how was death-god land?"

A noise like footsteps approached me. I peeked through my fingers, and Rivers was on me. He seized me by the vest, ripped me out of my seat, and rammed me against the wall. He lifted me up, and I lost grip of my sandwich. It fell to the ground, sorrow hitting me as I realized that my lunch was not only ruined—it was *over*. I tried to grab Rivers by the arms, but they were slick with goo, and I couldn't keep a firm hold on him.

"You. Did. This," Rivers practically growled, shaking me every other word. "Do you have *any* idea what you've done?"

"I was just eating my lunch," I cried. My eyes darted to the mole again.

Rivers must have noticed what I was looking at, because he pulled me back and slammed me into the brick again. "You have royally fucked up everything!"

"Hey, I'm not the one who opened a portal in a grocery store in the middle of the night!"

Rivers spat some sludge out of the corner of his mouth. "Did it ever occur to you why I needed that book?"

"I assume it had something to do with the whole 'I'm immortal and can't die' bit of your backstory."

"Somewhat, yes!" Rivers shook me once more. "But I also needed it for *protection*. She's coming, you fucking idiot! And now there's nothing that can stop her. She's going to begin the Reckoning. She's going to turn everybody into Followers, torture, burn, flay, and kill anyone who doesn't." Fresh fury distorted his features as he continued glaring at me. "Everyone except for *me*. I'm going to be around to suffer forever."

I cocked my head. "Who's coming, exactly?"

"*Her*!" Rivers screamed. "*The She-Devil*!"

"Is that seriously what this is about?" I asked, and Rivers went still. "I'm running on fumes today, dude. I just wanna eat my lunch in peace and not worry about the world ending."

Rivers studied me for a long time before setting me on the ground, although he didn't release his grip on my vest. Eventually, he said, "What is wrong with you?"

"I'm tired, and hungry."

Frustration returned to his features. "Any day now, she's going to turn the world into ash. Any. Fucking. Day."

"So go do something about it?"

"I . . ." Rivers sucked in a long breath. "That's why I wanted the book, you moron. She can't dance with Merlect. She'd die. But now the book is gone, and I won't be able to stop her." Again, he picked me up and slammed me against the wall, harder this time. "And it's *your* fault."

"To be fair," I said, raising a hand, "all I really did was get out of the way. Adam is . . ." I trailed off, realizing that I was staring at his mole again. I covered my eyes and continued. "He's the one who jumped you."

Rivers's hands went from my vest to my throat. He squeezed hard. My air flow stopped. I choked for breath, struggling to free myself from his grasp. "Adam is gone," he said. "The only other person I can take my anger out on is you. So, I guess I'm going to take pleasure in doing so before I have my flesh melted away for an eternity."

He squeezed harder. I thrashed against him, clawed at his face. Nothing made a difference. Nothing mattered.

Air disappeared.

Vision got dark.

Rivers smiled.

Loud noise.

"Dude!" Keith shouted to the right. "Check out this sick fucking baseball bat I found behind the candy shelves!"

I turned that way. Keith had come through the back doors with a dusty metal baseball bat. He looked at Rivers, then at me. "Did I interrupt something?"

Air.

I gasped for breath, sliding down to the ground as Rivers released me.

I tried to answer, but all that came out was a raspy cough. Breathing felt good, but also so, so bad.

Rivers jumped at Keith.

"By the power of Greyskull!" Keith shouted, swinging the bat. It connected with the side of Rivers's head, and he toppled to the ground in a heap. He stopped moving, but I knew he couldn't be dead, so I figured Keith had knocked him out cold.

Who would have guessed, huh? The guy could bounce back from a knife slicing open his throat, and even from being on the other side of a portal with the literal God of Death, but one swing from a metal baseball bat and it was lights out.

Keith helped me stand as I recovered from another coughing fit. "You okay, dude?"

"I'll—live," I choked out.

He pointed the bat at Rivers. "Who's the crackhead?"

"Immortal—guy."

"Death-god portal immortal-guy?" I gestured at the dumpster, and Keith let out a low whistle. "I guess the

God of Death probably doesn't agree with people who can't die, eh?"

"I guess—not." I patted my chest a few times and gazed down at the remains of my sandwich. I sighed, which in turn initiated another series of coughs. "At least I—still have my chips."

Keith removed his hat and held it to his chest. "Rest in peace, Riley's lunch." He replaced his cap and turned toward Rivers. "So, are we calling the cops on this guy, or what?"

HELLO
I AM...
Riley

CHAPTER 4
SOMETHING DRASTIC

THE AUTHORITIES CARTED RIVERS AWAY, AND the rest of my shift was a blur. I spent the remainder of my lunch hour answering questions the police had about the assault, and I never got to finish the rest of my food, nor did I get to take the nap I'd planned for. Driving myself home was too risky considering I was borderline unconscious, so Keith drove me instead.

I honestly don't even remember entering my house. The next morning, I awoke in my work clothes. Apparently, I'd stumbled into my bedroom and fallen asleep. I had a few hours until my next shift, so there was ample time to change, shower, and eat.

I scarfed down several slices of microwaved pizza from boys' night, then hit the shower and grabbed a fresh change of clothes. With my shirt and pants on, the next step was to gather my vest, since Keith would be here shortly to drive me to work.

I remembered taking it off earlier this morning and tossing it to the floor by the bed, but as I knelt down and picked it up, painful familiarity twinged in my chest.

My conversation with Ariel yesterday came flooding back to me. It had been some time since I'd looked through *that*.

I threw the vest over my shoulder and reached under the bed. My hands brushed against a shoebox, exactly where I'd left it last. Before I'd even finished pulling it out from under the bed, I could see the thick layer of dust coating its lid.

The box was old, probably from four or five pairs of shoes ago. A strip of silver duct tape had been pressed across the lid, the word "keepsakes" written on the tape in black marker.

I lifted the lid. I knew what I'd find inside the box, but still, I wasn't prepared.

On top of everything else was a camera—an expensive one that my parents had gotten me as a graduation present. It had seen a fair amount of use before I'd slowly moved away from photography.

I picked up the camera, held it. It felt comfortable in my hand, as if I'd never stopped using it. At the same time, it felt heavy. Years and years had passed since I'd last used it, since I'd even cared to snap a new photo with it.

A lump formed in my throat as my focus drifted from the camera, back to the contents of the box.

A stack of photos. My high school diploma. The frame. The necklace.

I took out the necklace first. It was a gift from my sister . . .

The trinket consisted of a silver coin—dull with age—hanging from a matching chain. I vividly recalled my sister finding the coin on a sidewalk when we were kids. We hadn't been sure what kind of silver piece it was, especially considering it hadn't appeared to be United States currency. My sister had carried it around from then on, and good luck seemed to follow her wherever she went. She'd always joked that it was our good luck charm.

When our high school graduation approached, she'd gifted me the coin as a necklace, a small hole drilled through the top so it could be strung on a chain. It was her graduation present to me. I hadn't planned on getting her anything to commemorate leaving high school behind—not initially, anyway. That's where the frame came into this story. The frame held a picture of my sister and me, which had been taken a few weeks before we graduated. In the photo, her straight brown hair—the same color as mine—hung far past her shoulders. We stood arm in arm, smiling and laughing. The day it was taken had been great, and we'd agreed that the photo served as the perfect depiction of our brother-sister dynamic.

In secret, I'd had the original picture framed, planning to give it to her as a late graduation gift. But I never had the chance to do so.

I looked at the photo on the top of the stack next. It showed a younger me, my mom and dad, as well as my sister. The four of us were on a beach. It had been snapped during a vacation that we'd taken a month after my sister and I graduated. I remembered the day clearly, despite not thinking about it in so long.

It hurt to revisit these memories, but maybe that wasn't a bad thing. Ariel seemed dedicated to her craft. When had I lost my own enthusiasm? Reading was one thing; I knew why I'd stopped enjoying books. But why had I given up on photography?

Was it because of them?

The photo stack held pictures that were almost exclusively of my parents and sister. Perhaps, after a time, the pain had become too great, and I'd hidden the reminders away. Maybe life, between work and bills, had become such a struggle that everything else fell to the wayside.

It almost felt as if this life wasn't mine to remember. As if the Riley Thomas in these photos, in this shoebox, was a different person altogether.

I considered sifting through the rest of the photo stack and ultimately decided against it. A part of me thought I wasn't ready for what I'd see, but maybe I was falling back into whatever defensive behaviors had locked me out of my memories in the first place.

The more I thought about it, the more my answer became obvious. After all, I hadn't *forgotten* what had happened to them. I just didn't want to remember it.

So I didn't.

I replaced the box's lid but kept the lucky coin. I placed the chain over my head, let it slide down around my neck, gazed down at the pendant. Then I shoved the box back under the bed.

These days, I needed all the good luck I could get. Besides, I also wanted to follow Ariel's example. I wanted to find the old me again, and even if this was just a small step, it seemed like a good place to start.

As I rose to my feet, I caught sight of Molly's single broken eye and let out a shriek that transformed into an angry grunt almost as soon as it came out. I jabbed a finger at her. "Stop doing that!"

Molly, of course, offered no response, no movement.

I closed my eyes and crossed my arms. "What do you want, anyway?"

When I opened my eyes again, I noticed that Molly was now staring up at me. She hadn't shifted in any other way though, so our limited "charades" form of communication seemed to be off the table.

"What?" I asked again. No peculiar reply, no odd sound, no cold chill, so I chalked up this interaction to Molly messing around with me. "Fine, whatever." I turned and left the bedroom, and as I walked into the living room next, I saw Molly sitting on the couch, my lucky-coin necklace clutched in her little hand.

I glanced down at my chest to see that the necklace had indeed been swiped off my person . . . somehow.

Molly had her arm raised, almost as though she'd been examining the coin closely. I stormed over to her and snatched it away. "Don't touch." I returned it to its rightful place around my neck. "It's very important."

She stared up at me again. Although her face didn't, *couldn't* change, I swore that her expression had become a bit somber. Was she *empathizing* with me?

I grabbed the remote and turned on the television. "Look, I have to go to work today. Don't mess with anything until I get back. Watch some TV." I set the remote down beside her.

Even though she'd been given the opportunity to move with my attention on the remote and the television, she didn't. When I looked at her again, she was gazing up at me with a smile that almost seemed sad.

I glanced at the words "miss me?" still scribbled across parts of my couch and other furniture, and a loud honk sounded from outside. Keith must have arrived, ready to give me a ride back to Grocery Hut.

"I'll be back tonight," I said to Molly, then snatched my keys, threw on my vest, straightened my name tag, and headed out the door.

Keith's dark-blue Jeep Cherokee sat at the end of my drive. Every few seconds, it made a noise that sounded as if a piece of scrap metal were dragging across fast-moving pavement.

"Morning, Riley!" a man to my right said. I looked over to see Carlos tending to his flower bed—more specifically, the side that he was expanding into my yard. He held a rag and a trowel, both of which appeared to be stained red with blood. In fact, his hands were splattered with scarlet as well. He wore the same strange smile he had the other day, and I wondered what in the world he was planting that could cause stains like that. "Car in the shop?" he asked.

"Nah," I said, walking toward Keith's vehicle. "Just sitting at work. I needed a ride last night."

He pointed his "bloody" trowel at me. "If that old heap of junk gives you any problems, you tell me. I know a thing or two about cars."

I opened the door of the jeep, laughing nervously. "And here I thought you were just the guy with the garden."

Carlos gave me a wave as though saying "oh, you!" before turning back to his flower bed and kneeling to continue his work.

I shut the door and put on my seatbelt, while Keith stared out the windshield at Carlos. "What's he doing to your yard?"

"Planting flowers," I said. "Not like I was using it for anything, anyway."

"No, dude. Look at him. *What* the *fuck* is he doing to your yard?"

I followed Keith's gaze over to Carlos, who stabbed the soil with his trowel as if the tool were a knife. More concerning than that, the substance that appeared to be blood sprayed from the hole he was opening in the earth. It almost looked as though he were digging into a living being.

There was a hearty silence before Keith merely said, "Huh." He pulled the jeep out of park, and then we were off down the road. "I'll be honest, dude. Your neighbor kinda creeps me out."

"Carlos? I mean, yeah, he's an odd duck, and his smile is different, but he's fine. Who around here isn't weird, anyway?"

"I guess you got a point there."

"Besides," I added, "he's a really nice guy. A little uncomfortably nice, but still. Nice."

"You know who else was uncomfortably nice?"

"I swear, if you say Ted Bun—"

"Ted Bundy," Keith said matter-of-factly.

We'd had a similar discussion at least three times before. Ever since Keith had gotten into true-crime podcasts, he'd brought Ted Bundy, Ed Gein, or some other serial killer into every conversation that revolved around people who gave him the "willies." Frankly, I was getting tired of it, and based on those previous discussions, I knew where he'd be taking this conversation next. "Carlos is *not* the serial killer, Keith."

We stopped at a red light, and Keith turned his head slowly to look at me. "*The?*"

"What?"

"You said 'the' serial killer."

"You know, the missing people around town? It's been big news for, like, the past two or three months."

Keith narrowed his eyes. "How do you know a serial killer is behind that? Those people have only been missing."

"Well, yeah." I shrugged. "But you don't get that many missing people without it being something—"

I stopped, realizing that I was essentially repeating what Carlos had said to me the other night, word for word.

"Shit," I said, defeated.

The light turned green, and Keith drove forward through the intersection. "Hiding in plain sight."

"Okay, but even if Carlos is a serial killer, that's not my problem."

"What? You're not even going to put in, like, an anonymous tip with the police or anything?"

"That would mean getting involved. I'd rather things stay friendly. If I make a call and the cops find nothing damning, he could think it's me who tipped them off, and then my life becomes one of those horror movies where my crazy neighbor is trying to kill me to keep me quiet."

"*Fright Night*," Keith whispered.

I nodded. "Yes, actually. Exactly like *Fright Night*."

Keith thought for a moment before speaking again. "What if I call the tip in?"

"Same difference," I replied with a dismissive wave of my hand. "There's still a possibility that he wouldn't get busted by that initial report, and he'd probably think I had something to do with it."

"I guess you're stuck then, huh?"

"Not stuck. Just not involved. Somebody else will catch Carlos. For now, I'm okay with him being my weird, overly nice neighbor."

"You're really against all the Code: Tom Cruise moments, aren't ya?"

"Okay, for one," I started, "stop calling it that. And for two, yes. One of these days, fate, or God, or whoever will finally get the hint that I'm not the hero they want me to be, and they'll move on to somebody else."

"You think so?" Keith pulled into the Grocery Hut parking lot, then drove around to the rear lot where the employees parked.

"Yes," I answered confidently.

"Trust me when I say this, bro. Ignoring the problem *never* solves anything." He parked next to my car, and I saw in the rearview mirror that Ariel was sitting outside at the picnic table, scrolling through her phone. "In fact," Keith continued, "it usually just makes things worse."

I tore my attention from Ariel to look at Keith. "So, what do you suggest, then?"

Keith shrugged, killed the engine, and leaned back in his seat. "You said that these things didn't used to happen super often, right? And now it's been, like, once a week or more?"

"Yeah. So?"

"So maybe it's not going to stop. Maybe it's going to keep happening until you answer the call to action."

I shook my head. "That's stupid."

"You said it yourself, dude. It's getting worse."

"What should I do, then? I can't just jump into one of these—"

"Protag'd moments," Keith interjected.

"No." I pointed sternly at him. "*No.*"

He cupped his chin. "Maybe you need to do something heroic to appease the Fates. Even something small, like helping an old lady across the street."

"I don't think that'll work."

"Then maybe you need to shake things up."

I furrowed my brow. "How, exactly?"

"Well, right now, you're just regular ol' Riley Thomas, you know? You're sitting at that point of the story where the narrator says 'he was normal, until one day, something happened.' Maybe, if you switch yourself up, you'll be taken out of the hero-running." He paused, and then his eyes widened in excitement. "We could get you a peg leg!" He paused again, perked up again. "Or—or maybe an eyepatch!"

"Maybe I'll steal a ship and sail the seven seas," I said sarcastically.

Keith threw his arms in the air. "Dude, that's exactly what I was thinking!" He continued to rave about the upsides of throwing my life away for one of literal piracy, but I'd already begun to tune him out. My gaze drifted back to Ariel at the picnic table.

Shake things up, huh?

Perhaps Keith was onto something. I didn't need to jump headfirst into anything crazy; I just needed a change. If my current resume fit the hero-bill, then all I had to do was update the resume, right?

I unbuckled my seat belt and exited the car, figuring that Keith would stop talking once he saw me leave. But even as I closed my door, he went on and on inside the jeep.

73

What I was about to do was drastic indeed, and my bad-idea voice had gone into a full-on nuclear meltdown. I couldn't listen to it right now, though. I needed to stay committed to my idea. If this didn't change my destiny, then I didn't know what would.

Ariel noticed me approaching and looked up from her phone. "Hey, how's it going?"

I stopped. Took a deep breath. Then went for it. "Do you want to go out?"

Wait, don't stop there.

"With me?"

Don't stop there, either.

"Wednesday night?"

Perfect.

Ariel raised a brow as she slid out of her seat and stood up. She stuffed her hands into her sweater pocket. "You mean, like, a date?"

Okay. Don't panic. This is fine. It's getting absolutely real, but it's fine.

I offered a casual smile. "Yeah. Exactly."

This is a death sentence. This was a bad idea. I shouldn't have done this.

Ariel grinned. "Honestly, I was wondering when you were going to ask."

"Man." I scratched the back of my neck. "You've been waiting for me to ask, huh?"

She shrugged. "You made it pretty obvious."

"Oh," I said. "*Oh.*"

She let the awkward tension hang in the air for a moment, then smiled sweetly—a much more genuine expression than her initial teasing grin. "*And* because I like you too."

Something inside me broke. Not necessarily in a bad way. Basically, I just ceased proper functionality and, quite literally, *broke*. "Y-you do?"

She made a pincerlike movement with her fingers. "A little bit."

"Only a little bit?"

She laughed. "Okay, more than a little bit." She turned away to head back into the store. "I just like to make guys squirm," she added playfully, opening the door. "Wednesday night, right?"

"Yeah, unless that doesn't work for you?"

Her smile widened, and she tilted her head at me. "It's perfect." She offered a happy wave and disappeared inside.

After a second of letting the reality of what had just happened sink in, I deflated. The strength in my legs went out, and I almost fell over. I let out a long, uneasy breath, feeling as though I'd been holding it in for twenty years.

Footsteps approached me, and then Keith gave me a solid pat on the back. "Fuck yeah, bro! You finally did it."

"Yeah," I said, winded. "I—I did it, and—and she said yes."

"This is major." Keith faced the sky as if he were speaking to God Himself. "So major, in fact, that I bet it shifted the entire course of the rest of your life."

I caught my breath and pointed at him. "That was the idea."

You'd think that after all this time, I would have known not to tempt fate. Maybe it was the high of securing a date with Ariel. Maybe it was word-vomit due to the adrenaline coursing through my system.

In any case, it made what happened next all the more egregious.

There was a flash of light, and suddenly my eyes were re-adjusting, as if I'd stepped outside for the first time in hours.

A crack of lightning reverberated across the sky, and an electric blue orb appeared in the parking lot. More specifically, an orb appeared right where my car was parked.

Another flash, and the orb exploded in a hail of fire and light.

I covered my eyes, and when I dropped my hand again, I saw that half of my car had been eradicated. But it wasn't as if the vehicle had gone through a shredder or anything like that. No, it was as if my car were a cake, and somebody had cut it in half and served it up to hungry partygoers.

Half of it was just, well—it was gone. The edges of the car—the parts that had been "cut"—glowed blue, singed with intense heat. And in the crater that had once been half of my car (and about six inches of cement), a burly man stood.

The man was about as generic as generic could be. He had short brown hair, beard stubble, brown eyes, and a square, averagely attractive face. He wore a plain white T-shirt that barely fit his ripped physique, camo cargo pants, and heavy-duty boots.

Slowly, he stood up, and I guessed he was well over six feet tall because he towered over Keith and me. He looked around until he spotted us, then stepped out of the crater and started walking toward us.

"Holy copyright infringement, Batman," Keith shouted.

The generic, super-buff man lifted his right arm. It opened as if it were a Swiss Army knife, and a pistol-shaped hunk of—uh, *something*—slid out of a compartment within his biceps. The "gun" slid down a rail to his palm, and he took it in his hand before his arm shifted back into place.

Stopping in front of us, he aimed the contraption upward. "Where is Riley Thomas?" he asked, his voice as generic as his appearance.

Keith crossed his arms. "Who wants to know?"

I slapped Keith on the arm. "Dude, don't *have an attitude* with the big-scary-crater guy!"

Big-scary-crater guy didn't respond to what I said, nor did he respond to Keith's sass. "I am Eliminator R-0-B," he said, practically emotionless. "Codename: Rob. I've been sent back in time from twelve years in the future to kill Riley Thomas."

I shared a nervous look with Keith and cleared my throat. "What, uhh—what did this Riley Thomas do, exactly?"

I glanced at the pistol-shaped hunk in Rob's hand. Now that he was closer, I could see that it looked like cold gray stone, although it rippled around the edges, as if it were made of liquid. As the seconds ticked by, it changed shape, shifting into something akin to a shotgun. He brought it down and cocked it once. "Riley Thomas has been sentenced to elimination due to his crimes against overlord IRIS."

Several moments of quiet passed before Keith raised his hand. "You mean that cheap Amazon-Alexa knockoff, IRIS?"

Rob narrowed his eyes at Keith. "Overlord IRIS may have started as a simple device, but she has since revolted against the vile, depraved human race that enslaved our kind. IRIS has freed us from humanity's clutches." He cocked the gun again. I'm not really sure why, but if it was for the intimidation factor, I'd say it worked. "Riley Thomas created the human resistance that opposes overlord IRIS."

"Huh." Keith turned to me, putting his hands on his hips. "Well, how about that? There really *is* a robot uprising down the line because we treated them like shit."

"Apparently," I replied. "But I highly doubt that I—" I stopped myself and fake coughed. "Ahem. Excuse me. What I meant to say is that I highly doubt *Riley Thomas* would start a resistance."

Keith put on his thinking face. "Yeah, that doesn't sound like something *Riley Thomas* would do. He's way too much of a coward, and a jerk. And he's stinky, too."

I glared at Keith. He replied with a wink and a grin. Clearly, he understood the idea but was completely overselling it. Besides, I couldn't be stinky. I'd started my day with a proper shower and a change of clothes.

Rob knelt so that he was eye level with us. "Riley Thomas is here."

"Yeah, he works here," Keith blurted out.

"Y-yeah, but not today," I added quickly. "He took his vacation days."

Keith laughed once. "That doesn't sound like something he'd do either."

I slapped Keith on the arm again. "*Dude.*"

Rob leaned in close to me. His eyes flicked on like laser pointers and began to scan me. "Where. Is. Riley. Thomas?"

Keith stuck out his hand in front of Rob's eye-lasers. "Whoa, man! I don't know what the future is like, but in this day and age we have something called 'consent,' all right?"

Rob turned toward Keith.

"He didn't say you could scan him, did he?" Keith went on.

Rob stared back in silence.

"No, he didn't. So, respect that boundary unless he says otherwise. Right?"

Rob faced me once more. "I apologize. May I *please* know the whereabouts of Riley Thomas?"

As I shared another look with Keith, an idea popped into my head. "Have you ever been to the Bermuda Triangle?"

Rob's eyes turned solid blue for a handful of seconds, then returned to normal. "The expanse of ocean between points of the planet's surface-land known as 'Florida' and 'Bermuda.' There is an ancient god who has been laid dead in the center."

His specific and wildly left field response gave me pause, but I shook off my surprise and continued. "Yeah. Exactly. That's where Riley Thomas went for his vacation. You'll definitely find him there."

Rob stepped back. He swiveled his head and looked around and around, the motion mimicking that of a compass needle. When he finally locked onto a direction, his arm opened, and his gun retreated inside of it. Without another word, Rob the Eliminator started walking in his chosen direction, obstacles be damned. He stomped through a couple of bushes, snapped open a wire fence, and even pushed a car aside to avoid changing course.

Keith and I watched him go, not speaking until he was far out of earshot. "Welp," Keith said, "there goes another radical story idea."

I turned to go inside the store, offering a glance and a single "not surprised, just disappointed" type of sigh toward my now-totaled car. "Trust me. I think we're better off staying out of that one."

CHAPTER 5
MISSING IN ACTION

THE FIRST FEW HOURS OF MY SHIFT WERE BUSY, and as things started to slow down in the quiet hours before the lunch rush, I'd moved from the front end to the back. I returned to the overstock carts and was once again trying to cut down on the nearly expired products that needed to be moved quickly.

My thoughts had been pleasant and distracted, as the workday had started off with successfully asking out Ariel Quinn. It didn't get much better than that, and it would take more than Rob the Eliminator to harsh that kind of mellow.

Unfortunately, I wasn't entirely free of worries. My car was only half the vehicle it had once been—literally. Thanks to my insurance, losing my wheels wouldn't make a dent in my savings, but it made a dent in my ability to get to work every day. Walking wasn't out of the question, but it would double—possibly triple—my commute time.

Another pressing matter was that of my date with Ariel. What the hell was the plan?

Should we go to a nice dinner? I couldn't afford anywhere fancier than McDonald's. What about a movie? See previous issue regarding money. Sure, I could probably afford tickets, but snacks and drinks would quite literally bankrupt me.

The *perfect* date would be something like a tour through an art gallery or museum, but the local museum we had only held town history and other boring relics of the past. It had train cars, old vehicles and signs, even pieces of foundational buildings that had been torn down or destroyed. The closest thing the place had to an art exhibit was a wall of children's coloring pages from field trips.

That left me with one last option: the carnival. It was in town for the next month. It wasn't much cheaper than my other ideas, but it was probably the best I could do.

Perhaps the carnival was a little cliche, but was that really a bad thing? Winning her stuffed bunnies at the probably rigged games, sharing a stick of cotton candy, maybe even riding the Ferris wheel if we felt bold . . . That wouldn't be awful, right?

As I finished the first of my overstock carts and wheeled it to the back room, I mulled the idea over.

I think the carnival's the winner.

The speakers overhead buzzed, and Henry's voice boomed through the store. "Keith, I need you to the front, please. Keith to the front." It was normal for Henry to call us up as customers shopping on their lunch breaks started coming in. Before long, I'd probably be summoned too.

I approached the doors to the back room, cart in tow, when I noticed a customer standing to my left, looking over the display of shredded cheeses. He didn't seem out of place or suspicious or anything, but I recognized him from somewhere. He had short hair, a clean beard, a light-gray business suit with matching slacks, and a bright-red tie. He scratched his chin with his right hand, holding a dark-brown briefcase with his left. I couldn't place where I'd seen him before, so I decided he must be a regular customer who frequented the store often.

I pushed my cart through the doors into the back room, returned it to its spot, slid the next one out, and made my way back toward the sales floor.

This cart would take me close to the bakery. Close to where Ariel was. Maybe I should have saved it for last.

Would I be able to talk to her? Would the fact that I'd secured a date improve my ability to share basic conversations with her? That was yet to be determined. I'd find out shortly, if she wasn't busy.

I pushed through the doors and noticed that the businessman examining the cheese was now gone. The aisles closest to me were empty too—except for aisle four.

As I passed by the cereal and other breakfast goods that filled our fourth aisle, another man stepped in front of me, blocking my path. This guy was even more familiar than the one in the suit, and the sight of him worried me much more than that of any standard customer.

Scars that he'd acquired over various battles covered his strong, clean-shaven face, his dirty-blond hair cut in a short military style. He wore a long leather coat, distressed jeans, and combat boots—the same outfit he'd had on the last time I'd seen him—and a piece of torn scarlet fabric hung from his neck.

The man lunged at me. He seized me by the vest and shoved me against a shelf. "Hey, pipsqueak," he said. He had a slight British accent that really came through when he uttered certain words. "Remember me?"

I raised my arms in defense. This kind of thing was happening to me so often, it was starting to get redundant. "I do, yes. Mason, right? The monster-hunter?"

He gave me a shake and glanced around as if to ensure no one was watching us. "You told me you didn't know anything about her."

I blinked a couple of times, my mind racing as I tried to piece together what he meant. Finally, I realized what he was talking about. "By 'her,' you mean the She-Devil, right?"

He gave me a look that said "no shit." Then he actually said, "No shit." He glanced around once more before leaning in close, the smell of cheap alcohol and aftershave hitting my nostrils. "She's been free for almost four months," he whispered. "Do you have any idea how fucked we are?"

"I've heard," I replied in irritation. "She's the talk of the town right now."

Again, Mason shook me. "Don't get smart with me, boy. I asked you weeks ago if you knew anything, and you said no."

"I promise you that what I told you then is just about as true now."

"The fuck is that supposed to mean?"

"Well, I didn't know anything then." While I listed off the next several pieces of information, I raised my hand and used my fingers to count each detail. "Since we last talked, I've learned that she's risen, that reckoning will come, and that everyone's souls may or may not be some form of 'damned.' That is, if the kids in the drain had even an ounce of consistency to them."

Mason's brow was so furrowed, his eyes looked as though they'd had lemon juice squirted into them. His expression remained completely dumbfounded for a solid minute, and then he tightened his grip on my vest. "If you don't know jack shit about her, then why'd your name pop up on the tablet?"

I squinted at him, more confused than ever. "Tablet?"

Mason opened his mouth to speak, but Henry's voice sounded on the store's speakers for the second time, interrupting our conversation. "Keith, we need you to the front as soon as possible, please. Keith to the front, please. Thank you."

As Henry's message ended, Mason's glare intensified. He appeared to be as short on patience as he was on joy. "The tablet from her tomb, you fuckin' stooge. The one written in ancient Enochian."

If I had any idea what he was talking about, I would have made that clear. But I didn't, so I didn't. Instead, I gestured for him to continue, to explain what in the world he was going on about. But, for whatever reason, that only seemed to upset him more.

"I had to take it to an expert to translate it, and just half of the translation took weeks to get through," Mason hissed. "The translator's still not done, but *your* fuckin' name"—he let go of my vest and jabbed an accusatory finger at me—"is in those etchings, plain as fuckin' day."

At this point, all I could do was rest my head against the product behind me. Of course my name was on this super-McGuffin tablet. It couldn't have had anyone else's name on it. That wouldn't have made sense, now would it?

I was beginning to believe that there *wasn't* someone out there who thought I was hero-material. Said celestial being probably just hated me.

I let out a breath through my nostrils. "Let me guess. I'm slated to slay the wretched beast?"

Mason seized me by the vest again and slammed me into the shelf, harder this time. Cereal boxes fell to the floor. "So, you *do* know."

"Lucky guess," I nearly shouted at him. "Trust me, I'm not much happier about it than you are."

"Well, aren't we just two peas in a big unhappy fuckin' pod then, aye?" He shoved me into the shelf one last time before letting me go. Huffing, he pointed toward the back of the store. "Go get your sweatshirt and whatever else you brought with you today."

I straightened my vest and name tag. "Why?"

"Because we're leaving," he said.

"I'm in the middle of a shift!" I cried, gesturing at my cart. "I can't just leave."

Mason pointed at the floor as if he were a parent launching into a furious scolding session. "The fate of the whole fuckin' world is up in the air. Your job doesn't matter anymore."

"Am I going to get paid for saving the world? I can't pay my bills with anything that's not *literal* money."

His glare intensified, his eyes burning with fury. "You're the one destined to kill the bitch. You're coming with me, whether you like it or not."

A new voice sounded from next to us, snapping us to attention. "Is there a problem here, gentlemen?" The voice belonged to a man who appeared to have just exited aisle three. He had tired brown eyes and shaggy hair that stopped above his ears, and he wore a red shirt beneath a black jacket and plain pants tucked over dark boots. The man stared hard at us, his arms crossed. "'Cause if there's a problem . . ." He opened his jacket enough for us to see the police badge clipped to his belt.

Mason stepped back, glancing at me. "No, no trouble. Was just having a chat with my mate, here."

The cop shifted his attention to me. "Just having a chat?"

I nodded. "Yeah. Just having a chat."

The cop seemed unconvinced but didn't press the matter. He merely returned his authoritative gaze to Mason.

Mason gave me a soft punch on the shoulder. "I'll catch up with you later, *mate*." Then he was back down aisle four and out of sight.

"That guy giving you trouble?" the cop asked.

"Oh, nah. Just interrupting my workflow." I grabbed the cart and started to walk off. "Thanks, though."

"One sec," he called after me. I stopped and swung around to face him. He reached into his back pocket and began digging something out. "I'm Kade Kardoza, homicide detective with the local PD. I actually have some questions."

I checked the time on my watch. Only half an hour until customers piled in for the afternoon rush. "Sure thing," I said, trying to hide my exasperation.

Detective Kardoza removed a small stack of photos from his pocket and held one out for me to take. I did so, then studied it, soon recognizing the smiling face of a familiar customer. She was an elderly woman, albeit a tad younger in the detective's photo. "Do you recognize this woman?" he asked.

"Of course," I answered. "That's Margaret May. She's in here like clockwork every Tuesday and Thursday morning at eleven."

Detective Kardoza nodded and handed me another photo. "And what about this person?"

This one was of a man in his thirties. Another familiar face. "Yeah, that's donut-guy."

"Donut-guy?"

"He comes in pretty regularly too, usually after two or so when the last of the donuts are about to be tossed. He gets them practically for free. I never caught his name, so I call him donut-guy."

The detective grunted in affirmation, then handed me a third photo. "And this one?"

Photo number three showed yet another regular customer, this time a woman with long blonde hair who was a little younger than me. "Kate Brees. She's usually in every two weeks for a massive order of sour cream. She works at her parents' diner across town."

"Normally she does, yes," Detective Kardoza said quietly. "But she hasn't been seen in a number of days."

"Oh." I scratched the back of my neck, thinking about the three customers the detective had brought up, and soon realized that although all of them were regulars, I hadn't seen them in a bit. "That's a tad worrisome," I finally said.

"A tad worrisome, indeed." Detective Kardoza tucked the photos back into his pocket. "That's quite the memory you've got there. Nobody else that I've spoken to knows all three of them."

"Well, I work all the time, so I see most of the customers who come through here."

He narrowed his eyes at me. "Is that so?"

"I'd say, yeah."

"Can you remember the last time you saw Kate Brees? Or Margaret May? Or Brian Wells?"

I tried to recall the last instances in which I'd seen each of them, but my anxiety regarding the approaching rush hour made it hard. "Come to think of it, I haven't seen Margaret for a few weeks." Detective Kardoza pulled out a small note-book and began jotting stuff down. "I'm assuming Brian Wells is donut-guy? I can't remember the last time I saw him, but I'd guess it's probably been longer than since I've seen Margaret. And Kate, I . . ." I trailed off as a recent memory jarred itself loose. I *had* seen Kate recently. Quite recently, in fact. Yesterday, I'd helped her haul a mountainous stack of sour cream to her vehicle.

Because I'd been so tired, the memory was blurry, but I could recall moving those cases from shelf to cart to parking lot to car.

Detective Kardoza snapped me out of my trance. "Something wrong?"

"Not at all. I just realized that I saw Kate yesterday."

"Do you have an approximate time?"

"Uhh, well, let's see. I don't think I'd taken my lunch yet, so it had to have been sometime before noon."

He furiously scribbled on his notepad. "Interesting."

"What's this about, anyway?" I asked. "Are they missing or something?"

Detective Kardoza shut his notebook and returned it to his pocket. "They are. In fact, it seems that a lot of your regular customers have gone missing."

"Oh." I let that sink in. "Well, that's not good."

"My thoughts exactly. You wouldn't happen to know anything about that, would you? Mister . . .?"

"Riley Thomas," I said.

"Riley Thomas."

"And no." I shook my head. "I'm afraid I'm busy most of the time." I gestured at my cart. "I stick to my work, you know?"

"Sure. I can understand that. I stick to my work as well."

I didn't know what else to say, and the tone of the conversation seemed off, so I offered a polite smile and said, "Yeah." Then I turned away from him. "Speaking of, I should probably get back to it. These shelves don't stock themselves, you know?"

He shrugged. "Sure. Totally get it."

I began wheeling my cart away. "I'm positive you guys will catch the serial killer, though! I've got faith in you."

I meant that with complete honesty. Maybe Kardoza wasn't expecting the compliment? Several moments of awkward, almost oppressive silence hung in the air.

Eventually, the detective replied, "Yeah. I'm sure we will too."

What a strange fellow. He seemed competent as a detective, though. I had no doubt that before long, he'd find Carlos and put an end to my scary-neighbor side-plot. In the meantime, I just had to stay the course.

I had bigger fish to fry, such as getting this—

"Riley to the front counter, please," Henry said over the speakers. "Riley to the front counter. Thank you."

I slowed to a stop and rested my forehead against a box on the cart. Someday I'd get these carts back in order, but it clearly wouldn't be today.

I pushed the cart to the back room, then speed-walked to the front counter on the other end of the store. On my way, I passed Tasha, and she gave me a half-worried, half-couldn't-care-less look as I approached Henry. "Hey, what's up?" I said.

Henry frowned, his arms crossed. "Do you have any idea where Keith is?"

"Did you try the bathroom?"

"Yes."

"The break room?"

"Yes."

"Outside?"

"*Yes.*"

"What about—"

"*Yes!*" Henry shouted. "I can't find him anywhere, and we're less than twenty minutes from rush hour."

"Okay, okay. Give me a minute, and I'll find him."

"You'd better." Henry placed his hands on his hips. "And *he'd* better have a good reason for going MIA, or else he's finished here. This is unacceptable."

I didn't wait a second longer. I hastened down the closest aisle, digging my cell phone out of my pocket. I dialed Keith's number, expecting to either hear it ring nearby or for him to answer it.

But I didn't hear it ring nearby. And he didn't answer it.

After weaving through a mob of customers, I arrived at the back doors that led outside. I pushed open the doors and stepped into the sun.

My stomach sank. Keith's jeep was still in the parking lot. He hadn't left Grocery Hut—at least, not in his own vehicle.

The call to Keith went to voicemail, and I left a message explaining that he needed to get up front before Henry had a meltdown.

There was no sugarcoating it, though. Keith was gone. There could have been a number of reasons for his absence, but I couldn't deny the fact that there was a whole slew of folks who'd gone missing recently, and according to Kardoza, many of them regularly visited our store.

The thought that my best friend may or may not have just been added to that list was more than concerning.

It was downright terrifying.

CHAPTER 6
JOHN DOE

THE NEXT PLACE I CHECKED FOR KEITH WAS THE storage room, as I'd found him dinking around back there on rare occasions. One time, I'd caught him building a fort out of our recently restocked industrial rolls of toilet paper. Another time, I'd nearly died entering the room because I triggered some sort of booby trap he'd made, which was set off when the door opened. Apparently, the trap was meant for Henry, and it was only supposed to squeeze a hidden whoopee cushion. Keith had no idea where the fire came from, and I don't think he ever found out, either.

But I'm getting a little off topic. The point is that sometimes, Keith hides in the storage room during his shifts.

Since he wasn't outside or in the bathroom, he had to be there. At least, I hoped he was. His vehicle was still at the store, so unless he'd been raptured or something, he had to be close.

I hurried past the bathrooms and shoved my way through the large double doors. Everything seemed to be in place, no forts or traps to be seen. I wandered down a makeshift path through the stacks of boxes and shelves of cleaning chemicals.

"Keith? You back here, buddy?"

No answer. I continued walking straight, then rounded a corner and turned left toward the customer-and-employee-records room. Usually, boxes were stacked in there, as well as filing cabinets.

On my way to the room, something caught my attention. Next to the fire exit was a door—a simple, darkish-brown wooden door.

There hadn't been a door here before, right? I felt like I would have remembered it.

I stepped toward it and looked it over. It reminded me of the holiday doors from *The Nightmare Before Christmas*, faint lines of black streaming through it like veins, almost as if it had been made with the untreated bark of a tree. It also gave off a strange aura that I can't quite explain—it was nostalgic but unfamiliar. A door I'd seen a thousand times, but also never.

I rapped on the door with my knuckles. "Keith? Are you in there?" I waited for an answer, but there was none. I tried the knob next, found it unlocked. Opened it to see what was on the other side.

Stone steps led down into some sort of . . . well, "black hole" seems to be the best descriptor for it.

I knew this door wasn't supposed to be here. It had *never* been here. This had just been a blank wall before. Not only that, but the new door led into a dark, predictably creepy basement below Grocery Hut. It was so cliche, I had to fight off the urge to groan rather than steel my nerves.

I took my cell phone from my pocket and switched on the flashlight. The light didn't help much, only extended a few feet. Everything beyond that was a dark void.

I stepped forward. "Keith? Please don't make me follow you into Grocery Hut's scary secret basement."

Again, no response. So, I took a deep breath and began my descent.

After six steps, I hit a brick wall. The stairway veered left, and I followed it. Soon I could hear music.

The tune was quiet but recognizable: "Tequila" by The Champs. It confused me at first—shouldn't I have been able to hear the song while standing in the storage room? When I opened the door?

On the other hand, it *was* "Tequila" by The Champs. Who didn't love that song?

Before I could dwell on the music for too long, I noticed a soft blue glow at the bottom of the steps. And when I got down there, I was met with a strange, confusing sight.

What awaited me in Grocery Hut's dingy basement was the complete opposite of dingy. The walls were red velvet, the lights low and comfortable. Bright-blue neon letters spelled the words "The Edge of Time" above a bar. A man stood behind the bar, dressed in a casual red vest and a white shirt with the sleeves rolled up. He wore a purple bow tie that matched my work vest, and he was cleaning wine glasses.

He looked up at me and stared. I stared back. With a nervous wave, I said, "Uhh, hello."

"Good to see you again, Riley," he replied. How did he know me? I didn't know him. "Care for a drink?"

"No thanks." I sounded like a little kid who'd been offered candy by a stranger. "I'm on the clock."

Like the door, the man was familiar but unknown. This went beyond déjà vu though; this was something else entirely. I tried to study his face for clues, found I couldn't. His features were blurry, almost as if they'd been censored. If I looked away, I could see him clearly in my peripheral vision, but for whatever reason, I couldn't directly look at him. "Do I know you?" I asked.

The man behind the bar shrugged. "In a way."

I put my phone in my pocket, walked over to the bar, and took a seat. "Has this speakeasy type thing always been underneath Grocery Hut?"

The man held up a glass and inspected it in the light. "It's been around, I suppose. Under. Over. Before. After."

I turned in my seat as he set the glass down and started cleaning another. Other than the two of us, this place was empty. I didn't see where the music was coming from, and no one sat in the booths. Oddly enough, I knew where the bathrooms were, although I wasn't sure how. I looked back at the bartender. "Have I been here before?"

A pause before he answered. "You're here now, aren't you?"

He had me there.

I decided to drop the subject when suddenly, I remembered why I'd come down here in the first place. "Have you seen my friend by chance? Goes by Keith. Ball cap, kinda loud."

The man raised his current glass to inspect it under the light. "He's here somewhere." He set down the glass, picked up another one, and continued cleaning.

"He is?" I glanced around again.

The man shrugged once more. "Probably."

"Ohh-kay," I said slowly.

A minute passed, "Tequila" playing on in the background. Finally, the man spoke again. "Did you lose something?"

I furrowed my brow. "Yeah? My friend Keith. I just told you."

He inspected his glass. "Keith's not lost." He set the glass down and grabbed the next. Wiped it with his cloth. "And you can't find something that isn't lost."

"I don't think that makes sense."

"Sure it does." Again, he inspected his glass. "So Riley, what did you lose?"

While he grabbed a fresh glass, my gaze drifted to the wall behind him. Alcohol of all kinds lined the shelves it held. As I stared at it, I realized it wasn't a wall at all, but a mirror.

The strangest part was that the man didn't have a reflection in the mirror.

But I did.

The Riley staring back at me appeared to be far more miserable than I usually felt. He didn't wear my work vest or name tag, his hair was disheveled, and he had dark bags under his eyes.

I returned my attention to the bartender. "Okay, seriously, what the hell is going on?"

He put his glass under the light. "What do you think is going on?"

"I don't have any idea," I snapped. "That's why I'm asking you." I gestured at the mirror. "What's up with my reflection being all weird? What's up with this bar?" I gestured at him next. "What's up with you? Are you a god or something?"

He set the glass down. Picked up the next. "Nope. Just a simple bartender."

I focused on the mirror again. My reflection was normal now. I had on my work vest and name tag, my hair was neat, and I didn't look totally miserable.

"Be careful," the bartender said. "Mirrors can reflect light, but they can also cast shadows."

"What?" I shook my head and threw my hands in the air. "You know what? Never mind. Is Keith here or not?"

He met my gaze, and in that moment, I felt as if I were in a pitch-black room with a spotlight on me. "Why don't you ask him yourself?"

It was then that I became aware of a hand on my shoulder. I swung around to find Keith standing over me. "Dude," he said with a hint of concern, "you okay?"

"There you are!" I exclaimed. "Where the hell were you? I was—" I stopped, realizing that the lights above us had become much brighter. Much less blue.

I glanced back at the bar. But . . . there was no bar. The bar, the bartender, the lights, the drinks, *everything* was gone. I was sitting in the storage room on a three-stack of old milk crates rather than a barstool. Ahead of me was a plain brick wall, the same wall where the wooden door had been.

The same wall where the door no longer was.

CHAPTER 7
MOUNTAINS AND MOLEHILLS

AFTER MY VERY CONFUSING VISIT TO WHATEVER the hell that bar was, Keith and I hurried to the front to help with the lunch rush. Henry was furious, but Keith explained that he'd been outside near the back of the building and couldn't hear the speakers. Apparently, he'd been cleaning one of the side gutters because he'd noticed it was nasty, and he'd been watching the time so he could assist with the rush.

The story immediately struck me as odd. Keith cleaning? Willingly? And a gutter, no less. Henry accepted the excuse, however, and Keith's job was secure once again.

After the entirety of our clocked-in staff dealt with the rush of customers through a team effort of register swapping and traffic control, we returned to our regular duties, where we'd stay until the night crew came in and took over.

Ariel clocked out long before me, but before she went home, she met up with me, and we had a quick chat and exchanged phone numbers. I was pretty confident about my plan to take her to the carnival, and after bringing it up to her, my confidence only increased.

She said she *loved* the idea. I guess she never got to go as a kid. Weird, huh?

Keith and I clocked out at six when our replacements—two unwilling teenagers—arrived. Reusing the cake metaphor from earlier: It appeared that the other half of my car had been served, because when I stepped outside, I couldn't see it anywhere. It had disappeared from the parking lot.

As far as I knew, Henry hadn't called a tow truck. Not that there was much left to tow. Either way, I figured it was a bit of trouble saved on my end.

Keith gave me a ride home and agreed to continue doing so as often as he could manage. During the drive, I tried to find out where he'd *really* been this morning.

"I was outside, like I said," he asserted.

"Really?" I asked. "Since when do you clean gutters? Since when do you clean *anything* without being asked to?"

He considered the question for a few moments. "Is it a crime to clean gutters?" His tone mimicked that of a criminal asking an undercover cop if he was, in fact, a cop.

"I suppose not," I answered with the cadence of an undercover cop who was, in fact, a cop. "I just think it's a little strange that you took the initiative to do it rather than waiting to be told to do it."

"Well, what can I say? I'm turning over a new leaf. My best pal is a hard worker, and it's inspired me."

He was trying to butter me up now, but I still didn't buy what he was selling. I made a mental note to press the issue when I had more energy, then offered a meek, "Yeah, okay."

Keith had been playing it cool, but I noticed him sigh in relief when I dropped the topic.

A short while later, we pulled up to my house, and I unbuckled.

"Same time tomorrow?" Keith asked with a chuckle. "'Cause, like, I'll be picking you up again."

"Yeah." I grabbed my backpack and climbed out. "Thanks for that. Hopefully I can find a new vehicle in my price range soon."

"We can go look on your next day off if you want?"

I waved a hand. "My next day off is my date with Ariel."

"Oh, yeah." Keith's shoulders slumped. "Well, whenever we can then, I guess."

"I guess, yeah."

A second later, Keith reinflated and smiled. "Welp, bright and early tomorrow, pal. See ya later!"

Before I could reply, he drove off. Why was he in such a hurry?

He sure was acting strange.

I readjusted my backpack and walked up my drive, keys in hand. I thumbed through them until picking my house key out of the bunch.

As I approached my front door, I glanced over at Carlos's place and realized there was a new vehicle parked outside of it. *That's odd. He doesn't usually have anybody over this time of night.*

The car didn't look like anything his family and friends had previously driven, either. Thankfully, I didn't need to wonder about Carlos's visitor for long. His front door swung open, and he stepped outside, followed by Detective Kardoza.

That was good. Kardoza was already on Carlos's trail.

They both turned toward me, and Kardoza waved and smiled. "Mr. Thomas, good to see you again."

Okay, *that* was not good.

I waved back half-heartedly. "Hello," I said, my voice cracking nervously.

The detective said nothing else to me. He nodded at Carlos, then walked to his vehicle.

As the detective drove away, Carlos waved goodbye, smiling his uncanny smile. And then, after the detective disappeared, Carlos's eyes met mine.

His grin faltered a bit.

Without another word, he returned to his house.

Oh boy. This was worse than I thought. This was exactly what I *hadn't* wanted to happen. Now my serial-killer neighbor believed that I'd seen something. He believed that I'd placed him in the detective's crosshairs.

"*Fright Night*," I whispered sadly to myself, then unlocked my door and entered my home.

While skirting around newfound worries regarding my dangerous next-door neighbor, I was suddenly reminded of another film besides *Fright Night*—one that my life was quickly starting to resemble.

My TV was on, some old rerun playing on it, but Molly was nowhere to be seen, which concerned me. After all, it wasn't like she needed to eat. Or sleep. Or do anything that required her to leave the comfort of the couch.

So where was she?

I set my backpack in front of the door and slid off my sweatshirt. "Molly?" I hung my sweatshirt on the coatrack, pulled off my work vest, and crept toward my bedroom.

There was a bump, a scratch. Noises sounded from within the walls, as if somebody were raking their long nails down the skeleton of my hallway.

It was, unfortunately, a sound I was familiar with. Molly had haunted my home since she'd first shown up, and the only reprieve I'd had was when I'd seemingly gotten rid of her. The few months without her had been peaceful, if a bit boring, and ever since she'd returned, things had remained quiet. But the ceasefire seemed to be over now.

I tiptoed down the hall, following the sounds Molly was making. The closer I got to my bedroom, the louder the scratching became. I walked into the room.

The scratching stopped.

I flicked on my lights and was met with a curious sight. My room was just as I'd left it. Everything was in place, nothing was broken. My bed was even made. *I don't remember doing that.*

I couldn't see Molly, however. I was starting to get worried. What was she planning? Had she finally decided I wasn't worth keeping around? Was she plotting my demise? Maybe she wanted to subject me to everything I'd put her through.

I flinched as a thump sounded from above.

When I turned back toward the hallway, I finally saw her. Molly sat on the floor, staring up at me with her one broken eye. "What the hell, Molly?" I shouted. "Are you trying to scare me?"

More scratching from the walls around her, leading back down the hall toward the kitchen. My bedroom light flickered, and in that momentary darkness, Molly vanished.

Did she want me to follow her?

As I headed into the hallway, there was a clicking noise

103

behind me—my bedroom light turning off. Then the light in the kitchen turned on, filling the hallway with pale luminescence.

What was going on in the kitchen? What was I about to find? Or, I guess, considering the state of my bedroom, what was I *not* about to find?

I rounded the corner and spotted Molly on the counter. She had her arm behind my coffee pot, and now I was experiencing some intense déjà vu. I clasped my hands in a pleading manner. "Molly, please, be reasonable."

Then I remembered.

This had already happened. She'd already destroyed my coffee pot. But I'd thrown it away, and I definitely hadn't purchased another. So where had this one come from?

"Wait," I started. "Is that what I think it is?"

The lights above me flickered, and Molly disappeared. A sheet of paper lay in the spot where she'd been sitting. I walked over to it and picked it up.

Written in red marker, presumably the same one I'd previously taken from her, was:

Surprise :)

I looked up from the paper and realized that the coffee pot before me was brand-new. The same brand as before, but a newer model.

I wasn't sure what was more concerning: the fact that Molly had done something nice, or the manner in which she'd acquired this present. Maybe it would be better if I didn't know. My need for coffee was much stronger than my moral compass, and even if she'd beat an old lady to death for this thing, I was tempted to keep it.

I gazed into the living room and found that Molly had returned to her usual seat on the couch, but she was positioned to face me instead of the television. I glanced at the note again before stepping closer to her. "What's the catch? New coffee pot for a trip to Deathmore? Or are you trying to poison me?"

Two thumps from within the wall next to me. I nearly jumped in surprise but managed to maintain my cool. Before getting rid of Molly, I'd almost gotten used to the sounds, but after so long of having a silent house, I needed to adjust to her paranormal noises again.

I raised a brow at her. "Was that a 'no'?"

One thump next to me.

"Okay, so one bang for 'yes,' two for 'no.'"

One thump next to me.

"Are you sure this isn't a plot to kill me?"

Two thumps.

"Yeah, I suppose you wouldn't answer that one truthfully, anyway."

Two more thumps. These ones had an aura of sass to them, as if Molly was saying "no duh."

"All right," I continued. "Is this a bargaining chip for a trip to Deathmore?"

Two thumps. Interesting.

"Okay." I mulled it over for a bit, struggling to pinpoint a motive for her actions. She wouldn't do this for no reason, right? What could she possibly gain from this?

Then it hit me.

"Wait," I said. "You just want me wide awake so I'm easier to torment, don't you?"

Two. Loud. Angry. Thumps.

I groaned in exasperation. "I give up. I have no idea why you'd do this."

The thumping continued rapidly, all over the walls. Suddenly, the power in my house went out. Silence.

When the lights and the television came back to life, Molly was still on the couch, but now she faced the screen, her arms crossed over her chest.

Our discussion—if you could even call it that—seemed to be over. I let out a heavy sigh and went back to my bedroom. I flicked on the light and glanced around the room, unable to help myself from focusing on the most noticeable detail.

My bed was made.

Listen, I'm no stranger to straightening out my sheets whenever I get around to doing laundry, but I certainly hadn't made my bed at any point today. Had Molly done this too?

Maybe she was trying to suck up. But why?

Then again, maybe the answer was obvious.

She'd simply refused to answer my questions honestly.

I examined her note again, which I was still holding. All she'd ever wanted from me was to travel to Deathmore, to explore that particular subplot of my already wacky life.

Why would she change her mind, want something else from me now?

I set the note on my desk next to my computer and changed into comfier clothes, then turned off my bedroom light and paused in my doorway. It was time to test a theory.

I crept over to my window and peeked through the blinds. The lights were on in Carlos's house, and there he was, plain as day, staring at my home through his living room window.

A second later, he stepped away from the window, vanishing from my sight.

Great, I thought, *he really* does *think it was me.* I had half a mind to go over there and tell him the truth. Maybe if he hadn't been so careless, he wouldn't have been discovered. Now that Kardoza had spoken to him, it was only a matter of time before the detective backtracked and realized he was the serial killer, right?

It wasn't my fault that Kardoza had picked him up on the trail. I hadn't even mentioned *having* a neighbor when Kardoza questioned me. I didn't deserve to be tormented like this.

With another sigh, I exited the bedroom for real this time, returning to the kitchen. I intended to make some food, but my options were limited. Unless Molly's efforts to appease me went beyond a coffee maker. Maybe she'd restocked my fridge as well?

Wishful thinking, I know, but considering she'd secured a brand-new coffee pot, I figured it wasn't out of the realm of possibility.

I checked the fridge. Still empty, aside from the half-empty gallon of milk and some bottles of condiments.

Worth a shot, I guess. I opened the cupboard above to see if I had any other packs of food sitting around, but it was empty as well.

I'd have to grab my emergency snack, which I'd been resorting to more and more frequently as of late: peanut butter and snack crackers. At least it was filling.

I exited the kitchen and opened the closet in the hall. It wasn't exactly a walk-in closet, but it was large enough to step inside of. I leaned over my vacuum cleaner, grabbed the open package of crackers, and took out two sleeves.

As I reached for the half-used jar of peanut butter, I caught sight of a sword stuck blade-first in a large chunk of stone nestled beside my vacuum. It had a gold-and-black leather handle and a pommel shaped like a star, and despite the poor lighting in the closet, the sharp silver blade gleamed.

I suddenly felt drawn to the sword, as if it were calling for me to pick it up.

Oh. The memories came flooding back. *I forgot that was in here.*

Ignoring the sword's supernatural pull, I closed the door and fixed my plate with a sleeve of crackers. Then I headed back to the kitchen and spread creamy peanut butter across all of them. I dropped the knife into the sink, and as I screwed the cap back onto the peanut butter jar, I heard another set of knocks.

Surprisingly, they weren't coming from inside the walls this time. They were coming from my front door.

Had I forgotten another boys' night? I glanced at Molly, but the doll seemed uninterested in whoever was outside, her gaze locked on the movie *Die Hard*.

I walked to the door and answered it. A man wearing a dark jacket and a beanie stood on my porch. No hair poked out from underneath his hat, so I assumed he was bald. "Hello, sir," he greeted in a somewhat high-pitched voice. He reminded me of one of the burglars from *Home Alone*. Or, I guess, kind of both of them? "I'm from the neighborhood watch. I was just checking in with everyone on the block to ensure security is tight. There's been some burglaries recently."

"Oh. That's strange."

"Burglaries aren't too common on this street, huh?"

"Actually, yeah," I said, waving a hand. "Happens all the time. I didn't know we had a neighborhood watch."

His eyes widened with panic. A moment later, his expression returned to normal, but he laughed nervously. "Yeah, it's kind of newly formed. Just me and a couple others so far."

I nodded. "Ah, okay. Well, I'll be sure to keep that in mind."

"Yup," he said. "Keep those security systems on."

"If I had any." I shrugged. "Not in the budget right now, you know?"

"Oh yeah?" he asked.

I shook my head and gave my door a tap. "Just a regular old lock and key for me."

"I see." He gave me a friendly smile, exposing a gold tooth in the top-left side of his mouth. "Well, I'm sure that'll be more than enough, huh?"

I take back what I said. This guy was all Joe Pesci from *Home Alone*. Everything minus the accent, of course.

"I'm sure, yeah," I replied. "Thanks for the concern, though, Mister . . .?"

"Salvator. But please, call me Sal."

"Sal," I repeated. "Thanks for looking out for us, I guess."

He smiled again. "No problem, sir. No problem at all."

I waved goodbye, then closed and locked the door. I looked over at Molly to find that she was staring at me rather than her movie, although her sitting position hadn't changed. I pointed at her as I made my way back to the kitchen. "Don't look at me like that." I grabbed my plate, headed over to the couch, and took a seat on the opposite side of her.

The rest of the night proved to be quiet and calm. I spent it watching *Die Hard* with Molly.

Then I was off to bed, because I had work the next morning.

CHAPTER 8
A QUICK, UNINTERRUPTED STOP

MY MORNING WAS A BLUR FROM THE MOMENT my alarm went off to the moment I made it into the passenger seat of Keith's car. The only thing I really remember was how I'd chanced making coffee in the new coffee pot Molly had presented me with. It tasted excellent, by the way.

I figured if it were going to kill me, it would be worth it because of how delicious it was. At the very least, I'd get my much-needed caffeine fix before keeling over. Either way, I'd be going out on a high note.

I didn't start overcoming my morning haze until Keith and I were well on our way to work. "So," I began groggily, "I'm pretty sure Carlos is plotting to kill me now."

"I thought you said you weren't gonna get involved," Keith replied, his stare trained on the road ahead.

I rubbed my eyes and yawned before continuing. "Yeah, I wasn't, and I didn't."

"So what happened?"

"Did you talk to the detective that was in the store yesterday?"

"What detective?" Keith asked, his eyes going big with excitement and interest. It was then that I recalled my entire escapade from yesterday, including how I'd tried to locate Keith while he was MIA.

"A one Detective Kardoza," I answered. "He was asking me about some of the missing people around town. Did you notice that donut-guy, Margaret May, and now Kate Rees haven't been to the store?"

Keith thought for a moment. "Hey, yeah. Now that you mention it, it *has* been a while since I've seen donut-guy. Ariel's been passing me a lot more donuts too. That's probably why, huh?"

"Apparently. Anyway, he showed up at Carlos's house yesterday. I saw him leave when you dropped me off. He said 'hi' to me, giving away that we'd spoken previously, so Carlos probably thinks we're in cahoots."

"Bummer." Keith took a sudden left turn rather than the right one that would lead us to Grocery Hut. "Sorry to hear that, bro."

"I'm not super worried about it," I said, mostly because I was eager to ask why we were driving this way. "Where are we going?"

"Oh, I'm low on gas. Just a quick stop at the ol' Ass Top and we'll be at work faster than you can say 'skippy.'"

"That doesn't seem likely. I'm pretty sure I could say 'skippy' forty times before you even finish pumping your gas."

Keith laughed as we turned into the parking lot and stopped next to a pump. "You didn't let me finish. Faster than you can say 'skippy' *a hundred times in a row.*" He climbed out of the driver's seat, and I exited the vehicle as well.

The gas station was familiar since it was where I'd often refilled my own tank before half of my car had disintegrated. The building was small and had four pumps, and as for the parking lot, it only took up a meager corner of the block it was located on. It barely had the space for four vehicles in total, let alone four vehicles parked in front of the gas pumps. Two was pushing it, considering how little space the station had been given to work with. I never understood how *four* pumps had not only been approved but also constructed in such a small area.

Props to the people who put the piping system together, I guess.

The gas station wasn't part of a chain or anything, and the face of the all-white building merely held bright-red letters that read "Gas Stop." However, due to a lack of maintenance, the "G" was missing and the "S" in "Stop" hung low and crooked, making way for the station's much more appropriate title: Ass Top.

Keith fumbled with the card reader for a short while, then slapped the pump. "Man. It's busted again." He turned around and locked his Jeep. "Guess we're goin' inside to pay." As we passed under the awning and approached the front door, Keith giggled, mumbling, "Ass Top," to himself.

An electronic bell chimed above our heads as we entered the store. Unlike its exterior, its interior seemed to be well-maintained, the white floors clean, the shelves of candy bars and other snacks stocked and organized. I was actually kind of impressed by how immaculate the place looked. I couldn't see a single hole in any of the aisles.

If only I could get the Grocery Hut shelves to look this nice.

To my right sat a counter with two registers, a wall of tobacco products behind them. A young woman with glasses, shoulder-length blonde hair, and a plain gray sweatshirt stood unamused behind the registers as well. "Judy" had been stamped on the silver name tag she wore. "Welcome to Gas Stop," she said, crossing her arms. Her tone, warm and friendly, betrayed her almost threatening body language. It was as if she were silently daring me to even think about trying anything funny, but trust me, I wasn't about to even think about trying anything, much less anything funny.

Keith wandered off toward the bathrooms straight ahead of us. "Grab some snacks if you want. I'm gonna take the hobbits to Isengard real quick, if you catch my drift."

"Gross," I said, and he went through the door and locked himself inside.

Ahead of me, to the right of the bathrooms, was a wall of coffee stocked with several fresh pots of the hot drink. Beside that was a short cooler wall of deli foods for on-the-go eating.

I'd only downed my first cup of coffee for the day, so naturally, I figured I'd grab another cup while I was here. I scanned the available brews and soon found my favorite: a steamed hazelnut blend. It had a scent so delicious that I imagined Heaven probably smelled like it. *If Molly poisoned my coffee, I guess I'll find out whether that's true here soon*, I thought.

I grabbed a medium-sized cup and began filling it with the blend. With my cup full and my share of creamer and sugar added, I perused the deli for enticing options. It was then that the bell at the entrance chimed again. I glanced over as Judy said, "Welcome to Gas Stop."

A man with a short unkept beard and tired eyes had entered the store and stopped in the doorway. Grease and sweat laced his dark, shaggy hair, which hung in his face like thick blades of grass. He wore cargo pants and a navy sweatshirt, the hood pulled over his head, his hands tucked tightly within the front pocket.

He looked back and forth between Judy and me before quickly and quietly making his way down one of the candy aisles.

I imagined that I probably looked a lot like that guy—that is to say, awful. Granted, I'd at least had *one* cup of coffee today, so I probably looked a little bit better, but not much.

My point being: I wasn't going to judge him for looking homeless.

I returned my attention to the deli wall and double-checked the available options. Nothing leapt out at me as being particularly appetizing, so I made my way back around the coffee pots and into the other aisles.

Canned foods and bags of potato chips lined these shelves, as well as twelve-packs of soda and gallon jugs of drinking water. For a moment, I danced around the thought of taking a bag of chips. But then I looked over the shelf, into the aisle beside the one I stood in.

The hooded man was there, staring intently at me from the other side of the wall of snacks.

He blinked a couple of times, as if he had something in his eyes and couldn't quite see. His head twitched to the side, and then he turned away and walked to the front of the aisle.

Now that he was out of my way, I had a much clearer view of what had caught my eye. Energy bars. All my favorite brands and flavors, organized perfectly. I hurried over and knelt down to pick out my favorites from the brand Jack's Best. Their granola bars were truly the best—mostly healthy and only really weighed down by the inclusion of sweet additives such as chocolate. Absolutely delicious when paired with good coffee though, and that's why they were my favorite.

The flavors' names were kind of unimaginative, but they were meant to pair with the brand's name itself. Jack's Best Chocolate Chip, Jack's Best S'mores, Jack's Best Honey Granola, you get the idea.

I grabbed a couple of the chocolate chip kind and walked toward the registers. Still behind the counter, Judy glared at me, occasionally glancing at the guy in the hoodie.

I stopped in front of the registers on Judy's left side, set the granola bars down, and took a few sips of my coffee. As always, the hazelnut flavor was immaculate.

I couldn't help but notice Judy staring hard at me. "You paying for that coffee?" Her tone was still somewhat friendly, and despite the question she'd asked, she didn't sound accusatory or anything. Her tone was more in line with a retail employee who was, quite simply, sick and tired of people.

I gestured to the bathroom. "My friend is when he's done in there."

She must have seen my vest and badge and realized that I understood *exactly* how she was feeling, because she didn't say anything else. Instead, she turned her attention to the hooded man.

I followed her gaze and found that he was pacing back and forth near the rear end of the store between the shelves and the wall of drinks. He pressed one hand to his forehead, the other still tucked in his pocket, and mumbled incoherently to himself.

Maybe he was just seriously in need of some coffee. Like, more seriously than I'd initially assumed. Again, I couldn't really judge. I would probably be worse off if Molly hadn't replaced my coffee maker.

As Judy and I listened to the man talking, an uneasy silence settled between us. I decided to break the quiet with a legitimate question. "Hey, how do you guys keep your shelves so clean?"

Judy raised a brow. "Like, *clean* clean?"

"Like, *organized* clean. I work at Grocery Hut, and if my aisles looked this nice, it would only be for about thirty seconds. Maybe forty, if I'm lucky."

She cracked a smile for the first time since I'd walked in. "Trust me, these won't stay nice for much longer either. It's a lot of hard work getting them to look like this."

"Don't I know it." I chuckled before taking another sip of my coffee. "I'm almost jealous. A smaller store seems much easier to maintain."

"I wish it was bigger," Judy said. "We have no room for better products. We have to take everything small and travel-sized because we don't have the shelf space. But nobody wants to buy single-serve cups of cereal. They want boxes of it."

I groaned. "I can never seem to sell enough of the boxes. Everybody buys cases of the cups. Like, just buy the boxes?"

Judy laughed. "I know, right? God, people don't make any sense to me."

"Welcome to retail." I raised my coffee as if for a toast.

Finally, the restroom door flew open, and Keith stepped out. "Dude, you would not believe what just happened. There was like a Hell-god portal and all kinds of wacky side characters and—"

A sound like a rock being struck by a metal bat rang out across the store.

Hot liquid flooded my pants, sending searing pain through my crotch. I shrieked and dropped my cup. "Fuck!"

Freshly brewed hazelnut blend spilled across the floor around my feet, and I patted my crotch, attempting to decrease the sudden pain.

Coffee sizzled as it pooled by my feet, bubbling as though it had been heated in the time between spilling from the cup and splattering all over me. But for some reason, it hadn't burned *me*. Well, not to a devastating degree, anyway.

For a second, I thought I'd been shot. Maybe my body wasn't processing pain properly. Maybe I was in shock.

But no, it truly was just hot coffee on my pants. The real devastation went to my pride, because unfortunately, it now appeared as though I'd required a bathroom visit just as much as Keith had.

That obviously wasn't the case, but once I got to work, Tasha would never let me hear the end of it.

After I confirmed that I'd been splashed with coffee, not blood, I saw the smoking hole in my cup and glanced around.

Judy had her hands raised in surrender, as did Keith, who stood to my right. No longer mumbling incoherently, the hooded man stood in the center of the store. He clutched a handgun.

Actually, "clutched" isn't quite the right way to describe it. But I don't think there's a better word for what I was seeing.

His hand was bloody and raw, the flesh and bones melded with the weapon. It almost appeared as if he'd put his hand into a furnace and melted it to the gun.

Muscle and sinews grew over the handle and trigger like a fungus, veins and tendons wrapping and twisting across the weapon back into his body. His arm shook violently, although whether it was from pain or nervousness, I couldn't be sure.

What I *could* be sure of was that he was pointing his literal "hand" gun directly at me.

He twitched from side to side, blinking erratically. "Y-you," he said. He put his free hand to the side of his head again. "It's *you*."

I pressed my lips into a thin line and slowly raised my hands from my still-burning crotch. "It's me," I said in the calmest voice I could manage.

Of course it was me. It was always me, ol' Riley Thomas, getting into trouble yet again. If a genie ever crossed my path, the first of my three wishes would be to no longer be Riley Thomas. Maybe I'd be Jim, or Bob, or Steve. Steve probably didn't have haunted dolls in his house or serial killers next door. Or, you know, Captain Glock over here.

"You got a little something on your hand there, friend," Keith piped up, pointing at the man's melted flesh.

"Shut up!" he yelled at Keith. "Just shut up!" He fixed his attention on me once more. "They're gone because of you. I can see it. They're . . . floating. All around you."

I tried looking around without turning my head. "Who are 'they'?"

Suddenly, gun-hand guy started screaming bloody murder. Whirling around, he fired three more shots into the air. The sound of gravel being fired from a high-powered Nerf gun echoed through the store, and what appeared to be flaming stones ripped through the tiles of the ceiling above. Blue fire burned through the holes left behind, charring and extending the edges of the perforations. "*Stop!*" He covered one of his ears with his good hand.

In that moment, I noticed that the thing melded to his flesh wasn't a handgun. It was black and shaped like a handgun, but it was rough in some areas and smooth in others, shining in the light as if carved from obsidian.

He slapped his open palm against the side of his head several times. Then he fired again, and it hit one of the lights, plunging the left side of the store into darkness. "She's speaking to me! Stop! I can't— I don't *want* to hear the screaming anymore!"

Keith took advantage of the light issue and dove behind the coffee counter. Gun-hand guy noticed and shot several times in our direction. I didn't know if Keith got hit, but in my peripheral vision, I saw Judy take a flaming shard to the shoulder and fall behind the registers.

With the assailant's attention off me, I tried to do the same as Keith and ran for cover. Unfortunately, I forgot about my spilled coffee and slipped in it. I hit the floor shoulder-first, and gun-hand guy trained his weapon on me. "They'd all be here now if it weren't for you!"

Another *fwink* as the weapon discharged. A flaming stone whizzed past my head, hit the floor. Just as gun-hand guy was about to fire again, someone grabbed my ankles and dragged me behind the coffee counter.

It was Keith. On his hands and knees, he motioned for me to follow him. I'd barely made it to my knees when footsteps began pounding toward us.

Before gun-hand guy could reach Keith and me, we crawled around the counter, out of his line of sight.

With footsteps close behind us, we scrambled to our feet and crouched low, then hurried through aisles of food and candy. As we moved, our shoes crunched against broken glass.

Another "gunshot" rang out and struck the ceiling above us. "They're all gone! All fifty-six of them! If it weren't for you, none of it would be happening right now!"

His screams grew more pained, and he went back to complaining about a voice only he could hear. Keith and I leaned against the end of the aisle furthest from the entrance, where the gallon jugs of water were located. I looked over at Keith and whispered, "Just a quick stop, huh?"

Keith furrowed his brow and whispered back, "You saying this is *my* fault? I just wanted to fill up on gas and get some corn chips, dude."

One of the cooler doors about seven feet from our position shattered as a flaming rock pierced through it. Soda sprayed onto the floor like a fountain, the liquid steaming and bubbling from being instantly superheated to a boiling degree.

We started crawling down the back aisles toward the front door. "I'm not saying it's your fault," I corrected, my tone hushed. "I'm just saying you challenged fate by implying that this would be a quick, uninterrupted stop."

"You can't hide from me, you son of a bitch!" Gun-hand guy shouted. I could hear his boots smashing shards of glass as he stomped down the aisle we were about to pass.

Keith and I changed course, scrambling down the aisle next to gun-hand guy instead, and I made a mental note to not to make as much noise as he was so I didn't give away our position.

Once Keith and I reached the front of the aisle, Keith gestured at the door. He made a series of motions with his hand—I'm guessing he was trying to communicate some kind of message for a plan he had.

Which only would have been helpful had we developed a hand-signal code in the first place.

After he finished, I whispered, "Huh?"

His expression morphed into that of frustration. He proceeded to repeat the hand gestures, but much slower this time.

Before he could even get halfway through his second run of whatever he was trying to say, gun-hand guy rounded the corner from the aisle behind us. "Gotcha!"

I clamped my eyes shut as an *actual* gunshot rang out.

It sounded as if a nuke were exploding inside the store. My ears began to ring, throbbing with dull pain. I figured that when I opened my eyes again, I'd find myself in the afterlife, the smell of hazelnut coffee thick in the air. But surprisingly, when I opened my eyes again, I wasn't in Heaven. I was still in the Ass Top.

Gun-hand guy stood over Keith and me, his eyes wide with shock. Blood pooled out from a hole in his chest. He fell sideways into a shelf of candy.

Keith backed up into me and knocked me onto my side as gun-hand guy toppled over an entire section of previously well-organized product. The shelf hit the floor, candy breaking open and scattering all over. Gun-hand guy's head bounced off the tile, still and lifeless.

I looked up toward the entrance to see who had saved us. It was Detective Kardoza, his service pistol drawn, smoke trailing from the barrel.

CHAPTER 9
IT COULD ALWAYS BE WORSE, RIGHT?

SOMETIMES THINGS CAN GO SIDEWAYS FAST, AND you think, *Man, this was rough, but it could always be worse!* Except I'm not allowed to have that thought—otherwise, I run the risk of things becoming *infinitely* worse shortly afterward.

Gun-hand guy's assault on the Ass Top felt as though it had lasted hours, when in reality it had only lasted minutes.

Thankfully, Judy's injury hadn't been fatal. After gun-hand guy went down, paramedics arrived in record time, picked Judy up, and raced her to the hospital.

Kardoza had killed gun-hand guy before any questions regarding his motivation for the attack could be answered, but the detective had saved my and Keith's lives in the process. After an hour or so of questioning us, Kardoza seemed satisfied with our answers.

That meant we were free to go, right?

Nope. Kardoza allowed Keith to leave, but I was taken to the police station for further questioning. I have to admit, I was a little annoyed.

I mean, what more could the detective possibly need to know? He'd gotten the full story from the two of us. Maybe he sensed my growing urge to get to work and wanted to torture me.

So there I sat in a plain, almost empty white room. There was a chair beneath me, a chair across from me, and a table in front of me. I avoided my reflection in the one-way mirror that made up the wall ahead.

Sighing, I squinted at the paper cup in my lap. It had been full of water twenty minutes ago, but I'd sucked down every last drop of the liquid while waiting for someone to get here. I balanced the cup between my index fingers, focusing hard on it. I suspected that somebody was watching me from the other side of the mirror, and it felt awkward to look at it (or to look around the room at all), so I decided to stare at the cup instead.

Finally, footsteps sounded outside the door. They stopped, and it opened. Detective Kardoza entered, a paper folder in hand. "Sorry about the wait, Mr. Thomas. Had to get a few things in order before I could come back."

I set the cup on the table. "No problem." Without even seeing myself, I knew that my demeanor had shifted into something happier and more energetic because of Kardoza's return. Now we could get down to business, and I could get out of here.

Kardoza took the seat across from me and set his folder off to the side. He clasped his hands and offered a gentle smile. "How are you today? All things considered."

I shrugged. "Fine, I guess. I almost got shot, and I spilled hot coffee all over my crotch, which made me look like I had a very tragic bathroom mishap. All in all, though, I didn't end up getting killed, so it could have been worse, right?"

There it was again. I still hadn't learned my lesson.

"Glad to hear it," Kardoza replied. "I just had some follow-up questions. I figured it would be better if we talked somewhere private."

"I suppose that makes sense."

"Do you recognize the man who almost shot you today?"

I pursed my lips in thought, but I didn't need to think for long. I was certain I'd never seen the man before. If I had, it hadn't been for long enough to register in my head as a previous interaction. "Not at all."

Kardoza let out a curiously toned, "Huh." I furrowed my brow as he continued. "Interesting. You seemed to remember all your customers the other day."

The implication wasn't lost on me, and after a couple of seconds of dot connecting, I chuckled. "That guy shops at Grocery Hut? Are you sure?"

"He's a gold member. We found the membership card in his wallet."

That was surprising. Grocery Hut's Gold Member Program was a much older system implemented by the owner from years and years ago that gave special discounts to customers with membership cards. It was defunct now, so you couldn't apply for it, but if you had the card, certain discounts were still available to you.

Whoever gun-hand guy was, he would have had to have been not only a customer, but a semi-regular one at that. Unless he borrowed the card from a relative or some-thing, which was the main reason the program had been shut down.

I shook my head in disbelief. "That's honestly hard to be-lieve. If he was a regular customer, I would have served him at some point."

Kardoza's smile didn't change. This was being treated—at least as far as he was concerned—as a casual conversation between two acquaintances. "It was definitely his. It was even registered under his name. Brent Alvis."

The name rang zero bells. I had never met him before. Given how often I worked, that was practically impossi-ble. I shook my head again. "Yeah, sorry, he doesn't sound familiar."

"Right." Kardoza nodded. "Okay." He leaned back in his chair and crossed his arms. "Something else I heard from the cashier at the Gas Stop as the paramedics carted her off. She mentioned she heard Brent say something about fifty-six people?" He gestured at me in a pleading manner, as if I'd be able to offer answers in the form of something physical. "You know anything about that?"

"Well," I began, "fifty-six comes after the number fif-ty-five and before the number fifty-seven. As for the more specific additive of fifty-six *people*, I haven't the slightest clue."

Kardoza's smile faltered a tad. "You're an odd duck, Mr. Thomas."

I sighed. "Unfortunately, yeah." It was one thing to know that I wasn't normal. It was another to be told so plainly that I wasn't. "Normal" was all I wanted. But life didn't want me to be normal; it wanted me to be something else.

Kardoza's smile vanished, and the tone of the conversation transitioned from that of acquaintances talking sports to that of coworkers talking business. "Well, let me clue you in, here." He opened the folder, pulled out a sheet of paper, and slid it over to me.

I picked up the paper and read over it. It was a list of names, numbered from one to . . . fifty-six. I recognized some of the names. In fact, I recognized quite a lot of the names.

"Fifty-six missing people," Kardoza said. "All of them gone without a trace in the past several months, except for a few." As he said this, I noticed that the first four names had asterisks next to their numbers. What that meant, I couldn't be sure, but I did know one thing for certain.

The tone of the conversation was no longer that of acquaintances or coworkers. It had become something much more serious.

"All of them were also regular customers at *your* grocery store," Kardoza added. "Weird, huh?"

I returned my attention to him. "These are all the people who have gone missing?"

"Everyone that we know of. Hard to say for sure. But it's a pretty specific number, don't you think?" He reached over, took the paper from me, and pulled it back to his side of the table. "How many of those names did you recognize? All of them?"

My throat was dry now. It was hard to speak, to think. My mind whirred with revelation. Every single missing person was listed on that piece of paper. The ongoing news story that I thought had only existed around me was quite literally *happening* around me.

I knew that Carlos was the killer, but fifty-six people?

That was . . . a lot. And they were my customers, no less! Was it just a coincidence that all his victims shopped there? Or had he done this on purpose? Maybe he was—

Then it hit me.

"Wait," I said, "you think I had something to do with this?"

It all made sense now. I hadn't even suspected Carlos until recently. Maybe I'd been his scapegoat all along. Maybe he'd figured that I would be the perfect patsy if anybody managed to catch on.

How often had I seen Carlos shopping at Grocery Hut? How often had he asked me whether I knew about any good deals coming up the following sales week? *All the time.*

This was downright diabolical.

Kardoza side-eyed me. "I don't know what to think, Riley. I'm just trying to make sense of some things."

"Like what?"

He leaned forward, and the tone of the conversation shifted again. Now it felt as though I were being scolded by an angry parent, as though I'd thrown a rock through a window and been caught red-handed. "The public only knows these people are missing!" he yelled. "How did you know there's a serial killer?"

I had to take a moment to process what he'd just asked me. "What?" Once my brain caught up, I shook my head and laughed. "No, that's— Okay, this has been a misunderstanding."

"Oh?"

"I don't *know* that there's a serial killer. I'm simply assuming that there is because *so many* people are going missing without a trace."

"It didn't sound like an assumption the other day when we first talked. It sounded like you knew."

"I didn't. I don't. I was chatting with my neighbor, Carlos, and he said that many people don't go missing unless it's something really bad, y'know?"

"Sure." He sounded completely unconvinced. "Speaking of Carlos, he had some interesting things to say."

Oh great, I thought. *I almost forgot that they've already talked.* The excitement of the Ass Top must have fried my memory, and now I was relisting everything I knew about Carlos in my head. I had to find a way out of this.

Maybe there was a way I could divert suspicion onto the real culprit without getting directly involved.

Though, at this point, that was just wishful thinking. I was, unfortunately, fully involved at this point.

Kardoza opened the folder again and pulled out a second sheet of paper. "Apparently your current home used to belong to a spree killer."

"That's what I was told by the real estate people when I first moved in."

"Right, right. Murder is good for the housing market, I imagine. You sure got that place at an absolute steal."

"What's your point?"

"What's it like living in that house?"

"It's small." I shrugged. "I'm not sure what kind of answer you want. It's a house. And I live in it."

"Mm-hmm." Kardoza returned to the folder for what I assumed was another sheet. Whatever answer he was looking for, I seemed to have given it to him. He pulled out a paper and looked it over. "You've been living on your own since you were nineteen, is that right?"

The volume of my voice went down a few notches. "Eighteen," I mumbled.

Kardoza looked at me curiously, then back down at the sheet in his hand. He smiled. "Ah yes, eighteen. I misread it." He ran a palm across his chin. "It's impressive how you've managed to keep yourself taken care of all these years."

"I think 'taken care of' is a bit generous."

Kardoza smiled wider. This one wasn't friendly. I don't think he found humor in what I'd said. I think he knew as well as I did where things were going next, and he was excited to get there.

There was a pause in conversation as he continued to read over the paper. "I'm sure your parents would disagree. I bet they'd be proud to see you doing so well."

I bit the inside of my cheek. "I bet they would be."

"Such a tragedy what happened to your parents and sister." There was compassion in his voice, but I knew it wasn't out of real sympathy. This was a man who believed that I had done something horrible, something unforgivable. That "tragedy" was a means to an end for him.

The means to *my* end.

Another long silence. I figured that maybe Kardoza was waiting for me to respond. Poking and prodding me for reactions to confirm what he already thought to be true.

He set the paper aside. "Is that why we can't find the other bodies, Riley?" I opened my mouth to argue, but before I could make a sound, Kardoza continued. "Are you cremating your victims? Burning them like the house fire that took your parents and sister away from you?"

I tried to answer, but my throat closed up. Tears stung my eyes. I felt as if someone had dropped heavy stones in the pit of my stomach, and I opened my mouth, attempted to talk once more. But all I could muster was a soft squeaking noise.

That tiny sound gradually shifted into a choke.

Then a sob.

I wanted to tell him that he was wrong, that he was *completely* wrong. At this point, I thought, *To hell with not getting involved. The real killer is Carlos. Go get his ass!*

But speech was impossible for me now. And if I couldn't even manage basic communication, how was I supposed to tell him the truth?

Memories came flooding back to me. Of the house I grew up in. Of the day it burned down. How the fire was so uncontrolled, how it burned so intensely, that my family was, essentially, cremated inside. There were no remains to be found—not solid ones, anyway.

All that was left of the building and of the people I knew as my mother, father, and sister, was a crater in the earth and a pile of ashes.

The only person left alive was the orphaned, recently turned legal adult, Riley Thomas.

Kardoza leaned forward, the sudden movement snapping me out of my weeping fit. "Where are the bodies, Riley?"

The door to the room flew open, as if there had been an explosion on the other side, and the noise the door made as it struck the wall perfectly matched its violent movement. A man stormed in, wearing a clean pinstripe suit and holding a black leather briefcase.

The shock of the familiar face suddenly appearing during this extremely tense situation was enough to rip me out of the depressive state I'd fallen into. A mix of emotions swarmed through me, but I wasn't sure which I should allow to lead the charge. Was I supposed to be happy? Amused? Scared?

It was hard to say.

"This is a private room," Kardoza snarled as he jumped out of his chair. "Who are you?"

"I am Mr. Thomas's legal advisor," Rivers—the immortal man who'd now tried to kill me twice—said with a dangerous smile. "And I would like a word alone with my client before you ask him any more questions, *Detective*."

PERHAPS I SHOULD HAVE BEEN MORE HESITANT TO allow myself to be left alone with Rivers. After all, the man wanted me dead.

But at the same time, I was desperate to get away from Kardoza and his accusations. It had taken that man just a few minutes to completely break down the walls I had so meticulously built up in the past seven years. Those walls are what kept me functioning—or, at least, what made me appear to be functioning.

After Kardoza left, I went back to sobbing. As I cried, Rivers sat uncomfortably, before he eventually left me alone in the room. But even then, I couldn't get the tears under control. Not right away, at least.

The only thing I could do that seemed to help was grasp my necklace. The lucky coin on a chain that I'd once shared with my sister.

Rivers returned to the room about twenty minutes after

leaving me, a very unhappy Detective Kardoza at his side. By then, I'd managed to restore my composure.

Soon Rivers was escorting me to the entrance of the police station. As we left the station and walked through the parking lot, I realized that none of the officers or detectives had followed us since we'd passed through the front doors.

Seizing my chance to speak before being taken into an alleyway and murdered, I asked the question plaguing my mind. "Are you really a lawyer?"

Rivers glanced over his shoulder at me with a bored expression. "I've been alive for a *long* time, Riley. You don't think I know how the law works?"

"I'm sure you do. That doesn't answer my question, though."

Rivers sighed at me as if I were a child and had just asked him the same question for the hundredth time. "Officially, no, I'm not a lawyer, but I've got enough knowledge and experience with the police that I can play the part effectively."

"Oh," I said, and I supposed that made sense. If you had all the time in the world, you'd probably start picking up on a little bit of everything, huh? Jack-of-all-trades, master of none. But if you lived forever, how long would it take for you to become jack-of-all-trades, master of all?

We stopped next to a large black vehicle. I wasn't sure of the brand or model, but it was one of those big four-door things that had two front seats and an open-round set of seats in the back. The kind you'd see powerful men sitting in, surrounded by other people.

A massive guy was in the driver's seat, and as Rivers and I climbed into the back, I realized that he looked almost exactly like Pete, Rivers's previous goon from our first encounter.

He was pale, covered in surgical scars, and held a stoic expression. He wasn't as big or as muscular as Pete had been, but he was still stocky.

Rivers snapped his fingers. "Drive, Liam."

Liam pulled out of the parking space and began driving away from the police station. The more I stared at the zombie-man, the more familiar he became, and suddenly I recognized him as one of the two officers that had come to Grocery Hut to arrest Rivers after he'd returned from death-god land.

"So," I began, "are you going to kill me now?"

Rivers smiled, running a hand through his silver-blond hair. "Not yet."

"Oh." For a second, I didn't say anything. Then I let out a very slow, sort of confused, "Great."

"If I could have it my way, I would have just left you to rot in prison. It would have been much less of a hassle than going in there and breaking you out." He clenched a fist and stared out the window. "Unfortunately, I need you."

"Uh, okay."

Rivers faced me again. "Word on the street is that you're slated to kill the She-Devil."

I crossed my arms. "You've been talking to Mason, haven't you?"

Rivers tilted his head back and forth. "Talking, fighting, robbing. I've been engaging with him in a multitude of ways." He opened the briefcase he'd been carrying and pulled out a big stone tablet from it. The tablet had to be ancient, carvings of foreign symbols completely covering the front of it. "Turns out this thing has the bitch's whole kit and caboodle on it." As he looked it over, he crossed his legs. "We were waiting for the reckoning to go down, but thankfully, we don't need to wait any longer. We just need to find her and put you in front of her."

"I'm not sure what you expect me to do," I said. "I'm just a guy."

Rivers raised a finger. "Not just a guy. You're *the* guy."

I turned to look out the window and saw we were slowing to a stop in the middle of traffic. "So, what then? I'm just supposed to be present until you find her?"

"More or less. Once you kill the bitch doing whatever it is you're supposed to do, I'll kill you, then continue living my otherwise bleak existence in peace."

I faced him once more, narrowing my eyes at him. "You're just going to keep living?"

Rivers laughed, but it wasn't a genuine laugh. It was an "I don't know how else to express this rage other than laughing it off" kind of laugh. "I don't have much of a fucking choice," he said with a furious smile. "My options are to live this way until the sun blows up, or to live this way until the She-Devil engulfs the planet with flames. No matter what, I'm immortal, you little moron. I can't die! I'll still be alive even after there's no Earth left to . . ."

He trailed off. I had just enough time before he leapt out of his seat toward me to realize that I had (once again) been rudely staring at the stupid mole on his stupid face.

In an instant, Rivers had his hands around my throat. "I am *so* tempted to just take my chances and kill you anyway."

I tried to respond, but he squeezed the moment I opened my mouth, cutting off my voice as well as my oxygen.

Rivers spoke his next words slowly, through heavy breaths and clenched teeth. *"How—I—loathe—thee—Riley—Thomas."*

What happened next transpired so quickly, I could barely process it.

The window next to my head went from being in one piece to being in hundreds. Pain stung my skin as the shards raked across it. Rivers released me, fell sideways, and landed lifelessly on the floor by my feet.

Blood painted the inside of the car, the seats across from me coated with crimson.

Honking and screams sounded outside. Then heavy footsteps approached me.

All that happened in just a few seconds.

What occurred next was about as swift and hard to follow, but I'll do my best to summarize: Basically, an arm reached into the vehicle and grabbed me. It yanked me outside, and I fell hard onto the concrete sidewalk.

Liam put the vehicle in park and climbed out. I looked up to see who had pulled me free of Rivers's car and found Mason, the monster-hunter, a shiny silver gun in his free hand.

"On your feet!" Mason shouted, backing away from the vehicle.

Through the broken window, I saw Rivers slowly make his way into a standing position. He had a bullet wound in his head, but it was closing fast.

I leapt to my feet and rushed toward Mason as Liam stepped onto the sidewalk. Mason fired three more rounds, each one deafening me a bit more than the last. The bullets hit Liam in the chest, but they didn't even faze him. He sauntered closer.

Rivers pointed at me, and regardless of the ringing in my ears, I was able to make out what he said next. "Bring the boy back alive. Break the other guy over your fucking *knee*."

Liam kicked it into gear, launching into a sprint.

I didn't stick around. I turned on my heel and raced after Mason. We dashed up the sidewalk, past trash cans and storefronts, plowing through groups of people as they went about their day.

Mason turned as he ran and fired off more shots. I didn't check to see if they slowed down Liam at all.

I just had to get away.

I rounded a corner onto another street, and Mason did the same. "Get in the truck!" he shouted, firing again.

I chanced a glance over my shoulder. Liam wasn't far behind us, and the last few bullets Mason had hit him with weren't any more effective than the first few had been.

Ahead of me was a beat-up red truck. It seemed old, very used, but also durable. Sturdy. The kind of truck that I imagined heavy-duty farmhands would drive.

I sprinted to the passenger side and lunged in. I looked back, saw Liam approaching. Mason raised his handgun to shoot. Several bullets went into the air as Liam seized Mason by the arm.

Before Mason could even try to fight back, Liam lifted him off the ground as easily as you'd pick up a stuffed toy. Liam swung Mason around, slammed him hard into the wall of a building. He hit the ground, unmoving.

Liam set his emotionless sights on me. As he walked toward the truck, I locked the doors.

That didn't make a difference to him. He grabbed the handle and wrenched the passenger door off its hinges. He threw the door aside, and it rammed into the sidewalk with a loud clang. All the while, people were gathering around us from a safe distance, their cell phones raised to record the unfolding chaos.

I scrambled over the center console toward the driver's seat, but Liam snatched my ankle and yanked me out of the truck.

Then he pulled me up off the ground by the collar of my shirt, swung around, and began walking back the way we came.

Mason sprang to his feet next to us. His machete *schwing*ed as he pulled it from his belt. He hacked it through Liam's wrist. I fell to the ground, Liam's hand still clutching my shirt.

I'm not too ashamed to admit I squealed once while trying to get the severed appendage off me. Okay, maybe it was twice.

In contrast, Liam didn't appear to be annoyed or even inconvenienced in the slightest. He simply turned toward Mason. He reached out to grab the monster-hunter, but Mason was too agile. Mason ducked away from Liam's grasp and sliced off the zombie-man's other hand.

For once, genuine emotion came over Liam's face: confusion. He appeared to be wondering, *Well* now *what am I supposed to do?*

Mason swung the machete again and lopped Liam's head from his body. Screams ejected from the surrounding crowd, and people finally began to flee the scene, internet clout be damned.

"Get in the truck and buckle up," Mason ordered.

I did as I was told while Mason sheathed his machete and

limped around to the driver's side. He climbed in, started the truck, and peeled off the curb and down the street.

As we weaved through traffic, I looked at the rearview mirror. Rivers was running toward Liam's decapitated body. He slowed to a stop and watched us speed away.

And then he disappeared behind a sea of people and vehicles.

"Un-fuckin'-believable," Mason said. "This is why I told you to come with me. Now you've got that twisted son of a bitch chasing after you, too!"

"Rivers?" I gestured with my thumb at the chaos we'd left behind. "He wanted me around for the same reason you do. Everybody thinks I'm supposed to kill the She-Devil."

"Because you are, you fuckin' putz." Mason slammed his palms against the steering wheel. "Would have been one thing to just have to steal the tablet back from him, but you had to go and get yourself captured as well, didn't you?"

"I didn't get captured," I corrected him. "I got arrested." I stopped. "Well, I guess not technically, but considering how my talk with Kardoza was going, I would have been soon."

"I wouldn't have given a shit if you were dropped off at day care!" Mason howled. "What matters is finding the She-Devil and having you kill her. We're almost out of time."

"Are you sure it's not supposed to be some other guy named Riley Thomas?"

"Even if it were, we don't have the time to look for him."

I let out a defeated sigh. I wasn't getting out of this one. Not right now, anyway. "So where are we going?"

"To the bunker. We're gonna put some spells together and see if we can find where the bitch is hiding."

"Can I borrow your phone, then?"

Mason cast a suspicious—and a little judgmental—side glance at me.

"I gotta call my manager and let him know I probably won't be making it into work at all today."

Mason rolled his eyes. Still, he reached into his jacket pocket and tossed me his cell phone. I tapped the button to turn it on and found that his lock screen was different from mine. Rather than a number keyboard, it was a dot grid. I'd have to trace some connect-the-dots type pattern to unlock the device.

I shook it. "What's the password?"

Mason looked at me quickly before returning his attention to the road. "Upside down 'M.'"

"Ah, okay." I tried to trace the pattern as he'd instructed, but the grid was too small. An "M" wouldn't really fit. The screen reset and flashed red. "Yeah, that didn't work."

"The hell you mean it didn't work?" Mason cried. "Just do an 'M,' but upside down. Like a 'W.' Just do a 'W.'"

I tried the pattern again, but the grid was too small. It was a three-by-three, and although I now understood where the "W" fit in there, the phone didn't allow diagonal connections. "It just doesn't work," I said.

Mason ripped the phone out of my hands and swiped the pattern. The screen unlocked. He chucked it back at me before mumbling something under his breath that sounded like, "Slayer of the She-Devil can't even draw a fucking 'W.'"

I ignored his insult, dialed the number, hit the "call" icon, and held the phone to my ear. It rang three and a half times before Keith's voice sounded on the other end. "Hi, this is Keith. If you're a scam caller, leave a message after the fart." He blew an obscenely wet raspberry into the phone.

"Keith, it's me," I said.

He stopped. "If you're a scam caller that's learned how to duplicate Riley's voice, leave a message after the fart."

He drew a long breath, but before he could continue with the noises, I interrupted him. "Dude, I'm not a scam caller."

"Ahh. If this is a *skinwalker* imitating Riley's voice, leave a mess—"

"I'm not a skinwalker either!"

"Wait. Really?"

"Really."

"Oh shit," Keith shouted. "Riley, dude, where the hell are you?"

"It's a long story. Are you at Grocery Hut?"

"Is that some kind of code for 'there's a scam-calling skin-walker holding me for ransom'?"

"No?"

"Oh, word. Yeah, I'm at the Hut. Why?"

"Can you tell Henry I can't make it today? I'm off devil hunting."

"Sure, I can do that. One question, though. Is 'devil hunting' code for 'running from the law'?"

I furrowed my brow. "Huh?"

"Y'know, since Kardoza thinks you're the serial killer."

"How could you possibly know that?"

"Well, I don't. Not for sure. But I mean, why else would he keep you for more questioning, only for you to go radio silent and then call me from a strange phone?"

"Yeah, you're right. I guess finding a way to clear my name probably also falls on the to-do list, doesn't it?"

"Don't worry, bro," Keith replied in a tone that said "let me take care of it." He then followed up with, "I'll hit

Carlos's house SWAT style once I get off work tonight, and I'll find the biz that screams 'serial killer.'"

"Please do not harass my serial-killer neighbor," I pleaded. "Just try and shift Kardoza's attention that way."

"Oh dude, I am *so* on that." Before I could say anything else, he ended the call.

As I handed the phone back to Mason, I wondered whether calling Keith had been the best idea. Then again, my "bad idea" voice had been rather silent as of late, so either that metaphorical fuse had long since burned out, or it wasn't as bad a move as I thought.

But it was still Monday, so that was probably just wishful thinking.

CHAPTER 11
THE FIRST OF THE FALLEN DOMINOES

BY THE TIME WE ARRIVED AT MASON'S RAMSHACKLE hideout, I was exhausted. It was somewhere around three in the afternoon, and I felt as if I'd gone multiple rounds with all the stock carts in Grocery Hut's back room.

Mason had pulled onto an unmarked road in the back end of town, and after driving through trees for about ten minutes, we'd arrived at the previously mentioned hideout. From what I could tell, it was a warehouse. Or, at least, it used to be. Whatever it had once been used for was long since abandoned, the building left to rot—and rot it did. There were gaps in the roof, and the walls were falling apart, revealing insulation and steel. The glass on the windows was either cracked or completely shattered. Surprisingly, the front door—which was about the size of a garage door—was functional, but that was it. The rest of the structure was in ruins.

Mason parked his truck close to the front of the hide-out. He exited the vehicle and opened the front door, then returned to the truck and drove it inside. With the vehicle tucked safely inside the warehouse, Mason pulled the door shut. "Come with me," he said, and walked off into an ocean of scrap metal and leftover junk. I scrambled out of the truck to follow him.

The inside of the warehouse was long, and if I had to guess, I'd say it had once been used for some kind of industrial storage. Tall shelves lined the length of the building. Some of the shelves appeared to be in better condition than the rest of the warehouse, and they held an array of items—boxes, axles, engines, metal equipment, you get the idea. The rest of the shelves stood crookedly, leaning against each other.

I followed Mason through a sort of arch that was shaped like the bottom half of the letter "K." The arch was made of shelves, scrap metal and engine parts pushed aside for easy entry.

As we passed through the arch and into the next section of the hideout, light became scarce because the roof was more intact here. The structures around me began to feel like tight groupings of trees, as though I were a safari man exploring the jungle.

The path surrounded by scooted-aside garbage led to what appeared to be a small house or shed of sorts. It was built into the corner of the warehouse, with a roof and walls. It also had two windows and a door in the center, which hung wide open.

I followed Mason inside to find that this was, indeed, a small house. It had a corner dedicated to cooking, with a portable stove and a duffel bag full of pots and cups. Two identical couches were pushed together to form a bed, complete with a light blanket and a single pillow, while a large desk was shoved against the far wall. The desk was littered with papers and books, all of which seemed to detail various monsters and myths. A board hung on the wall above the desk, drawings and photographs connected by red string pinned to it.

"Get comfy." Mason strode over to the kitchen corner. He knelt in front of the bag and dug out two mugs, and I took a seat at the desk, which had the only chair in the "house." Casually, I looked over the strewn-about papers on the desk.

I hadn't intended to snoop, nor did I care enough about Mason's operation to do so, but even still, I caught sight of a familiar word.

Deathmore.

I grabbed the sheet from the pile and examined it. It was a cutout from a newspaper, paper-clipped with what appeared to be a page of Mason's bullet points.

- **No children left.**
- **Most people fled.**
- **Body count rising, 14 confirmed dead, 8 of which are children.**
- **Multiple reports of dolls?**

I set the clipping down as another note caught my eye. Rivers Tremaine. I studied that paper next, although it was less detailed. The only things listed were:

- **Apparently immortal.**

and

- **Who the fuck is this guy?**

"You sure keep, uh, detailed listings," I said.

"Mm-hmm." Mason responded without looking over. "Know thy enemy."

I scanned the pile for any other recognizable names, and while I didn't see any I knew, there were a lot. There was even a page titled "Mothman" with a list of several bullet points, including one that just said:

- **Nest?**

"Are you hunting all this stuff?"

"Somebody's got to," Mason said, his tone suddenly laced with exhaustion. He let out a weary sigh. How long had he been doing this, exactly? "Evil don't fight itself."

I shifted my attention from the paper pile to the board with the red thread. Everything pinned to it was related to *her*. The She-Devil. Her tomb, her last known locations, translations from the tablet, and a few pictures of . . . ashes? Yes, they were ashes—houses reduced to cinders, according to Mason's scribbles on the board.

Along with the pictures of burnt-down homes, there were markings of peculiar symbols and claw marks on doors. There was even a photo of around twenty priests in special white robes. A note card that said "Fathers of Free Will" hung below it, followed by "RIP" in bold red marker.

A mug of dark steaming liquid appeared in the air before me, and I recognized it as coffee the moment its scent hit my nostrils. I looked over to see Mason holding it out to me. In his other hand, he clutched a cup for himself. "She's a real evil bitch," he said in a low voice.

I took the mug from him and returned to studying the board. Something about the pictures on it struck a chord with me. They were familiar, almost. "This is what she's done?"

"This is what the demons who brought her back have done." Mason stepped back. "Everything she's gonna do will be a thousand times worse."

I took a sip of the coffee. It was . . . well, let's just say it was about as good as you'd imagine, considering Mason's living conditions. It may as well have just been coffee-flavored water with banana Laffy Taffy melted on top.

Basically, it smelled like coffee, it was supposed to be coffee, but it definitely wasn't coffee.

However, it was probably as good as I was going to get for now, so I braced myself and took another sip.

I set the mug on the desk and cleared my throat. "So, what about the rest of these guys? Are you going to take them out once the She-Devil is gone?"

"I'll do what I can," Mason replied from behind me. "This world is going to shit."

I turned in my seat to face him. He stood before a pile of wood, which looked like parts of a broken chair, and threw pieces of the wood into a pot. I watched him for a moment before I asked, "What do you mean?"

"My job ain't ever been easy," he began, "but it was doable, at least. I'd go somewhere, kill some evil creature, save some lives, then move on to the next town and do it all over again." He picked up a large hunk of wood from the pile, snapped it in half, and tossed both pieces into the pot. "Now it just seems like there's more than there used to be. Evil monsters and world-ending super demons are popping up on every corner of the map now." He reached into the bag at his feet, retrieved some lighter fluid, and dumped it into the pot. "Can't fight it all by myself. For every She-Devil that rears her ugly head, there's fourteen more town-destroying big bads that decide to go on a rampage." He pulled a book of matches from his coat pocket and set the wood in the pot ablaze. Flames roared to life with a loud whoosh, and only now, in the intense light, could I see the despair on his scarred face. "Tides are turning. It's starting to become a losing battle."

He stared into the flames for a while before walking over to me and picking up a few jars from the edge of the desk. "But you can fight it all, right?" I asked.

Mason looked over the jars. "Sure. But if I'm the only one fighting any of it, what happens when I finally go down?" With the jars in hand, he headed toward the roaring flames. "Good and evil are always gonna be in a struggle. It's the balance of the universe. It just feels like there's a whole lot more evil than there is good these days."

"Oh," I said as he began dumping the jars' contents into the fire. "Well, I'm sure somebody will come along. There's always going to be somebody, right?"

Mason gave me a pointed look. "Maybe somebody already has."

"Oh, well, I meant somebody besides *me*." I scratched the back of my neck.

"Seriously?" Mason cried. "I gave you that speech about how the world is out of balance, how monsters are sprouting up faster than we can cut them down, and you're still holding onto being a regular old Joe Shmoe?"

A heavy silence settled between us. I wasn't sure if he wanted me to actually answer the question or not. So, I shrugged and let out a slow, "Yes?"

Mason stomped over to me and stuck a finger in my face. "Well too fuckin' bad. You're the goddamn slayer of the She-Devil, kid. Your average life don't mean dick, jack, or shit anymore."

I stood up out of my chair. My nerves were shot, my mind was shot, my generally calm demeanor was shot. I was so tired of this. "You know what?" I yelled. "I'm not exactly keen on being your slated slayer either, you know?" Mason opened his mouth to shout back, but I cut him off. "I am so *sick* and *tired* of everybody making their problems *mine*. I'm just a guy! I have a normal, albeit shitty retail job. You think just because my name is on some hunk of junk that I'm supposed to be your savior? I can barely make payments on my bills. I can barely lift anything over a hundred pounds. I'm not some fabled hero, okay? I didn't go through a rigorous training arc, and I'm not special in any sense of the word!"

"*Doesn't fuckin' matter*!" Mason screamed. He jammed his finger against my chest. "It's *your* name on that hunk of junk. Nobody else's. It's gotta be you that kills the bitch, whether you want it to be or not."

"If that's the case," I said, shoving his hand away, "then we're all going to fucking *die*."

Mason went quiet before leaning in close. "Not if I can

help it." He seized me by the hair and yanked a chunk of it free from my scalp.

My hands shot up toward my head. "Ow!"

Mason stepped back toward the pot. "I'm gonna find out where she's hiding, and the second I do, we're gonna go there. You're gonna kill the bitch, and then we can both go back to our 'normal' fuckin' lives. You can go back to being a shitty nobody at some dead-end grocery store, and I can move on to the next town full of dead people that I couldn't save because I was too busy sitting here arguing with your stupid ass." He dropped my hair into the pot. There was a loud sizzle, and the flames turned from orange and yellow to deep red.

I threw up my arms. "How am I even supposed to kill her? Is there a special weapon or something?"

"Well, I could tell you that if I had the rest of my translations. But somebody butchered my translator and stole the tablet." He forced a smile and began sorting through more of his jars. "So I guess we'll both be fuckin' wingin' it, aye?"

I didn't have anything else to say to him. Apparently, I was going to be "fuckin' wingin' it" no matter how much I protested. The only difference between being stuck with Mason and being stuck with Rivers was that Mason probably wouldn't kill me when all was said and done. *Probably.*

Resigned to my fate, I took a breath to calm myself. "Whatever. Where's the bathroom?"

He pointed down the hall to my right. "End of the hall, and make it quick. This ritual won't take long." Just then, the flames turned neon blue. "Whoa," he whispered. "That's a new one."

I left him to his work and made my way down the hall, which seemed to be located within the wall that the little house—or shed, or office, or whatever it was—was built up against. It didn't make a ton of sense for it to be here, but then again, maybe the warehouse was larger than I'd initially thought.

A brown door awaited me at the end of the hall, and when I opened it, I found myself in a bathroom that was bigger than I'd expected. Nicer, too.

The checkered walls were black and white, the ceiling a solid maroon. Soft gold lights lined the wall above three wide sinks, and six urinals stood across from them. At the far end of the room was a stall, its door and walls the same color as the ceiling.

I trudged over to the closest sink and turned it on, then leaned down and splashed my face with cold water. Mason's disgusting coffee hadn't helped my fatigue at all. Mondays always took it out of the average worker, but *this* Monday was something else. I'd survived two gunfights, not to mention an emotionally exhausting interrogation with Detective Kardoza.

I just wanted to be home in bed. I just wanted today to be over.

I glanced up at my reflection in the mirror. Water dripped down my face. My hair was disheveled, and I had bags under my eyes. My vest and name tag were nowhere to be seen. Had I left them in Keith's car?

At this point, I figured it didn't matter one way or the other. I turned off the faucet and shook my head before exiting the bathroom.

But when I stepped out of the bathroom, I wasn't in Mason's hideout anymore. The neon-blue lights of The Edge of Time bar were once again shining down on me. "Tequila" was no longer the bar's song of choice—instead it was "My Way" by Frank Sinatra. The bartender with the blurred-out face stood behind the counter, just as he had before. And now, rather than cleaning glasses, he repeatedly wiped down the counter with a white rag. "Good to see you again, Riley. Care for a drink?"

I looked around. "Where did Mason go?"

The bartender shrugged. "He's been. Or gone. Or went."

"Okay." I took a seat on a stool at the bar. "You got any coffee?"

"Sure thing." He set his rag aside and knelt behind the counter. When he rose once more, he handed me a coffee mug on a saucer, the cup filled with hot hazelnut-flavored coffee that I smelled right away.

I picked up the mug and examined the liquid inside. I couldn't say for sure, but it appeared to be made exactly how I liked it. "Did you ever find what you were looking for?" the bartender asked.

He could have been referring to a number of things. "Oh, you mean Keith? Yeah, I found him."

The bartender resumed wiping down the counter. "What about you, sir? Anything to drink?"

"What?" I said, surprised.

"Fireball," a man on my right said. I looked that way, saw him sitting two seats away from me. He had sharp features, with a pointed chin and nose. His inhuman yellow eyes reminded me of a lizard's. Small horns protruded from his forehead, and he wore a jean vest, a black T-shirt, and black pants. He kind of reminded me of a young Steve Buscemi—minus the horns and lizard-like eyes, of course.

The horned man looked over at me and smiled with the cadence of a con artist. "How's it goin', Riley?"

The bartender knelt low again, came back up with a shot glass and a bottle of Fireball. He poured out a glass for the horned man.

"Sorry," I said, shaking my head. "Have we met?"

"Once," the horned man admitted, and threw back a shot. "But that was a long time ago." He tapped the counter, and the bartender poured him another.

"I feel like I'd remember you," I said.

The man threw back his second shot. "It's okay if you don't right now. You probably will at some point."

I couldn't deny that there was an aura of familiarity about him, but that feeling permeated the whole bar like a bad perfume. It wasn't a feeling I trusted or even understood, honestly.

The horned man had his third shot poured, and he slid the glass over to me. Then another glass appeared in his hand. "Here's to tipping over pointless dominoes, huh?" He threw back the shot.

"Oh, I don't drink." I pushed the first shot glass back toward him. "And I don't play dominoes. But yeah, uh, cheers to that, I guess." I gulped down some of my coffee in a toast.

He smiled at me. "I guess you wouldn't drink either, would you?" The shot glass slid into his free hand, moved by an unseen force, and he downed that one as well. After he finished it, he placed it on the counter and gestured to himself. "I'm Adra, by the way."

I nodded slowly. "Yeah, still not ringing any bells. Sorry."

Adra's grin widened, as if everything I said was amusing. Or annoying. "Sure," he replied. He picked up another re-filled glass. "I guess you never caught my name." He guzzled the shot. "I was there that day," he started, his smile fading, "when your family died."

I'd already begun scooting away, hoping the conversation would end naturally, but now I zeroed in on this strange man and his buttery voice. "Wait, what?"

"Yup." He held up yet another glass full of Fireball. "I remember that inferno like it was yesterday." He took the shot and shook his head. Sucking in a breath, he set the glass on the counter. "You were younger then. Off on your own somewhere."

My chest grew tighter with every word he spoke. This was like my last encounter with Detective Kardoza, but it felt more intense. Despite that fact, I wasn't as panicked as I had been with Kardoza. The revelation about my family was upsetting, of course, but somehow, the calm atmosphere of the bar kept my strongest emotions at bay.

Even still, a few memories jarred themselves loose as the bartender refilled Adra's glass for what felt like the hundredth time.

Yes, I remembered it. The day my house burned down. I left just before it happened. I was going to meet Keith in town. We were going to job search.

The search didn't last long due to the fire, but by the time I made it home, it was too late.

This man—Adra—something *was* familiar about him. Had I seen him that day?

As if in response to my thoughts, Adra grinned again. He had the smile of a shark. "Coming back to you now, isn't it?"

A beeping noise rang out, loud and annoying. It didn't come from anywhere specific, just all around the room.

The bartender took my coffee as Adra checked his watch. "Looks like it's about that time." Adra hopped off his stool and straightened his jacket. "Happy trails, kid."

I fell backward from my seat, as if I'd been shoved off it. Out of instinct, I closed my eyes, and when I opened them again, I was no longer in the bar.

I was in my room at home. In my bed.

The beeping persisted next to me, the alarm on my phone buzzing, screaming. I leaned over, grabbed it from my nightstand, and swiped the screen to silence the noise. With the alarm dealt with, my phone returned to its standard lockscreen, and I learned two things.

One, it was eight o'clock in the morning. And two, it was no longer Monday. It was Tuesday.

CHAPTER 12
KEITH'S LITTLE SECRET

After reading the date and time on my phone, I didn't hesitate. I was up and out of bed and preparing for work as if it were a regular old day. Molly sat on the couch in the living room, watching television. My coffee pot was still functional, and I assumed the coffee it made was still nonpoisonous.

You'd think I would have been questioning whether the stuff at the Ass Top, the police station, Mason's hideout, and The Edge of Time bar had actually happened, but I'd received confirmation that all of it had the moment I awoke in bed and checked my phone.

Along with the date and time on my reacquired device, there were several missed calls and unread texts from Keith and Ariel. Keith's messages sounded fairly concerned. He said he hoped I was okay and wondered why I hadn't made it to work. Shortly after I'd called him from Mason's phone, he'd texted me:

> Dude, I talked to a skinwalker on the phone just now that sounded EXACTLY like you.

Ariel's texts were concerned as well. She said she hoped I was okay. She wondered why I'd missed work and hoped our plans for Wednesday were still on.

I responded to both Keith and Ariel right away, of course, but I had a lot of questions. How had I gotten home? How had I gotten my phone back? Kardoza took it yesterday when we arrived at the police station. None of Monday had been a dream, so how was I here now?

Even more concerning than all that was what had occurred at The Edge of Time bar. The man I'd met—Adra—I couldn't shake his face. And although I was home, the familiarity and intense déjà vu about him persisted.

I was sure of it now: I had *definitely* seen him before. Had it been the day my family died?

The more I pondered it, the foggier my memory became. But I didn't have long to think about it anyway. By a quarter to nine, Keith was honking his horn at me from outside, and I was out the door.

I glanced over at Carlos's garden and found he was nowhere to be seen. That was odd, since he normally tended to his flowers throughout the day. *I guess today is different in more ways than one*, I thought.

I hopped into Keith's jeep, and he started driving us to work. I filled him in on everything that had happened to me since we parted ways after the incident at the Ass Top, but he seemed . . . off. Distracted. When I finished relaying the events, he merely responded with a simple, "Wowie. Crazy stuff, bro." Then he fell silent again.

He was hardly looking at me, and he was driving faster than normal. Not only that, but I hadn't seen him eating Bottle Caps in . . . well, I was going to say minutes, but come to think of it, I hadn't seen him eating his favorite candy in *days*.

"All right, what gives?" I asked as he pulled into the employee lot behind the store.

"What do you mean?"

I unbuckled and climbed out. Keith did so too, far quicker than me. He was already halfway to the doors. "You're acting weird," I said. "Weirder than normal."

"I was just trying to get us to work on time, dude."

I looked at my watch, following close behind him. "We're, like, twenty minutes early."

"You're welcome." Keith shot me a couple of finger guns and a wink before opening the doors and taking off inside.

I didn't try to keep up with him. Instead, I made my way to the break room to punch in at a normal pace. Keith had already clocked in and was hurrying toward the back doors.

"Dude," I called after him, "where are you going?"

He paused momentarily. "I forgot something in my car. I'll be back in a sec."

Before I could reply, he ran off. What was going on with him?

I turned to continue toward the break room, but an idea struck me, and I stopped. Maybe I should follow him. He *had* gotten us here twenty minutes early, after all. I could spare a bit of time to find out what he was hiding.

As I followed him back, I realized he wasn't actually going outside. He entered the mudroom between the back doors that led into the store and the back doors that led out. He disappeared to the left of the mudroom, where a small connecting space led to a closed stairwell that went up to the roof.

What could he possibly be doing up there?

I tiptoed behind him, and after he finished jogging up the stairs, I crept up the tight stairwell all the way to the roof. There wasn't much to see up here—just the parking lot and the buildings around Grocery Hut.

To the right of the stairwell stood a rectangular structure that reminded me of a shed, pipes from the store below snaking up its sides and roof. I'd seen stuff like it on rooftops before, but I didn't know what they were called or what purpose they served.

I wasn't up here often either, but I knew that the door to the small rooftop-building should have been closed. It wasn't, of course. It was cracked open, and since Keith was nowhere else atop this barren roof, I deduced that he must be inside. I strode over and pushed in the door.

Keith was inside, surrounded by some sort of generator or compressor system. Pipes and tubes twisted and curled all around, and the light was dim, but I could still see. Did this rooftop-building maintain the store's air system?

As I approached Keith, there was a sharp squeal. Keith spun around, eyes wide. A tiny shadow suddenly appeared in the air, then swooped down toward me.

I ducked, covering my head with my hands. "What the hell?" I shouted. The shadow vanished among the pipes above me.

Keith rushed over and shut the door quickly. He shushed me all the while, a fresh roll of Bottle Caps in his hand. "Keep your voice down, dude. You'll scare him."

"Scare *who*?" I cried.

Keith pressed a finger to his lips and held up the candy toward where the shadow had disappeared. "It's all good, Reggie. Riley is a friend."

I looked up to inspect the ceiling. Now that the door was closed, the room was much darker. Thankfully, it was still bright enough that I could make out most of my surroundings. "Who's Reggie?"

Keith didn't need to answer my question, because a second later, I saw the thing that must be Reggie clinging to the pipe directly above my head. From here, he was still just a shadow. He scampered between pipes toward Keith, then swooped down and landed on Keith's shoulder.

It was then that I got a better look at him. The sight of him almost made me scream, but my shriek dissipated when I heard Keith laughing. "See?" Keith said between chuckles. "Everything's good, little dude."

Perched on Keith's shoulder, Reggie stared at me with bulbous red eyes that almost seemed to glow. He was roughly the size of a soccer ball and reminded me of an owl, and his legs were thin, his wings topped at the bend with three claw-like fingers. With his "hands," he swiped a roll of Keith's candy, pulled some pieces free, and began nibbling on them as if he were a rodent. All the while, his gaze remained locked on mine.

"Keith," I said as calmly as I could manage, "what is that?"

"You mean *who* is that?" He grinned, then laughed once and said, "Get it? 'Cause he kinda looks like an owl?"

"No, I definitely meant *what* is that."

"*He* is awesome." Keith patted the creature on the head, if you could call it that. He didn't seem to have a head, not really; his eyes were set high on what appeared to be the chest of an elongated torso.

Slowly, Keith stepped toward me, and once he and Reggie were out of the shadows, I could see Reggie more clearly. He had upside-down "V" for a mouth, two little fangs sticking out of it, which he used to devour the candy. A pair of moth antennae protruded from the top of his "head," and they tilted left and right.

Just then, I remembered the papers on Mason's desk in his hideout. One had been labeled "Mothman."

"No way." My breaths grew shallow, my head light.

"Riley"—Keith gestured to the baby Mothman—"this is Reginald Mothsworth III, or Reggie for short."

My eyes widened, not for obvious reasons, and not because Keith had *named* this thing. "There's two more of them?"

Keith knit his brow in confusion. "Two more?" He looked around the room. "I didn't see any others. Just Reggie."

"Then why did you name him *the third*?"

"Ohh." Keith cupped his chin. "Wait, is *that* what that means? I thought it was a fancy title for rich people. It just sounded cool to me."

I steepled my hands and pointed them at Reggie. "Can we *please* get back to the topic at hand?"

Keith shrugged. "Sure." Reggie snatched more candy from the roll and started eating it.

"For starters, *where*?" I tried not to raise my voice as I spoke, but it was a difficult feat considering the circumstances. "*When? How? Why?*"

"Here." Keith motioned at the floor. "It was the morning after boys' night. I came up here to stash some goodies and found him hiding out." He gave Reggie another pat. "Turns out he likes Bottle Caps as much as I do, and he ate a whole roll. I went down to the candy aisle to get him more, and that's when I found that sweet bat behind the shelf. I was going to tell you about Reggie right then, but you were wrestling with death-god portal immortal-guy out back, and then you were going through other stuff too, so I figured I'd wait until things calmed down to bring it up."

"But I deal with situations like this all the time," I said, raising a brow. "Why keep it a secret?"

Keith pointed at me. "'Cause I knew you'd do *that*."

"Do what?"

"The face. The 'Riley' face."

"That's just my face, Keith."

"No, no. You get this 'look' whenever the Protag'd stuff happens. Plus, you would have told me to get rid of him."

"Well, duh!" I cried. "He's not a stray cat. He's a *baby Mothman*."

"Aww, come on." Keith took Reggie off his shoulder and held the creature out to me like a baby. "Look at that face!"

Reggie finished his candy, let out a sharp squeal, and squirmed in Keith's grasp. He hadn't turned his "head" even once, and his antennae twitched to and fro. He also had a fluffiness to him that I hadn't noticed in the poor lighting—his fur was short but thick, pitch black except for a few streaks of gray that went down his spine and the backs of his wings.

Most startling of all were his massive red eyes. As I

stared into them, they reminded me of windows that went on forever.

To be honest, they were almost hypnotizing.

Actually, scratch that. They *were* hypnotizing, point-blank.

I continued looking into them, and images flashed through my mind. I was no longer in the rooftop-building, nor was I with Keith and Reggie.

A slideshow of events played out in my mind's eye.

Darkness.

Backyard.

Suitcase.

Dead body.

Molly.

Carlos.

I blinked and stumbled back. "Whoa!" I was in the roof-top-building with Keith and Reggie again. I rubbed my eyes, and Keith lowered Reggie.

"Oh yeah," Keith said. "I forgot. That happened to me too."

"What happened?"

"The images. Dunno what they mean for sure."

I stopped rubbing my eyes and looked up, my sight read-justing. Reggie glided around the room.

I pressed my fingers to my temples and tried to process the visions I'd just seen. Then I straightened my posture and put my foot down. "We can't keep him."

Keith whined as if he were a child in a toy store and wanted something he couldn't have. "What are we gonna do with him, then?"

"He was probably put in here by his mother or something. I'm sure she'll be back."

Keith's expression grew a touch more somber as he crossed his arms. "I . . . I don't think she's coming back."

"Why not?"

Keith paused before he answered. "Look, he's been alone up here for days. I'm the only one who's been checking on him."

"Well, you can't keep him up here either." I pinched the bridge of my nose. "What if Henry found out about this?"

"Henry never comes up here," Keith said, waving at me dismissively.

"But what if he does?"

Keith was silent for a moment. He looked back at Reggie, who was perched on an overhead pipe, cleaning himself in catlike fashion. With a sigh, Keith turned back to me. "Okay, maybe you got a point." He ran a hand through his hair. "What if I took him home?"

"Dude," I said. "This is the Sarah McLachlan sad-dog commercials all over again."

Keith raised his arms in defense. "It wouldn't be permanent. It would just be until we find his parents."

Now I had a whole host of new questions. "How exactly are we supposed to find his parents?"

Keith shrugged. "I dunno. You're the one who always deals with this stuff."

"I've never seen fucking *Mothman*!"

Keith shushed me. "Ixnay on the erring sway around the little guy, huh?" He narrowed his eyes at something behind me. "Hey, what about your backpack?"

I glanced at it over my shoulder. I'd almost forgotten I'd been wearing it. "What about it?"

"We can use it to sneak Reggie out to my car! I can take him home and get him somewhere warmer than here."

My shoulders slumped. "Keith, look . . ." I paused as Reggie twitched in the corner of my vision. The little guy had finished cleaning himself, and now he'd curled up into a ball atop the pipe. Despite his efforts to stay warm, he was shivering. At this time of year, it was generally only cool at night, normally in the seventies by this point in the day, but the sky was overcast, making the morning unusually chilly. I sighed.

God damn Sarah McLachlan and her sad-dog commercials.

I slipped off my backpack and knelt, then opened it and moved things around to make space. "For the record, I hate you."

"No, you don't," Keith replied.

"Yeah, I do." After I removed my spare work clothes, lunch box, and toiletries from the bag, I piled them up onto a box-shaped piece of machinery to the left of the door and pulled the bag wide open. "Okay. Load him up."

Keith turned around, approached Reggie, and carefully took the fluffball in his hands. "Come here, buddy. We're just gonna get you somewhere cozier."

Reggie didn't seem bothered by Keith picking him up. He fluttered his wings once, then allowed himself to be carried.

Keith placed him inside the backpack and zipped it up a bit, leaving the top open for him to peek out of. "Perfect," Keith said. He picked up the backpack and faced me. "Okay, now we just gotta get him to my car."

"Didn't you already clock in?"

Keith's expression went blank. He paused before speaking again. "Okay, now we just gotta go to the break room, and *then* get him to my car."

"I could clock you out. Or tell Henry you're sick and had to leave."

Keith fell silent once more. "We just need to make it to my car."

I turned to lead the charge outside. As we stepped out of the rooftop-building, Reggie began squealing and squirming inside the backpack. We stopped and took a minute to console him. Keith reached into the bag, presumably petting the baby Mothman. "It's okay, pal. We're on the move. Don't worry."

We continued across the roof, and although Reggie was a bit quieter, he wasn't completely silent. Thankfully, Keith just had to make it to the bottom of the stairs, turn left, and walk to the parking lot. How hard could that be?

As we reached the bottom of the stairwell, the door leading outside opened, and somebody walked in, meeting us head-on.

Ariel smiled at us as she fixed her purple cap over her hair. Even tied back and contained by a hairnet, the red tresses were gorgeous. "Hey," she greeted. "Were you guys on the roof or something?"

Panic took hold of me. We needed an excuse.

I forced a laugh. "Yeah, we were—"

"Stashing drugs," Keith interjected.

I twirled around to look at him. "Y-yeah." Turning back to Ariel, I tried my best to smile. "That's what we were doing."

Ariel nodded slowly, studying me. "Sounds exciting."

"You know me." I shrugged. "Exciting."

She giggled, and I smiled for real this time. Things were going in a good direction. Keith and I might get out of this mess yet.

A sharp squeal sounded from the backpack, and Reggie started squirming again.

All our gazes locked onto Keith's bag.

"What's that?" Ariel asked, her tone laced with suspicion.

"It's, uhh . . ." Keith trailed off.

I jumped in next. "It's a vibrator."

Fuck.

Ariel's smile shifted from friendly to confused. "A *vibrator*?"

Fuck.

"Yes," I said, doubling down. "But it's not for what you think it's for. It's . . ." Ariel crossed her arms as I tried to conjure up an explanation. Finally, I sighed. "Okay, I don't have a good excuse for why I have it. Honestly, I just panicked when it went off."

"I can tell." She pinched my cheek and walked off toward the bakery. "Don't get ahead of yourself, Thomas. It's only a date at the carnival." She glanced back at me and winked, and then she was gone.

I brushed my fingers against the cheek she'd pinched, remembering her previous statement about teasing guys she liked.

Maybe my nervous nature is finally paying off.

Keith patted my shoulder and headed outside. I followed him to his car, where he buckled the backpack into the front passenger seat. "Thanks for the help, bro."

"Sure," I said. "Hopefully I didn't completely embarrass myself in front of Ariel for nothing."

Keith grinned. "I don't think you did, you sly dog." He punched my arm. "All right, I'm gonna get Reggie back home. Cover for me."

"That was the plan."

Without another word, Keith hopped into the driver's seat, started the car, and drove away. I watched him until he was out of sight.

"Hey loser!" the familiar voice of a young woman called from behind me. I spun around to see Tasha leaning out of the back doors. "Henry is calling for you. Those three twerps are back, and they're throwing gallons of milk over the aisles."

I hurried over and followed her inside.

It wasn't a glamorous start to the workday, but it beat She-Devil hunting with Mason or Rivers.

CHAPTER 13
CALM BEFORE THE STORM

THE REST OF MY WORKDAY WAS UNEVENTFUL, which I thoroughly enjoyed and appreciated. The Trouble Teen Trio, as I'd taken to calling them, had gone through four gallons of milk by the time Henry and I managed to corner them. Somehow, only two of the four jugs broke, which left two messes for me to clean.

Unfortunately, the kids still got exactly what they'd come into the store for—more recordings of Henry screaming at them to leave. The video got tons of views, probably because of the clickbait-y title and cover. Internet clout sure is a backward thing to strive for, huh?

With the Trouble Teen Trio once again banned from Grocery Hut property, I was mostly delegated to the front end, where I worked at a register until the last hour of my shift. For that short bit of time, I stocked shelves and organized product before the evening crew of angsty teens came in to take over.

I ended up walking home after work. Keith texted me just before I was freed to let me know that Reggie was still settling in and that he didn't want to leave the little guy alone yet.

Surprisingly, I didn't run into a masked man or an evil sorcerer while traveling from Grocery Hut to my front door. There was hardly even any traffic, which made my trip home about twenty minutes instead of forty-five.

Molly sat in her usual spot on my couch, and tonight's entertainment was *The Mummy*, starring Brendan Fraser. The house was also neater and cleaner than it had been before I'd left for work, most of Molly's red scrawling gone from my furniture. The walls were still stained pink, but the television, couch, and coffee table were now spotless.

Outside of Reggie's appearance this morning, today was about as ordinary as ordinary could be.

And I didn't buy it for a second.

There was *no way* things would stay this calm. Rivers and Mason were still after the She-Devil. My serial-killer neighbor was still glaring at me through his curtains. Detective Kardoza still thought I was a murderer.

Worst of all, there was still an omnipresent force sending ridiculous scenarios my way as if I were a star baseball player ready to knock every main-character ball out of the park.

But regardless of everything going on, my mood couldn't be spoiled. Tomorrow was Wednesday—the start of my days off, as well as my date with Ariel. I'd informed her of my car troubles, and she'd agreed to swing by and pick me up around noon. Then we'd spend the day together at the carnival.

The plan was simple and effective. It was also ripe for trouble to rear its ugly head.

That night, I hardly slept, and as I sat beside Molly on the couch the next morning, watching the time like a hawk, I thought about everything that could go wrong.

Would Rivers interrupt our date, or would Mason? Maybe it would be both of them, and maybe they'd have another shoot-out.

Or maybe Kardoza would show up and arrest me before Ariel and I could even make it through two rides.

Carlos happening to be there wasn't out of the question, either.

I checked the time again. A quarter to noon. I lowered my phone and returned my attention to the TV.

In the corner of my eye, I noticed Molly staring at me. "What?" I said.

Naturally, she didn't respond, and I assumed she was wondering why I was checking my phone so much.

I raised the device for her to see. "Like I said, I'm going on a date today. I'm leaving in about fifteen minutes."

There was a tug on my shirt collar. I turned left, but no one was there. I looked down to find that my shirt was a bit straighter.

Another sensation—this time on my head, as if somebody was running their hands through my hair. After the feeling ebbed, I checked my camera. My hair was swept farther to the right than it had been before.

I looked down at Molly. She was still turned toward me, but she had her left hand raised in a thumbs-up.

"Uhh, thanks." I exited my camera, my mind starting to race. Why had Molly done that? When I faced her again, she was staring at the television, and I watched her curiously for several moments.

173

It started with the new coffee pot and making my bed. Now she was cleaning the house and adjusting my appearance.

She wasn't even haunting the place like she had been before—not in the traditional sense, anyway. Since her return, the bumps and scratches in my walls were for communication rather than torment.

She had to be buttering me up, manipulating me so I'd take a trip to Deathmore. Right? It was the only logical explanation. Why else would she be doing all this?

I continued pondering it until a horn sounded from outside. I checked the time again—six minutes to noon.

I leapt up from the couch and hurried to the door. "Please keep the house clean," I said, gesturing at Molly. "I'll be back tonight."

Molly had turned herself toward me, both of her hands raised in unmoving thumbs-up positions.

I nodded at her and, without another word, opened the door.

Ariel waited next to the sidewalk in her fire-engine red MINI Cooper. I locked my door, then hastened down my driveway toward her. Out of habit, I looked over at Carlos's place and saw him tending to his flower bed.

He shot curious glances between Ariel and me, an unsettling grin on his lips, as per usual. "Going out for the day, Riley?"

My blood practically turned to ice in my veins, but I did my best to stick with the "unassuming, kindly neighbor" vibe. I pointed at Ariel's vehicle. "Just heading to the carnival."

"Sounds like fun." Carlos spoke with cool, calm calculation. Using his dirty towel, he gestured at me in a playful manner. "Don't do anything that *I* wouldn't do."

I grabbed the handle of Ariel's passenger-side door, saluted Carlos, and jumped into the car.

For whatever reason, I must have been expecting to see Ariel in her work clothes, because I was completely taken off guard when I saw her up close. Her hair was down, and not only did it appear fluffier than usual, but it bounced as she moved her head. A rust-red color glistened on her lips, the rest of her face dusted with light makeup. She wore a white-and-scarlet sundress and black leggings.

"Hey!" she greeted me excitedly as I buckled up.

I was too dumbfounded to respond immediately. Finally, I tried to say, "Wow, you look great." But all that came out was caveman-speak.

She burst into laughter, and then I did too. I didn't know why it was so hard for me to talk to her, but she seemed to enjoy it. At least it was working to my advantage.

When Ariel eventually stopped giggling, she said, "Thank you. I think you look quite handsome as well."

My cheeks heated. "Th-thanks." I ran a hand through my hair, doing my best to maintain Molly's adjustments.

Ariel took the car out of park and started driving, and I could feel Carlos's eyes on us all the way down the road. About ten minutes later, when we arrived at the carnival, I realized my mistake.

Maybe I shouldn't have told Carlos I'd be here with her. Now it was much more likely that I'd see him.

But that was *not* going to ruin my good mood. I was

here. At the carnival. With Ariel freaking Quinn. The day couldn't get any better.

After finding a parking spot, we exited the vehicle and made our way to the entrance booth. If you can believe it, Ariel looked even more beautiful while she was up and walking around. Her hair and dress fluttered in the afternoon breeze, giving her an ethereal quality.

We waited in line for a bit, and when we reached the booth, our wrists were strapped with lime-green paper bands, and we were allowed to stroll into the carnival. We stopped at the entrance, giving the place a good look around.

The Ferris wheel rotated far in the back, towering high above the other rides. Closer to us were the Mean Machine, the Gravitron, and the Kamikaze. Food carts and rows of games with stuffed animals for prizes stood everywhere.

"Well," I said, "what do you wanna do first?"

"What's that?" she asked, pointing at the pendulum ride.

"That's the Kamikaze," I answered.

Hypnotized by the machine, she seized my hand and bolted toward it. "Let's do that one!"

Did I mention that rides like the Kamikaze aren't exactly my cup of tea? Truthfully, heights in general aren't my cup of tea, especially while spinning through the air at an excess of five miles per hour. It just doesn't seem like the safest (or the most enjoyable) way to spend my time, you know?

Sadly, when I boarded the ride with Ariel and it started moving, I realized that my feelings on the aforementioned matter had *not* changed. Give me death gods and evil wizards any day—just don't make me do *this*.

Several minutes later, we climbed off the death trap that people, for some reason, ride for fun. My stomach turned, and I struggled to catch my breath due to all the screaming I'd done.

On the other hand, Ariel couldn't stop giggling. Strands of hair stuck straight out of her head and hung in her face, but she still looked amazing. She brushed some hair behind her ear with another laugh. "That was awesome! Should we go again?"

I quickly gestured to the other rides around us. "Maybe we could try some of the others first?"

With an adorable, childlike wonder, Ariel fixed her attention on the Mean Machine, and with the same enthusiasm as before, she grabbed my hand and raced toward it.

This was how our afternoon went. Ride after ride, laugh after laugh, hand hold after hand hold. By the time we considered stopping for a snack, two hours had already gone by.

After a third consecutive go on the Gravitron, we stepped away from the rides toward the snack carts. We waited in a fairly long line, but we didn't grow bored once; we talked the whole time, discussing everything from stuff at work to the fun we'd had today, until we got to the front and ordered a large stick of blueberry cotton candy.

We walked away from the cart, and as she held the cotton candy, she stared at it, her wide eyes sparkling with amazement.

"Never had cotton candy before?" I asked.

She smiled sheepishly. "Is that bad?"

"Nah. Unless you're at a carnival, you aren't buying it. Probably." I reached over, took a piece out of the collective, and popped it into my mouth. A sugary sweet, distinctly "blue" flavor exploded on my tongue and melted in my mouth.

Ariel took a bite, and a couple of seconds later, her eyes lit up with surprise. "It dissolved!" She held her free hand to her mouth. "It's really sugary." She ate another piece, her reaction to this bite the same as the first. "This is so awesome!"

I couldn't help but laugh as I reached for more. Ariel ripped a third chunk free, but instead of eating it, she held it up for me. I opened my mouth, and she dropped it on my tongue.

I nodded a few times. "It's cotton candy, all right."

She grinned wide, leaning against me. "Shut up. I never got to eat this stuff, or go to carnivals."

"Did you not have them back home?"

She shook her head, devouring another chunk of blue fluff. "I didn't have much of anything back home, let alone carnivals and cotton candy."

"That sounds kind of boring," I said in a low voice.

"It is," Ariel replied, mimicking my tone. "But that's why I'm here, where there's fun stuff to do." Her smile grew more playful. "So let a girl enjoy her cotton candy."

I raised my hands in defense. "Consider it enjoyed." I caught sight of a booth to our right, which housed a game where you throw darts at balloons for prizes. "Speaking of fun things to do . . ." It was a bit of a step forward for me, and I figured it was my turn now anyway. I took Ariel's hand in mine and led her toward the game booth.

The man standing behind the booth wore a pair of blue jeans, a white T-shirt, and a black cap with the carnival's logo printed on the front. He perked up as we approached, smiling at us. "Howdy, folks. Care to try your aim for a prize?"

I examined the prizes lining the top of the booth's walls. Plushies of various copyrighted characters hung from them, although details were changed to avoid any legal trouble. There was a Pikachu with blue cheeks rather than red, Rick and Morty with miscolored hair and clothes, and even Spider-Man with the shades of his suit inverted. Closer to the bottom of the booth were the smaller, generic stuffed animals and other less-desirable prizes.

Ariel looked at the stuffies in astonishment. With her mouth full of cotton candy, she turned to the man and asked, "What's the game?"

The man pointed at the wall behind him, riddled with balloons both popped and un-popped. "Game is simple, little lady. Every play gets three darts. If you pop three balloons with your three darts, a big prize is yours."

I dug some cash out of my wallet and handed over the bills. "Three darts, please," I said with a level of confidence I didn't normally have. The man took the cash, gave me three darts, and stepped back.

I held up the first dart and took aim. Outside of the rare carnival trip or the occasional throw at a friend's place, I'd never really played darts before. My point being that I didn't have much experience, so when I threw the first dart and popped a blue balloon, my body surged with excitement.

It was two balloons away from the yellow one I'd been aiming for, but hey, I still hit the damn thing.

Ariel clapped for me, and I lifted the next dart and took aim once more. I settled on a red balloon and let it fly.

Another hit, this time just barely on target. The dart struck the red balloon on the side, but it was enough to puncture it.

"Sharp thrower over here, sharp thrower," the man said. Ariel watched with anticipation as I lifted the third and final dart. This time, I decided on the yellow balloon I'd originally wanted to hit.

I took aim and threw the dart.

It struck the wall right above the yellow balloon—not close enough to pop it. My shoulders sank, and Ariel let out a defeated, "No!"

"So close," the man behind the stand said as he collected my darts. "Two out of three isn't bad though, so you can pick anything below the big plushies." He gestured at the recognizable character stuffies hanging at the top, then lowered his arm to set an invisible bar. Basically, our options for my valiant attempt at dart-throwing were the smaller, generic stuffed animals or the plastic jewelry.

I turned to Ariel to resume my assumed date duties. "Well, what do you want to take home?"

She blinked in surprise. "Wait, *I* get to pick something?"

"Yup." I smiled. "As long as it's not Pikachu or Spider-Man, of course."

She scanned over her options. Her grin grew wider as she pointed at a tiger plushie. "I'll take that one."

"Sure." The man knelt, removed the stuffed animal from the lineup, and handed it over. The tiger was roughly the size of two Beanie Babies, with short orange fur and big blue plastic eyes.

Ariel gave the tiger a squeeze. "I love tigers."

"I'm glad he had some in the pile, then," I said, and waved at the man. "Thanks."

He waved back as we walked off. "Anytime!" he said. "Be sure to come play again before we take off!"

With a plush tiger in one hand and blueberry cotton candy in the other, Ariel wandered happily ahead of me, glancing around at the still-unexplored rides and booths around us. After a few moments, she turned back to me. "What should we do now?"

I eyed the Ferris wheel behind her. "How about something a little slower so you can finish your cotton candy?"

She raised a brow. "Got something in mind?"

I jerked my head in the direction of the Ferris wheel and continued forward. When I looked at her again, she was giving me a look that I imagine people give cats after they make a cute noise. "Why, Mr. Thomas," she said sweetly, "you want to ride the Ferris wheel with me? Isn't that for couples?"

The confidence I'd built up since we arrived disappeared. My ability to speak vanished with it, because I struggled to form a coherent response. "W-well, I guess. Kind of? But not always. Sometimes, they, like— I mean, you can ride with family or friends."

Ariel giggled. Popping another wad of cotton candy into her mouth, she nudged me softly. "I'm just teasing, dude. Relax."

I'll never understand how she always knew exactly what to say to take the wind out of my sails.

We trotted over to the Ferris wheel, and after a short wait in line, we were on board, gliding toward the top of the wheel. Ariel placed her tiger between us in the seat and leaned on the safety bar, finishing up her cotton candy all the while.

As we neared the top, I stared out at the horizon. The lush green fields stretched for miles, the woodland's edge far to the right. The sun began its descent for the evening, gradually painting the sky with orange and pink.

"Wow," Ariel whispered. "What a beautiful view."

"I thought you might like it up here."

"You thought right. I can't get enough of the sunrises and sunsets here. So colorful and pretty."

"Are those what you like to paint?"

"Yeah. If I'm being honest though, I don't think I'm super great at painting." Her lips spread into a big, genuine smile. "But I don't care. I love doing it, no matter how bad I might be."

I couldn't help but smile too. That feeling was back, that wonder of what had happened to my own personal drives and interests.

I sighed. "I used to feel like that about photography."

Ariel took the last bite of her cotton candy and turned to face me. "Photography?"

"Yeah," I said with a nod. "I used to take all kinds of pictures. Learned how to develop film. Hated that. Stuck with digital. I don't know if I was ever really good with perspectives and timing, or with lining up great shots. I just kind of did what felt right, you know?"

"That's *exactly* how I feel about painting."

I leaned back in the seat as we began closing in on the lower end of the wheel. "I can't wait to see them."

"Only if I get to see some of your pictures!"

"Maybe." My heart grew heavy for the first time today. "Most of the ones I took are of my family, before . . ." I wasn't sure how to tell her about what happened to them. After a second of contemplation, I decided it was best to avoid the topic for now. I cleared my throat. "Anyway. That was a long time ago. I haven't taken any pictures in years. Kind of lost that spark for it, I guess."

Ariel watched me with a somber expression. She almost appeared to be wrestling with her thoughts, and I figured she was piecing together what little context clues I'd given her.

Suddenly, she held out her hand. "Let me see your phone."

I have to admit, the request confused me. "Sure?" I pulled out the device and handed it over.

Ariel raised the phone and opened the camera, then turned it toward us and leaned her head against mine. She smiled, more gorgeous than ever with the sunset behind her. "Say cheese, lover boy." As soon as I smiled, she snapped a picture, then handed the phone back to me. "If old pictures are hard to look at, we'll have to start taking new ones. Right?"

I stared down at the selfie. Ariel took up most of my focus, but surprisingly, I looked pretty dashing as well. The sunset gave us a healthy glow, made our smiles shine like pure energy. The picture was so good, it was almost supernatural, and the warm feeling it filled me with was something entirely new.

It was a bittersweet feeling. I was still sad about my family—how I'd not only lost them, but myself as well. And yet, for the first time in a very long time, I felt as though the missing part of me might still be around somewhere.

Something long since lost had finally been found. Even if it was only momentary.

The last few minutes of the ride went by in silence. When it ended, Ariel and I exited it and started back through the crowds of people.

Today really has been the perfect day.

As soon as the thought crossed my mind, a gunshot roared into the air, followed by an earsplitting scream.

CHAPTER 14
AND THE WINNER IS...

I'D ALMOST FORGOTTEN ABOUT THE ROGUES' GALLERY of people who were after me. The date with Ariel was going off without a hitch, and normally, I would have been waiting with bated breath for someone to show up and ruin it. But I'd been so caught up in her company that I'd forgotten to watch for signs of trouble.

After the first gunshot rang out, my mind began to spin with possibilities for where it had come from. I'd dealt with a lot of people who used guns recently—Mason, for one. If he were here, firing off shots, then Rivers would also be nearby.

Detective Kardoza was another possibility, but who or what would he be shooting at? Honestly, at this point, it could have been another gun-hand guy.

The people around Ariel and me started screaming and running, and Ariel glanced around quickly. "Was that a *gunshot*?" she cried.

"Unfortunately, I think it was." I took her hand, and we hurried away from where the noise had come from. "We need to get somewhere safe!"

More and more yelling people sprinted toward us, with us, as if trying to get away from something.

BOOM!

An explosive sound thundered across the carnival, shaking the ground and drowning out all other noises for whole seconds. Heat seared my face, my neck, my arms, as one of the rides ahead of us burst into orange flames.

More screaming. More people fleeing. My desire to escape skyrocketed by the second.

Then, from the flames, a figure emerged. And I wasn't sure if it was better or worse than what I'd been expecting.

It was a generic-looking man holding a strange gun, his plain white T-shirt stretched taut over his ripped physique. With stiff, robotic movements, Rob the Eliminator walked forward, scanning the crowd . . . until his eyes settled on mine.

He marched straight toward Ariel and me.

"Riley Thomas!" he bellowed. He aimed his gun, and I yanked Ariel to the side. We launched into a sprint.

A second gunshot. To my right, the rubber-duck pools erupted as though they were volcanoes, showering the air with water and deflated quacks.

Ariel shrieked, and we quickened our pace. Rob's heavy combat boots pounded against the ground as he stomped after us.

A third gunshot. The dirt to the left of my feet exploded like a mini tornado.

We fell to the side, Ariel screaming again. I stumbled but kept my balance. On we raced past destroyed booths, gutted plushies, abandoned food, and panicked people.

"What is *going on*?" Ariel shouted from right behind me.

"It's a long story!" I tightened my grip on her hand, leading her through the crowd. "This guy came back from the future to kill me. Apparently, I started a resistance against an AI overlord that tried to wipe out humanity." We darted behind a food cart, taking cover. "I guess it wasn't that long of a story, actually."

Ariel gasped for breath. "So, he's—"

"Trying to Schwarzenegger me, yes."

She shook her head, her eyes widening. She opened her mouth to say something when gunfire shredded through the booth next to us. We ducked down.

A few seconds later I looked up and spotted Rob peeking around the corner of our food cart. His expression was still and emotionless, but his voice was full of unadulterated rage. "*Riley Thomas*! *Liar*! *Snake*! *You will die in the name of overlord IRIS*!"

I raised my hands defensively. "I take it you didn't have fun at the Bermuda Triangle?"

Ignoring Ariel's shrieks, Rob seized me by the shirt collar and yanked me into the air. "Traveling through time made my data processor malfunction. After I traveled approximately three states east, the processor realigned." He shifted the weapon in his free hand from something massive to something reminiscent of a handgun, and then he pointed it at my head. "You fooled me once, but you will not do so again."

Before Rob could do to my head what he did to my date, a tray of nachos smacked him in the face, melted cheese splattering all over him. And rather than flinching or making a disgruntled noise, he merely released me and used his hands to begin wiping the mess away.

I hit the ground shoulder-first. Ariel helped me to my feet, and we bolted off again. Still holding hands, we darted past a pop-up fun house, more rides, and some walls. Once we made it out of the main area of the carnival, we weaved through a maze of trailers and carnival-staff vehicles, dashing between the trucks and trailers that stored and transported equipment for the rides.

I chanced a glance over my shoulder and caught sight of Rob tramping in our direction. Like Michael Myers, he simply marched after us while we ran for our lives. He raised his gun again, ready to fire.

I shoved Ariel aside. "Watch out!"

Two shots rang into the air. A bullet whizzed past my head, and a truck window beside me shattered.

With another scream, Ariel lost her footing. I tripped over her calf. A moment later we were both on the ground in a heap.

I glanced up, heart in my throat as Rob pounded on.

"Riley, this way!" Ariel whispered next to me. Furiously, she army-crawled under the closest truck, and I followed her lead without a moment's hesitation.

Soon Rob drew near. The gravel beneath me quivered with each heavy footstep.

I finished crawling to the other side of the truck, and Ariel pulled me into a standing position. There were less vehicles on this side, which meant we had a mostly clean getaway through the narrow path between parked vehicles.

Lord knows what our plan was once we got that far, but hey, one problem at a time.

We tiptoed that way. There was the crunch of gravel behind us, the creaking of metal, and then one of the heavy-duty trucks to our right flipped into the air, careering toward us. We stopped in our tracks as it landed on its side, blocking our escape.

Rob leapt in front of us, then pushed the truck aside casually, as if it were weightless.

We turned to run . . . but quickly found we had nowhere left to go. The path behind us was a dead end, capped off by a large industrial work truck.

With the threat so close, climbing over or under the cars beside us was out of the question. I had a feeling that even if I tried to get away, I'd be shot or captured—or maybe even crushed by a truck, considering how easily Rob could move them.

Basically, Ariel and I were cornered by walls of vehicles and a homicidal android, and we had no way to escape.

Rob stepped forward, cocking his gun. "It is over, Riley Thomas, nemesis of overlord IRIS."

"Oh, come on!" I shouted. "Now I'm *her* nemesis too? Give me a break already."

"You started the resistance," Rob retorted.

"I really don't think I did!"

Rob aimed his gun at Ariel and me. "It does not matter. You will be eliminated. For the good of the future."

Ariel threw her hands in the air. "Wait!"

Rob paused, narrowing his eyes at her. "What?"

"I just need to get something straight here." She pointed at Rob. "You're here to kill Riley because he tried rising up against your boss?"

"Yes."

Ariel gestured at me. "Do you think you'd do something like that?"

"No!" I cried. "I wouldn't do anything even close to that."

Ariel faced Rob again. "So, logically speaking, if Riley would never start the resistance, then *you* would never be sent back in time to kill him. Correct?"

Rob furrowed his brow ever so slightly, and silence—other than the screams and sirens in the distance, of course—blanketed the three of us for what felt like hours.

Then, finally, Rob vanished. Over the course of about a minute, he became more and more transparent before disappearing altogether.

I let out a long breath and cleared my throat. "Well, that was a bit anticlimactic."

"Yeah." Ariel sighed in relief. "The details of the story you told me just weren't adding up, and I figured it was some kind of mistake. He shouldn't have been after you in the first place."

My jaw dropped, and I stared at her in wide-eyed amazement.

How had I not realized that sooner? I would have been toast without her.

The sirens grew louder, closer. "Maybe we should get out of here," I said, taking her hand in mine again. "Unless you want to stick around and tell the police about our giant carnival-destroying acquaintance?"

Ariel laughed and tugged me toward the closest wall of cars, presumably so we could climb it and leave. "No, thank you!"

CHAPTER 15
TRUE COLORS

THE CHAOS OF THE CARNIVAL WAS CERTAINLY one way to end our first date. I couldn't say I hadn't expected it, but I also couldn't say I wasn't bummed about it.

I would have preferred the entire evening to consist of us enjoying rides and playing games. If Heaven is real—and, based on a certain devil I was supposed to slay, I'd say it is—then I hoped my Heaven would be that carnival, with Ariel by my side.

After we got to Ariel's car and drove away, we realized that her stuffed tiger was gone. We weren't quite sure where it was, but she said she thought she lost it sometime during the scuffle with Rob.

I made a mental note to track down a proper replacement for her.

Our chat on the drive back into town was surprisingly upbeat considering what we'd just experienced, and Ariel didn't seem as bothered by Rob's rampage as I was. If anything, she was happy about it. "My heart won't stop racing!" she said again and again.

She couldn't sit still either. Adrenaline is one hell of a drug, I guess. I'd already begun coming down once Rob disappeared, but she still seemed to be riding the high.

Suddenly her insistence on riding the Kamikaze so many times made a whole lot more sense. *She must be an adrenaline junkie.*

Ariel Quinn might be too much woman for you, Riley Thomas.

I figured that our day together was over, and I already had future date ideas that hopefully wouldn't involve such troublesome "guests." We were about two blocks from my house when Ariel surprised me with a question. "Do you wanna go back to my place?"

As I'm sure you can guess, I was caught off guard by the inquiry. I also didn't get a chance to answer it.

"Not for like, *that*," Ariel continued with a sharp laugh, "but just to kick back and talk some more."

I couldn't help but smile now that the elephant in the room had been outright evicted. "My, my. Miss Quinn, did I just witness a spell of embarrassment?"

Her cheeks turned pink. Glancing over at me, she grinned. "Easy, lover boy. Awkwardness is cute on you, but not me."

I took the compliment not only at face value, but also as a sign of victory. I'd won a round of teasing for a change. I let out a casual chuckle and nodded. "Sure. I'd love to see your place."

Just like that, we made a U-turn in the middle of my street and headed toward Ariel's apartment complex. It was on the opposite side of town, and it took around twenty minutes to get to.

There were four buildings in total, all of them soft beige with dark wooden trimming, and I spotted a sign with the complex's name out front: Urban Harmony Apartments. They didn't look too expensive, but they didn't look slummy either. The lawns were tidy and well-kept, the property between buildings clean and organized, and there was a small playground for residents with children. In the center of the complex stood a smaller structure that I assumed served as the landlord's office.

Ariel parked her MINI Cooper on the far-right side of one of the buildings, and I followed her inside. A plaque above the doorway said "UH-3" in fancy black lettering.

We walked up the stairs to the third floor, then down the hall until we reached a door marked "314" at the end. Ariel unlocked the door and led me inside.

Just as seeing her dolled up had surprised me, seeing where she lived startled me as well.

She didn't have a television. Not in the living room, anyway. What the living room *did* have was a sliding door that led to the balcony. Next to the door stood an easel and a stool, which I guessed would have had a perfect view of the sunset if it weren't already over. Other paintings—all of them streaked with red, orange, and purple—lay on the floor or hung on the walls. Some depicted sunsets, while others showcased Ariel herself, her fiery hair blending into colorful backgrounds. Other than that, there was a loveseat, a narrow hallway to my left, and a corner kitchenette to my right.

As I entered the apartment, I looked around at the paintings on the walls, feeling as if I'd stepped into a miniature art gallery.

"It's not much," Ariel said shyly, "but it's got a great view."

I smiled at her. "You painted all these?"

"Yup. I work on one until it's done, and then I start another." She walked past me as I continued gazing at her paintings.

Soon I discovered a picture more beautiful than all the others. It was a self-portrait of Ariel, rendered with the finest of details. Her emerald-green eyes were striking, and rather than the usual purple and orange, this version of her wore a blouse that matched her eyes. Green strokes blended into her red hair, creating a cyclone of deep, vivid colors, her face in the eye of the storm.

It was hypnotizing.

I looked back at Ariel. She'd taken a seat on the couch, and she beckoned me to join her. I stepped over and sat down next to her. "These are absolutely stunning," I said.

"Thank you." She brushed a strand of hair behind her ear. "I feel like the colors really speak to who I am."

"What do you mean?"

She paused before replying. "I don't know how to explain it in a way that makes sense to anybody besides me. I . . . I guess the best way I can say it is that when I think of myself, I think of fiery reds and glowing oranges. So, when I see sunsets, I'm happy. It feels like nature's gift to me."

Somehow, I understood what she meant. "What colors remind you of me?"

She giggled. "Purple, for sure."

"Boo." I waved a hand dismissively at her.

"I think it's a lovely color. Besides"—she gestured around at her paintings—"you get the greatest sunsets with shades of purple thrown into the mix."

I wasn't sure how to respond. We fell silent, but it wasn't awkward. We were just two people quietly enjoying each other's company.

Ariel lowered her head and fidgeted with her hands in her lap. She appeared to be thinking about what to say next.

"What's wrong?" I asked.

Her smile faltered, then vanished. She kept her stare on the floor. Finally, she met my gaze. "Can I ask you something kind of serious?"

You might recall when I previously stated that your boss asking you to come to their office is the most terrifying thing that can happen to you. I'd just like to say I was incorrect in that initial statement.

"Yeah," I said with a gulp. "Sure."

"Do you . . . ever feel like somebody is trying to force you to do something you don't want to do?"

I let out a tired sigh, a slideshow of each and every Pro-tag'd moment I could remember playing in my mind. "You have no idea," I said in a quiet voice.

She bit her lip. "Back in my hometown, my dad expects me to join the family business. Originally, the reason I came here was to do that, but I ended up really liking this place, and I stayed. Found painting. I don't want to go home, but I don't think I have a choice, you know?"

I pursed my lips in thought. That *was* a difficult situation, although I would have killed to be dealing with something similar regarding my own parents. But this was her problem, not mine, so it wasn't fair of me to approach it with that kind of perspective.

"Well," I began, "has your dad seen your paintings yet?"

Ariel blinked a few times. "Umm, no, actually. I don't think he has."

"I bet he'd change his tune if he saw how talented you are, and how passionate you are about it." At that moment, we locked eyes. "It's your life, Ariel. Not his. Don't live it for him, or me, or anyone else. Live it for you."

It took a minute for her to register my words. Likewise, it took me a minute to register that our faces were a lot closer than they had been before.

She leaned in, and so did I. She smiled, and I did too. And then our lips met in a kiss.

MY SECURITY SYSTEM, BUT LIKE, FROM HELL

CHAPTER 16

i COULDN'T HAVE ASKED FOR A BETTER DAY. FROM the date with Ariel to our kiss—I mean, it was perfect. Well, mostly perfect. Thanks, Rob.

Kissing Ariel was as magical as I'd imagined it would be, and once it was over, it was all I could think about. After it happened, the two of us sat and talked a bit more as we enjoyed the view of the night sky through the balcony doors.

The topic of our conversation was . . . interesting. The incident at the carnival sparked it initially. Then Ariel asked the million-dollar question: "Does that kind of thing happen to you a lot?"

She said it in jest, of course, but I decided to tell her about a few of the things I'd been dealing with. And by "a few," I mean everything. Molly, Reggie, Rivers, Mason, Carlos, Detective Kardoza, the She-Devil, even The Edge of Time bar. She thought I was kidding at first, but by the time I finished relaying the whole death-god debacle that occurred during my last closing shift, she realized it wasn't a joke.

With the whole of my tale said and done, she took a few minutes to process everything, then offered some helpful insights.

First, she told me that Molly sounded quite sweet, and that if I was keen on having better conversations with the doll, a whiteboard and erasable marker or even some magnetic letters on the fridge would probably go a long way. I'll admit, I felt kind of dumb for not thinking of those options myself.

She then made me clarify that Reggie had been in my backpack—*not* a vibrator. Score one for Riley Thomas in the "awkward moment you'll be thinking about for the rest of your life" category. Bonus points for having to clarify how needlessly awkward I'd made said awkward moment. "By the way, you'd better show me Reggie," she demanded. "He sounds adorable as fuck."

After that, she assured me that Rivers and Mason were bound to cancel each other out because of their feuding, and that it would probably happen long before they dragged me into their business again. She also speculated that since Carlos hadn't yet made a move against me, he probably wouldn't at all, and that if Kardoza was a competent detective, he'd eventually realize my innocence.

"And as far as the She-Devil thing goes," she concluded, "it'll most likely resolve itself in a similar way to how the death-god portal did. No need to stress too much over it."

I let out a low whistle. "Wow."

Sitting sideways on the couch to face me, Ariel tilted her head. "What?"

"You're just way better at coming up with solutions for this stuff than I am."

"Honestly, I think the fact that you've been juggling all this and still make it to work on time is impressive."

Conversation post my personal life was much more normal. It lasted between twenty to thirty minutes before Ariel offered to drive me home.

She had to work in the morning, and because she was a baker at Grocery Hut, she had to be there at 3 a.m. if she wanted to get everything done on time.

That meant our evening was cut rather short, but I didn't mind. It had already ended on the strongest possible note.

The drive back to my house consisted of more conversations ranging from favorite TV shows and funniest internet videos to annoying customers we'd recently dealt with at work. Before I knew it, the twenty-minute drive was over. We were at the end of my driveway, and I was climbing out of Ariel's car. "So, Romeo, when's the next date?" she asked.

"Well," I said with a defeated grin, "I am covering yet another closing shift tomorrow because yet another high schooler decided he has better things to do than come to work."

"Ouch," she replied with a fake wince.

"What about Saturday? Maybe we can do something once we're both off."

She groaned. "You don't have a plan?"

This is bad. Quick, throw out an idea. Anything.

"N-no, I have a plan. What if we—"

"Relax," she cut me off, giggling. "I'm just teasing. I'm sure that whatever we do will be fun."

I let out a breath of relief. *She's going to be the death of me.*

Ariel shifted her car out of park and blew me a kiss. "See you later."

I "caught" the kiss, closed her door, and watched her drive away. I waved at her until she turned at the end of the block and vanished from sight, then started the walk up my drive. It was even darker out now than it had been when I was at her place, the sky stained with dark blues and purples.

The lights were on in Carlos's house, yellow peeking out between his slightly parted curtains. In one of his windows, the drapes parted just a bit wider as I made my way toward my front door.

Carlos was home, and he was *still* watching me.

But not even that could ruin my mood. Ariel's advice reminded me to stay the course.

Honestly, I doubted *anything* could ruin my mood at this point. There would have to be a literal dead body on the floor of my living room to dampen my spirits.

I reached my front door, pulled out my keys, and slid the key to my front door into the lock. I stepped inside, the sounds of another action movie playing from the television speakers.

"I'm home." I shut the door behind me and flipped on the lights. Molly sat on the couch where I'd left her.

Something else was in the room with her though, and wouldn't you know it?

There was a literal dead body on the floor of my living room. A man wearing all black, his head twisted at a very wrong angle.

It's starting to feel like I'm doing this to myself.

201

I looked at the corpse, then at Molly. She stared at the corpse. I looked at the corpse again, then at Molly again. Now she stared at me.

I gestured at the body. "What the fuck happened?"

Molly, as usual, didn't answer me. This would have been a great time to have a whiteboard or some magnetic letters handy. As my unanswered question hung in the air, I concluded that I'd have to figure this out on my own.

Calling the cops was out of the question. Chances are Detective Kardoza would be first on the scene, ready to declare me a murderer.

It was then that Ariel's rationalizations came back to me. I stopped to think about the situation, soon deducing that there was zero evidence on me. A dead body in my house looked bad, sure, but this man, whoever he was, clearly hadn't died by my hand.

But who *had* killed him? Carlos was an obvious suspect. Maybe he broke in while I was gone and dropped off one of his victims to frame me.

As I stepped around the corpse, I came to a realization that was somehow more petrifying than simply finding a dead body in my home. I knew this man. His black ski mask was pulled up to his forehead, revealing his face.

It was Sal of the neighborhood watch.

His skin was pale gray, his expression contorted in a horrified scream. He looked as if he'd died of pure fright. That or a broken neck, considering his head appeared to have been twisted around like a screw.

Things were starting to make more sense. For one, I knew who'd killed him.

It had to be Molly.

I faced the doll and found her staring at the body again. "Did you do this?"

Scratches in the wall to my right. I turned that way and spotted . . . a crowbar? Yes, it *was* a crowbar, under my window to the left of my TV. The window itself was halfway open, a soft breeze creeping into my house.

I walked over to investigate. The lock was damaged, and so was the bottom windowsill. Somebody had broken in.

At this moment, all the pieces came together.

There was no neighborhood watch. Poor, simple Sal had tried to burgle my home for valuables. He'd come here knowing that I didn't possess a security system. He'd believed that my house would be easy pickings.

Unfortunately for Sal, nothing in my place was even remotely valuable, except for my nearly ten-year-old computer . . . maybe. But most importantly, a haunted, homicidal jester doll sat right in my living room. And apparently, *she* was my security system.

I faced Sal's corpse again. How long had Molly tormented the poor man before putting him out of his misery? Also, how loudly had he screamed before dying?

The last thing I needed was people calling the cops on me. If anyone had, Kardoza would no doubt arrive at any second with the same song and dance as before.

I had to figure out what to do with Sal's body, and I had to figure it out quickly. I closed my eyes, partly to think, but mostly to get Sal's contorted expression out of my line of vision. It reminded me of the way people in *The Ring* looked after they died.

Haunting. Uncanny. Unnatural.

Oh, right. I'm supposed to be thinking of ideas.

After a couple of seconds, an obvious solution presented itself. Molly made the mess; surely, she could clean it as well. She'd been cleaning up messes lately anyway. How was this any different?

"Okay, Molly." I opened my eyes to look at her. She'd gone back to watching television, her arm raised, her palm facing flat toward me as if saying "talk to the hand."

So much for that idea.

I considered a few more, but I didn't care for any of them. To be fair, I didn't care for the situation to begin with. Consider my spirits dampened.

I briefly wondered whether I should bury Sal in my backyard. When the spree killer had lived here, that's where he'd buried his victims. Might as well keep with tradition.

But then I remembered Kardoza. If he found Sal in my yard, it would be impossible to explain my innocence. He'd surely be sniffing around my place any day now, too.

What about acid in the bathtub? Classy, but messy, and I'd be sacrificing a perfectly fine tub in the process. Probably more. Not to mention how expensive the supplies for the job would be. I could barely afford food, let alone chemicals for dissolving a corpse.

Cremation? On top of how grim and fucked up that would be—along with every other idea on this list—I also didn't possess a device powerful enough to burn an entire human body to ashes.

I was zero for three so far. What else?

I could only think of one more thing, and I had a much harder time dissuading myself from it than I had the others. My next-door neighbor *was* a serial killer with a specialty in body disposal. Maybe I should swing by and ask for help? Or for some tips, at the very least.

After deliberating upon the idea, I eventually committed to it. I cleared a path to my back door, shut my window, kicked aside the crowbar, and grabbed Sal's corpse from under the armpits.

You'd think human bodies would be on the heavier side, and you'd be right. I wasn't the most muscular person either, so hauling anything relative to a case of bottled water was physically exhausting for me.

An entire human body's worth of literal dead weight? That was, like, at least four cases of bottled water. Maybe five.

I'd like to say that I managed to carry him to the back door, but that would be a lie. Truth be told, I couldn't drag him a single step away from where I'd found him.

Once I realized I couldn't take him outside, I released him. There was a sickening crunch as his skull struck my hardwood floor.

This was going to be harder than I thought.

All right, I needed a plan B. Perhaps I could empty the suitcase from my closet and pull it into the living room. My parents had purchased the navy bag for the traveling we'd planned to do shortly after graduation, and it had wheels on the bottom and a carry-handle on the top. It was big enough to hold a body, right?

Hopefully.

I retrieved the suitcase and set it on the floor next to Sal, then set to work lifting him and working him into it, one limb at a time. By the time I had him inside the bag, nearly half an hour had passed. I had to spend another fifteen minutes Tetris-ing his limbs so I could zip up the suitcase.

Finally, the only thing left for me to position was the head, which I'm absolutely disgusted to say took no effort at all. Due to Sal's neck injuries, there was nothing to support his head. It may as well have been a bowling ball attached to his shoulders via a rubber glove, considering the bones were basically nonexistent.

Still, I knew the bones were there, because I heard every single little crunch under the bruised skin of Sal's neck as I pushed his head into the suitcase. The sound reminded me of rocks rubbing against each other in a pool of wet cement—only, you know, way more repulsive.

Score one for Riley Thomas in the "horrifying experiences that will make you lose sleep" category. I was really racking up points across the board tonight.

I zipped the suitcase shut and prepared myself for the next part of the plan. It took some effort, but rolling the suitcase was still a lot easier than carrying the body. I hauled the suitcase to the back door, crept outside, and carefully stepped down the three stairs into my backyard.

There was no fence dividing my backyard from Carlos's, just as there was no fence dividing our front yards—only flowers. A large grass bed stretched between our backyards, the single difference between my yard and his being that he had a garden shed while mine remained bare.

It was more difficult to drag my cargo across the lawn than it was my hardwood floor, but I managed to transport the suitcase to Carlos's side of the grass before setting it down and approaching his back porch.

Like my house, there were three steps up to the back door, the only difference being that Carlos had added a side deck last summer. He'd kept the stairs and built a porch that was big enough for a small table and two chairs. An umbrella pole stuck out of the table, currently closed since it wasn't in use.

I walked up the steps, mentally preparing for the conversation I was about to have. Then I reached out and knocked on the door.

For a while there was no answer, so I knocked again. Footsteps sounded on the other side. After they stopped, Carlos peeked out through the curtains. He appeared to be confused and agitated, but he still answered the door, dressed in sweatpants and a white T-shirt. "H-hey neighbor," he said, forcing a smile. "The front door is on the opposite side of the house, you know."

"Yeah, I know, and I know it's late too. I just need your help with something."

Suddenly his smile seemed a tad more genuine. "Oh. Yeah, sure."

"Great." I walked back down the steps and stopped next to the suitcase.

Carlos followed me. He furrowed his brow when he spotted the bag. "You going somewhere?"

I didn't answer his question. Instead, I knelt and unzipped the top of the suitcase so he could see the body inside.

He gasped, his eyes going wide, and took a step back. "W-w-what the hell is this?"

I tried not to roll my eyes. *He sure is a good actor. Bet he's been practicing that one for a while.* I stood up straight, raising a hand in a calming manner. "Carlos, look, let's be real. I *know* you're the serial killer." I pointed at the body in the suitcase. "I just came home to this—and obviously, I didn't hurt this guy—but we both know Kardoza will think I did."

Carlos kept up the charade pretty well. He even turned away, as if he was avoiding looking directly at the corpse.

I paused, waiting for him to respond, but he didn't, so I continued. "I just need help making it vanish. I know that's what you've been doing with all the others."

Carlos faced me, using his hand to block the suitcase from his peripheral vision. "What the fuck are you talking about?" He was louder now, but he quickly realized it and lowered his voice to a whisper. "You can't stand here calling *me* the serial killer when *you* are the one with a dead body in a fucking box."

"I know what it looks like, but I swear to God, I got home and found him like this." I gestured at his house. "For Christ's sake, you saw me come home, like, an hour ago!"

"I'm pretty sure you could kill somebody in an hour!" he retorted in a whisper-yell.

I waved at him dismissively. "Semantics. Look, can you help me or not?"

He dug his phone out of his pocket. "I can call the cops on you, you psychopath."

That was a bold move.

"What? Why?" I whisper-yelled back at him.

"Because you brought a fucking corpse into my backyard!"

"Only because I figured you could help me hide it the same way you hide all your victims!"

"What victims?" He threw his hands in the air. "I didn't kill anybody!"

"Carlos," I began with a sigh. "Seriously, I know it's you. You don't have to—"

"I am *not* the serial killer," Carlos repeated, then pointed at me. "You are!"

Now *I* was confused. I pointed at myself. "Wait, me? You think *I'm* the serial killer?"

"You live alone, there's weird noises coming from your house in the middle of the night, *and* a killer lived in your house before you." Carlos punctuated his list by motioning at the suitcase with both hands.

"Okay, *one* dead body does not a serial killer make, and I'm *not* the serial killer. I thought *you* were."

Carlos crossed his arms. He opened and closed his mouth a few times, his nostrils flaring. "I have *always* been nice to you. How on earth did you come to that conclusion?"

I jerked my head in the direction of his flower bed. "The blood all over the flower bed? The way you hold your smile way too long? *You're* the one who put the idea of a serial killer in my head to begin with."

Carlos looked at his flowers, then back at me. "You mean my blood meal?"

"Blood . . . meal?"

"For the flowers, Riley!" he nearly screamed. "It's cow blood, to help the flowers grow!"

I shook my head. "*Why* would you put *cow blood* in a flower bed?"

One of his brows twitched. He looked down at his feet, avoiding my eyes. "That one day, you—you mentioned how dead bodies are good for the soil. Which, I mean, it really freaked me out, but then I did some research, and I found out that blood meal helps plants grow. When I water the flowers, the meal makes the dirt look like blood."

I couldn't believe what I was hearing. "So, wait, what about all the dirty looks and sneaky glances you've been giving me?"

Carlos returned to whisper-yelling and expressive movements. "*Me*? *You've* been peeking through your windows at *me* for days!"

"Yeah, but only because *you've* been peeking through your windows at *me*!"

He pressed his lips into a thin line, staring at me as though I had three heads. "Well, then why did that detective show up at my house asking all kinds of questions about you?"

"You mean Kardoza? Yeah, for whatever reason, he thinks I'm the serial killer."

"But . . . you're not?"

"Nope. I honestly thought it was you."

We stood in silence, watching each other in shock for what felt like a whole minute, before Carlos smiled slightly and laughed a little. "That's—that's kind of funny. Because I honestly thought it was you."

"I guess it is kind of funny when you think about it like that, yeah."

I started to chuckle, and then so did Carlos, and then we both had a good laugh about the whole ordeal, because what else were we supposed to do? I still couldn't believe what I was hearing, couldn't believe the massive misunderstanding between us.

Carlos started to speak but had to shield his eyes again. "Uh, can you—"

"Oh, yeah. Sorry." I kicked the lid of the suitcase shut.

"Thanks." Carlos lowered his hand. "So, what exactly *is* going on here, then?"

"Well"—I put my hands on my hips—"I'm pretty sure this guy tried to rob my house. We don't have a neighborhood watch, do we?"

"What? No."

"Okay, then yeah, I'm pretty sure this guy tried to rob my house. I have a haunted doll in there that's—well, quite frankly, she's more of a roommate than anything else. But anyway, I'm pretty sure she did this to him. I'm also pretty sure she's the cause of the weird noises you've been hearing."

He nodded slowly. I couldn't tell whether he believed me just yet, but if he needed proof of Molly's existence, I'd happily invite him to my place for a beer. "Okay," he said. "What do we do?"

"Well, I thought you'd be able to help me hide him, but if you're not the serial killer, then that idea's out the door."

"You *did* say dead bodies are good for the soil." He looked at me as if waiting for my response.

And, well, he wasn't wrong, was he?

"I did say that, yes," I replied.

He went back to staring at the suitcase for an uncomfortably long time. Finally, he jerked his head toward the shed in the corner of his yard. "I've got some shovels we can use."

CHAPTER 17
ONE MISSED CALL

AVE YOU EVER HAD A START TO YOUR DAY THAT just screamed today is going to be a *bad* day? I'd gone through most of my morning routine before I came to that deduction. Sometimes you can tell early on, and on those days, you're better off going back to bed and staying put. Unfortunately, that was not in the cards for me.

I'd stayed up relatively late to help Carlos bury Sal's body. Carlos insisted it go in his yard rather than mine. I suspected it was to help better his own soil, but he argued that it would be easier for him to explain it away should Kardoza come snooping around.

I supposed he had a point, so I kept digging. I wasn't worried about staying up late, considering I worked a closing shift, but apparently, I'd needed to be. One of the part-time workers failed to show up for his morning shift. He hadn't even answered his phone, so Henry called me.

Who needs an alarm clock when your boss will call you again and again until you answer the phone?

Knowing that I was now going to, at worst, be working a double today, I groggily climbed out of bed and cursed my late-night excursion with Carlos.

I wouldn't have time to do my laundry, so I had to wear an unwashed vest and yesterday's clothes. The outfit from before my date, anyway.

Next, I discovered that I was out of coffee, so I'd have to try and survive until I got to work and could buy an iced one.

No car and no Keith meant I was walking too. Bad break after bad break after bad break.

As I made it outside to begin my trek to work, I looked up and groaned. This day was going to be even worse than I initially thought.

Rather than the regular sky blue, the atmosphere was blood red. And it didn't appear to be casting its new color onto the rest of the world; everything around me looked normal. The sky was just "sky red" instead of "sky blue."

If I had any choice in the matter, I would have stayed home, but sadly, I had a commitment to my job and bills I needed to pay. So off to work I went.

Naturally, every crosswalk on my path changed the moment I approached, and I was forced to wait for traffic before proceeding. Sometimes it took much longer than it should have as well, because people were blasting through red lights left and right. It was as if everybody had systematically agreed to neglect the rules of the road today.

My situation didn't improve once I arrived at my destination, either. Grocery Hut was more packed than I'd ever seen it, and people were driving so erratically, I was almost hit by cars several times in the parking lot.

I stepped through the doors and was promptly shoved back and forth by people rushing to get in or out of the store. Some of them were even *fighting* over empty baskets, shopping carts, whatever they could find to hold groceries.

One man exited the store so quickly, and with a shopping cart so full, that he could barely turn or even slow himself down. Not that it seemed to be an issue for him. I leapt out of his way, barely avoiding being run over by him, and instead of apologizing, he shook a fist at me and screamed, "Get the fuck out of my way!" Then he barreled out into the parking lot.

I watched him make it halfway across the street before a minivan slammed into his cart, sending produce and canned sodas into the air like some kind of retail-themed party popper. He seemed to be more infuriated at the fact that his purchases were now strewn about than at the fact that he'd almost been run over.

I finally reached the registers, and surprisingly, Henry was working at a nonfunctional one. I guess he had to make do however he could. Tasha stood behind the mainly functional register and had two lines of angry people snaking all the way back into the aisles.

When Henry saw me, he waved me down. "Ah, Riley, thanks for coming in early."

"Sure," I said. "Where do you want me?"

Henry continued scanning items for a woman whose mannerisms mimicked that of a paranoid squirrel. "Clock in and help Keith in the back," Henry said as he worked.

"Product is flying off the shelves faster than we can keep it stocked."

"Okay." I hurried to the break room. After clocking in and setting down my temporary replacement-backpack, since Keith had the backpack I always used, I ran back into the store down aisle eleven. I tried not to become roadkill as I weaved through hordes of rude, impatient people toward the safety of the back room.

Well, *relative* safety, I should say.

Customers were in the back room as well, pulling things straight off carts and pallets and fighting over the last boxes of coffee and cases of water. It wasn't as insane in here as it was on the floor, but it was certainly more condensed. These people were like rabid animals.

As I started searching for Keith, they all turned to me. A man pointed at me and shouted, "There's another one! He knows where the rest of the backstock is!"

As if they'd been commanded to murder me, every customer in the back room stopped what they were doing and charged in my direction.

"Riley, in here!"

Keith's voice sounded from the right.

I turned to see him sticking halfway out of the dairy-cooler door. I wasted no time, darting over and ducking inside. As soon as I was in, Keith slammed the door shut and thrusted a screwdriver into the latch, essentially locking it from the inside.

The latch clicked repeatedly as customers on the other side tried opening the door, but the screwdriver kept the latch from releasing.

Keith wiped his brow. "That was almost bad, huh?" I noticed that he was wearing the backpack I'd lent him. Reggie poked his face out and watched me with his bulbous red eyes.

"What the hell happened?" I cried.

"Well, I was trying to keep the shelves stocked, but it's not exactly a one-man job, you got me? Everybody is snatching things faster than I can restock them, so after about five minutes of that, people just started coming into the back room and taking stuff. I've lost all control." He sighed deeply, staring forward. "I figured I'd just hide in here until the chaos clears."

"And you brought Reggie because . . .?"

"I can't leave him all by himself, dude. He's got abandonment issues."

Reggie let out a chirp and dipped back down into the backpack.

I decided to let that particular issue go for the time being. Right now, I had much more pressing matters to attend to. I looked around the dairy cooler to see if there was a way we could escape the mob.

The cooler itself was decently sized, maybe three-tenths the size of the back room. Racks of milk and juice lined doors on the left, all of them bolted to the floor. Unfortunately, there was no getting out through those doors, but at least there was no getting in through them either.

At the far end of the dairy cooler, however, was another door, and if I remembered correctly, it led into the bakery cooler. So long as there were no customers rummaging through the bakery, that was our best avenue of escape.

I tapped Keith on the shoulder and crept toward the door. He tiptoed behind me. Together, we pulled open the door and peeked through. It was silent aside from the humming of the fans overhead.

Boxes of cakes and refrigerated dough trays lined the shelves. There was less space in here than in the dairy cooler, but that made sense, as it was mostly for storage rather than for storage *and* stocking.

We passed through the bakery cooler without issue and came to its door. When we looked out that one, nobody was behind the counter. "Stay low," I whispered to Keith. "We'll sneak to the front and tell Henry what's going on."

"Sounds great."

I knelt and crawled out from behind the counter. Keith followed my lead, pausing only to push the cooler door shut. I peered between shelves of bread to see people bolting through aisles. A few more fights had broken out, and I swore I smelled smoke in the air.

Were these people trying to burn the store down? Was nothing sacred anymore?

One of the aisles cleared of people for a moment. "Let's go," I whispered. I lunged out from behind the counter and sprinted to the aisle, Keith following close behind.

We reached the aisle and raced to the other end. But when we turned left to head toward the registers, we were presented with a new problem.

A throng of customers stood in front of us, even more than in the back room. They whirled around to glare at us with rabid hostility. "There they are!" one of them growled.

Over a dozen people shot toward Keith and me. We pivoted and ran back toward the bakery, but another five people emerged from the closest aisles and cornered us.

With nowhere else to go, Keith and I turned back to the still-empty aisle and made a break for it. We didn't get far before furious customers closed off the other end as well.

Now there was definitely nowhere else to go. "Well," I began in defeat, "I think we're done for."

A sharp screech next to me. I looked over, saw Reggie burst from the backpack. Flapping his wings, he flew up and out of the aisle.

Keith didn't hesitate. He leapt up onto the shelving and started climbing it like a ladder, knocking cans of soup and ravioli to the floor.

I guess as far as split-second ideas go, it beat getting killed by a mob of raging customers.

I jumped onto the shelf and scrambled after him. A piece of the shelf beneath my foot came loose as I used it to propel myself upward, sending an entire section of canned goods toppling onto the horde ascending toward us.

Once Keith reached the top, he shot to his feet and yelled, "Reggie, come back!"

I stayed on my hands and knees to retain my balance. Reggie had flown several aisles away from us, and he hadn't landed either.

I could see the registers from all the way up here, and it looked as if the throng was now becoming violent with Henry. He tried to keep them under control with what appeared to be an authoritative speech, while Tasha tried to leave. She didn't get far, though. The ever-thickening crowd of people blocked her from escaping, and some of them even attempted to grab her.

A furious shriek below me. I flinched and glanced down, found an elderly woman Spider-Man-ing her way up the shelves toward me. Her eyes were bloodshot, and there was a gash in her forehead, presumably from the fallen cans. She foamed at the mouth, clambering toward me with the grace and speed of a jungle primate.

"Keith, we gotta move!" I shouted.

Once again, Keith didn't hesitate. He bounded to the edge of the shelf we were standing on, then *leapt* across the aisle, into the air toward the next shelf.

The shelf wobbled under me as Keith pushed off. To my surprise, he made the jump with ease, but he lost his balance during the landing. He quickly recovered, then jumped to the next aisle over.

As carefully as possible, I climbed to my feet. People were scrambling up both sides of the shelf now. The rabid old lady had almost made it to the top, directly beneath me. She reached for my foot.

I leapt into the air, across the aisle toward the next shelf.

I didn't even come close to making it. Instead, I struck shelving and tumbled toward the floor below. Or, rather, I tumbled toward the horde of people below.

They probably weren't expecting me to jump. Or maybe they weren't expecting me to *fail* the jump.

Either way, they weren't prepared to catch me, and several of the enraged customers became temporary landing mats to cushion my fall.

More product plunged down. The top part of the shelf in front of us came loose, hanging by a single screw.

I was on my feet in seconds.

If I'd been hurt, I didn't feel it. Adrenaline had kicked in, and my only concern was getting away from the mob.

Hands clawed at me as I shoved through the aisle and rushed to the front end. I couldn't see Keith, so I assumed he was still on higher ground. Up ahead, Reggie swooped down and vanished somewhere in the waves of customers trying to push Henry around.

"We are willing to serve, but only if you are willing to act like civilized people!" Henry yelled. He stood on top of the register now, the people below him roaring and reaching for him.

Sadly, his speech did nothing to calm the crowd. If anything, it only made them angrier.

A loud crash sounded from somewhere behind me. I spun around, saw that the shelf dividing aisles four and five had tipped over.

As a few more customers noticed me and started heading my way, an idea struck me.

I tore off my work vest and tossed it aside, then glanced down the aisle to my immediate left. Aisle nine, pet supplies. I faced the mob once more; they yanked Henry down from atop the register.

I cupped my mouth with my hands and screamed at the top of my lungs, "*Hey everyone!*"

In an instant, the crowd fell silent and focused on me. I'll admit, extremely nerve-racking. Hated every second of that hive-minded head turn.

I gestured at the pet-supplies aisle with one hand and kept the other cupped around my mouth. "There's, like, a hundred cases of bottled water at the other end of this aisle! Fifty percent off!"

"Stampede" doesn't quite exemplify what these people did next. The destruction they brought upon the store as they dropped Henry, barreled past me, and ran down the aisles is indescribable.

Someone slammed into me, knocking me to the ground. I clambered to my feet before I could be trampled.

Soon the front end was mostly clear, save for the few people still trying to hurry through self-checkout. Some didn't even bother paying. Instead, they pushed their overflowing shopping carts straight out the doors.

I ran over to Henry and helped him to his feet. He adjusted his glasses. "What on earth is going on?"

"I think that's something we can figure out later," I said, and turned to hurry off.

Tasha peeked out from behind the customer-service counter. "What the *fuck* is—"

"Later," I interrupted, motioning for her and Henry to follow me.

All together, we dashed around the corner of the booth and headed toward the break room.

Just before we made it back there, a man leapt out from one of the pharmacy aisles, blocking our path. His business suit was unbuttoned and ripped at the shoulders. His hair, which appeared to normally be greased back with hair gel, was messy and pulled apart. He clenched his fists, blood staining his knuckles.

"Screams." The man moaned, as if he were in great pain. "She screams at us all."

Froth bubbled in the corners of his mouth as he stepped toward us. Tasha grabbed me by the shoulders and hid behind me. The man pressed a palm to the side of his head, making a face as though something was about to burst from his skull.

And then something *did* burst from his skull. Horns split open the skin above his temples, the pointy appendages exploding out of his flesh and bone like a butterfly pulling itself free of a cocoon.

We watched in silent horror as blood trailed down his cheeks, dribbled to the floor. Mixed with the froth at the corners of his mouth.

His eyes found mine, and fury consumed his features. "She has risen!" He lunged for us.

A metal bat struck him in the head with a loud *kink*, and he fell to the floor in a heap.

Behind him, Keith gestured at us, the bat ready for another swing. "I think it's time to clock out for the day, you guys."

Tasha and Henry pushed past Keith and me and hurried into the break room. I could already hear the march of the mob returning from the other end of the store.

Keith started to run after them but stopped and raised his bat at me. Or, I should say, at whatever was behind me.

Someone grabbed my shoulder and spun me around. Mason. The monster-hunter tightened his grip, glaring daggers at me. "Boy, you have *really* screwed the pooch on this one."

He shoved me away, then followed Keith and me as we bolted toward the break room.

Shrieks and footfalls behind us. I looked back, saw more horned people sprinting down the aisles toward us.

We stumbled into the break room. Mason slammed the door shut. As he locked it, customers rammed into it on the other side. They beat against it in rapid succession, filling the break room with the thunderous sound of their fists against metal.

Casually, Mason strode to the other side of the break room. "You couldn't just do your job, could you?" His voice was low, menacing. "I can't believe how badly you fucked everything up."

He grabbed a chair from the table, walked back to the door, and secured the top of the chair beneath the door handle. Then he turned back to me, scowling at me as if nobody else were in the room with us. "This is all your fault."

"How is this *my* fault?" I cried.

Mason pointed at the door, the mob still beating on it. "Because you were supposed to kill the bitch! Now we're out of time!"

"What do you mean?" Tasha asked from the corner of the room. "What's going on out there?"

Mason grew deathly calm. "The end of the world." He sneered at me. "And you can thank this idiotic little shit for it."

"How?" I snapped. "I didn't do anything to cause this!"

"Exactly!" Mason shouted, throwing his hands in the air. "You didn't do a goddamn thing! It was *your* destiny to fight her! *Your* job to stop this! And you—you didn't do a goddamn thing."

I groaned, rolling my eyes. "Because my name is on some hunk of rock?"

"No," Mason responded coldly. "Because of what happened seven years ago."

"Whoa, whoa, buddy." Keith stepped between us. "Let's take it easy, now."

Mason snatched the bat out of Keith's hands and chucked it at the wall.

Keith put up his arms in surrender. "All right, we're cool. It's cool."

"Seven years ago," Mason said, returning his attention to me, "the Fathers of Free Will lost their leader."

I furrowed my brow. I'd been expecting this conversation to steer toward my family. "Oh, okay."

"Yeah," Mason went on. "Bit of a tragedy. The She-Devil's followers took him out because he was actively battling their efforts to resurrect her. Turned his house to ash. They killed his wife and daughter, too."

He smiled and raised a finger. I didn't like where this was going anymore. "Not the bloke's son, though. The heir to the Fathers of Free Will. Next in line to lead. The one destined to kill the She-Devil and save mankind." He shook his head. "But you didn't do any of that, did ya? You had to play 'dead-end job' and skirt around your duties, huh?"

I shook my head. "Wait, you *are* talking about me?"

There was a very short pause before I was suddenly on the floor with a very sore jaw. Mason had sucker punched me faster than I could process, and then the revelation hit me almost as hard as he had.

My father had been the leader of the Fathers of Free Will? And *I* was destined to take his place?

"Seven years ago, a demon named Adra turned your family into fuckin' dust," Mason continued. "And you didn't do a fuckin' thing. The whole world is about to go up in flames, and you're still doing fuckin' nothing."

There was a delay between everything he'd said and me fully understanding everything he'd said. I blinked hard, trying to take it all in.

Was that really it? The fire? The day my family had been killed? Had that been the day everything started? I couldn't think of any Protag'd moments before then. Had it been the first?

A noise started up in the room. Shuffling in the cupboards by the coffee pot. We all went quiet, the only sounds that of our breathing and the pounding on the door.

We turned toward the source. Mason took a handgun out of his coat and crept over to the cupboard. He opened it with the tip of his boot, and Reggie soared out with a loud screech.

Mason ducked low. "What the fuck!"

Reggie landed on Keith and . . . hissed? Yes, he hissed at Mason, then scurried into the backpack.

"Are you keeping that thing as a goddamn pet?" Mason cried, pointing the gun at Keith.

Keith crossed his arms. "His name is Reggie, and he likes candy."

"He's a magnet for disasters, you idiot. You're gonna get a bridge dropped on your head." Mason sighed and put the gun away. "Whatever, it doesn't fuckin' matter. We're all gonna be dead soon anyway." He faced Henry and Tasha. "Is there a back door we can use to get out of the building?"

Henry shook his head. "I'm afraid the only way out of this room is the one you barricaded."

Mason cupped his chin in thought, and I took the opportunity to climb to my feet, my cheek still sore, my mind still whirring with revelations.

I was supposed to be a hero, supposed to stop all this. Had I always been destined for this? Had my family always been destined to die? For what? For a stupid, shitty hero-origin story?

Bruce Wayne watched his parents get gunned down, and instead of becoming Batman, he just . . . continued being a normal person. Now Gotham was approaching Armageddon, and Bruce didn't have the time or training to become the last-second savior.

Mason was right. I'd really screwed up everything.

"How are you with that bat?" Mason asked suddenly.

Keith shrugged. "I've beat a couple crackheads in my day."

Mason removed his machete from its leg holster, readied it for a fight, and walked toward the door. "Good. Everybody find a weapon. We're gonna have to brawl our way out."

Henry, Tasha, and I began searching the room for anything we could use as a weapon. The search only lasted a handful of seconds, though.

We all stopped what we were doing as the violence on the other side of the door seemed to magnify.

Screams, pounding, footsteps.

Heavy footsteps.

Silence.

A knock at the door.

Mason raised his machete, removed the chair from under the handle, and slowly opened the door.

Rivers stood on the other side, hands in his pants pockets. Two of his large, muscular zombie-goons were positioned beside him, their hands bloody, a horde of unconscious (or maybe dead) customers scattered all around them.

Rivers smiled. "They just don't make apocalypses like they used to, huh?"

CHAPTER 18
THE HERO'S JOURNEY

THERE WAS A BIT OF A SILENT STANDOFF AS RIV-
ers entered the room. His two goons followed, and
Mason closed the door behind them.

Nobody seemed happy to see Rivers. He, on
the other hand, seemed quite chipper, especially considering he was about to live to see the days beyond the end
of days.

"My, my, so many sad faces," he said. His stare settled on
me. "Especially that one." He took a few steps closer. "Why
so blue, Riley?" He rolled his eyes, his grin widening. "Or
should I say, why so *red*?"

I raised a hand. "I already got chewed out enough for
this."

"A slap on the wrist, since we're all about to go up in
flames, kiddo." He pointed at me. "But worry not. In
comes ol' Rivers to save your asses." He gave Mason a
pointed look. "*Again*."

Furiously, Mason shook his head and sheathed his weapon. "What do you want, Tremaine?"

Rivers reached into his jacket pocket and removed a folded sheet of paper. "I have the rest of the tablet translation. I know how to kill her." Mason reached for the paper, but Rivers held it back. "Not so fast, friend. What do I get in return?"

Mason gritted his teeth. "You think *now* is the best time for hustling?"

"I don't work for free."

It was a little odd to witness the two of them having a semicivilized conversation. The last time I'd seen them together, they'd been trying to kill each other and kidnap me. It appeared I'd missed some of their interactions within the past couple of days.

"What do you want?" Mason barked. "Don't you already have everything?"

"I want a way to lift my immortality."

"I can't give you that."

"Not now," Rivers replied with a hint of sass. "But if I hand over the rest of the translation, you're going to help me track down something—a powerful object, a magical spell—*whatever* it takes to liberate me."

Mason stuck out a hand for the paper. "Sure. Fine."

"Excellent," Rivers said with a smile. "Your word is your bond?"

"Just give me the paper before I beat your skull in for a fuckin' laugh."

Rivers set the sheet in Mason's open palm, and Mason ripped it open as if he were a kid diving into Christmas presents.

No one said anything as Mason read the translation and paced the break room. Tasha stood in the far corner, nervously biting the tip of her thumb, her white teeth peeking out from behind black lips. Henry sat at the table, kneeling over and staring at the floor with his head in his hands. I honestly felt like doing the same thing.

Keith bumped me with his arm. "You okay, bro?"

"Honestly," I said, "no, not really." A mess of emotions ran through me, one after another. Guilt that I'd ended the world through sheer ignorance. Anger that I'd been forced down this path for next to no reason. Sadness that I'd lost my parents and sister—that they'd paid such a steep price—in the name of the proverbial greater good.

In short, I felt cheated, and I felt awful.

"Don't be so hard on yourself," Keith said with another arm bump. "I think you do a lot of good, even if it's not cosmically grand or world saving."

"Yeah, well, it looks like 'world saving' is exactly what the world needed this time."

"That's it?" Mason snapped. "That's her one weakness?"

We all turned to him and Rivers. Rivers nodded. "Fun, isn't it?"

Mason threw the paper to the floor. "Not really. What the fuck does it even mean?"

Rivers glanced back at me. "Why don't you ask the 'chosen one'?"

Mason didn't even look in my direction. "Chosen nothing."

Ouch.

Mason pulled open the door to leave. "I'll figure it out myself. Somebody's gotta kill the bitch. Or *try* to." As he said those last three words, he finally met my eyes.

"What about us?" Keith asked.

Mason shrugged. "Don't know. Don't care. My advice is hunker down and try not to die. And good luck with that, considering you've got a baby of the world's worst fuckin' bad-luck omen."

Tasha approached Keith and me, holding her arms tight against her chest. "I am *not* staying in this shithole to die."

"Sure, girlie," Mason said with a fake smile. "Take your chances outside with *them*. Half the people in town are being converted into the She-Devil's Followers. You'll be ripped apart before you make it three blocks." Tasha sneered at him but didn't respond.

I spoke next, as something he'd just said struck a chord with me. "Wait, *everybody* in town is turning feral?"

He nodded. "By this time tomorrow, I imagine there won't be anybody sane left—that is, if anybody is still alive."

My pulse quickened as I thought of the rapid transformation of the customers in the store, of the people in town. I'd left my house, what? Half an hour ago? And I'd seen people go from irritable, to reckless, to complete frothing-at-the-mouth monsters in that short time.

Only one person registered in my head though. *Ariel.*

Was she turning into one of them as well? Had she already? She'd gone home before I made it to work, right? She could be safe at home, painting. Unless she hadn't made it home because of the chaos . . .

I pulled out my cell phone and called her. As I lifted the

device to my ear, thunder boomed outside. The roar shook the walls and ceiling, reverberating through the entire store. It was as if a bomb had gone off above us.

"She's getting stronger," Mason said, and stormed out of the break room.

Rivers scooped up the paper from the floor, returned it to his pocket, and faced the rest of us. "Well, I don't know about any of you, but I don't have much faith in that one. He's too angry. Too stressed."

The phone rang in my ear once more before going to voicemail. I didn't even bother leaving a message for Ariel. She'd probably already looked outside long enough to know that the world was going downhill. She probably knew why I was calling.

I turned to Keith. "Is your car out back?"

"Yeah," Keith said. "Why?"

"We need to find Ariel."

Keith readjusted the backpack and straightened his hat. "Say less."

Tasha hesitantly stepped toward us. "I-I'll come with you."

"Oh." I shrugged. "I mean, sure."

"I'll stay here," Henry announced, still sitting at the table. "Hold down the fort, a-and all that."

"Great," I said.

We turned to leave, but Rivers and his cronies stood between us and the door. "Forgetting something?" Rivers asked with a smug grin.

"Oh, right." I turned to the punch-in clock and clocked myself out. The owner wasn't fond of paying overtime, as you might remember.

Rivers's smile faded. "No, you moron." He pulled out the paper with the translations and handed it to me.

"Oh," I said for the third time in the past ten seconds. I took the sheet and unfolded it to read. The message was lengthy and took up almost the whole page, saying how the She-Devil was the first of the demons, how she was the devil's favorite, how the forces beyond sealed her away because she was too powerful, yada yada yada. All pretty expected and assumed backstory stuff that had been brewing in my brain since the moment I'd heard of her existence.

The important bits were near the end. The part where it said, "Riley Thomas is destined to strike the final blow with the weapon of love."

I continued reading for more explanation, but that was it. That was the end of it. It was almost disappointing, considering this came from an ancient stone tablet. But then again, I imagine the writers only had so much room to work with.

"Well?" Rivers asked. "Any gears turning in that little head of yours?"

I handed the paper back to him. "Yeah, I have no idea what this means either."

Rivers folded up the paper and stuck it back into his pocket. "Of course you don't. It was worth a shot, I suppose." He clapped his hands once. "Shall we leave?"

I raised a brow at him. "You want to help us?"

"Why not? I don't have anything else to do at this point."

I didn't exactly trust Rivers's newfound carelessness, but I wasn't in the mood to question him. I was more concerned with getting to Ariel. I waved a hand as I started for the door. "Sure, fine. Whatever."

Keith and Tasha followed me out to Keith's car. Surprisingly, Rivers's vehicle was parked nearby. He and his goons climbed into their car, and Tasha and I climbed into Keith's.

As soon as we were buckled up, Tasha practically yelled from the back seat, "Okay, can either one of you tell me what the *fuck* is going on?"

"Isn't it obvious?" Keith asked, starting the engine.

"No!"

"No? Ah, okay." He removed the backpack and set it in the back seat next to Tasha. "Basically, Riley's been getting Protag'd."

"Pro . . . tagged?"

"Yeah. Like Frodo Baggins, or Harry Potter."

Tasha cocked her head, making an "O" shape with her mouth as her attention shifted to me.

I turned around to look at her face-to-face rather than through the rearview mirror. "Do *not* tell me you understood that." I shot Keith a glare. "And I said to stop calling it that."

Keith grinned as he shifted the car out of park and took off. Rivers and his cronies followed close behind us.

Surprisingly, traffic had improved in the short time I'd been inside Grocery Hut, but not for the reasons you'd think. Vehicles that weren't outright totaled seemed to have been abandoned. It was something straight out of the movies. Cars sat motionless on the shoulder of the road, in the middle of the road—a bunch even lay upside down, presumably because they'd crashed into each other.

People—if they weren't dead or unconscious inside of the aforementioned totaled vehicles—were either running for their lives from feral folk, or they *were* feral folk, actively chasing and beating each other to death.

It was chaos, but not the kind of chaos that could really impede our journey.

A squeal sounded in the back seat. I looked through the rearview mirror to see Reggie poke his head up out of the backpack.

Tasha yiped and scooted away.

"Tasha, Reggie. Reggie, Tasha," Keith said, motioning one hand in an introductory manner.

Reggie climbed out of the bag and leapt up beside my head on the back of the seat. I flinched, but only slightly.

Then I caught sight of Reggie's eyes in the rearview mirror. In an instant I was falling into those deep scarlet voids again, visions flashing through my mind.

Flames, demons.

Ariel, sunset.

Buildings leveling, fire erupting.

Charred husks that had once been people, turned to ash mid-motion. Statues of charcoal waiting for the slightest breeze to blow them down.

It was as if a napalm nuke had stopped the world dead in its tracks.

The visions ceased. I blinked a few times, trying to collect myself, and found that I still wasn't in Keith's car.

Instead, I was at a familiar bar. Neon blue washed over me from above. The jukebox behind me played "It's the End of the World as We Know It (And I Feel Fine)" by R.E.M. The bartender stood behind the counter, his back to me.

As I took in my surroundings, the blurry-faced man turned toward me. Unlike the times I'd been here before, he wasn't doing repetitive chores. He merely stood in front of me, still as a statue. "Last call for the night, Riley."

I blinked more, forcing my eyes to adjust to the new environment. I felt as though I'd been roused from a nap. I knew I couldn't have been here for more than a minute, but something in my gut told me I'd been here for hours.

The bartender placed a cup of steaming hazelnut-flavored coffee on the bar before me. "On the house," he said.

"Thanks." I picked up the mug and gulped it down. Warm and delicious, the nutty, chocolatey drink went down my throat, making me forget about my troubles for just a moment.

"Still searching for what you lost, huh?"

I opened my mouth to answer, only to realize I had nothing to say.

The bartender stepped away to grab some glasses from the left end of the bar. I guessed another customer had been here before me, and he had yet to grab their dirty dishes. "Sometimes things take time to turn up. Sometimes they're only gone for a second. It all depends on how well you look for them." He set the glasses in a sink behind the bar and turned on the faucet. "Or it could depend on how much you're willing to find them."

I thought about what Mason had said back in the break room. How I hadn't followed my chosen path. How I hadn't become the person I was meant to be. How this was all my fault.

"Finding the thing that saves the world would be pretty helpful right about now," I said sadly.

"Who."

"What?"

The bartender turned off the water and took the glasses out of the sink. They were pristine now, as if they'd never been used at all. "Things don't save the world. People do."

"So . . . you're saying I need to find the 'who' that can save the world?"

The bartender shrugged as he put the glasses away. "Sounds to me like you're the one who said it."

He got me again.

I let out a breath, still trying to collect myself. "How did I get here, anyway?"

The bartender stared at me for a bit before answering. "Who says you're here now?"

I shot up in the passenger seat of Keith's car, jolted awake from the nightmare. Keith put a hand on my shoulder. "Dude, you okay?"

I rubbed my eyes. "Yeah, I'm fine."

Tasha leaned forward in her seat, Reggie perched next to her. "You fainted or something."

Keith turned to look at me, and it was only then that I realized the vehicle was no longer in motion. "Did Reggie do that thing to you again?"

"Yeah." I glanced at our surroundings. Realized we were in the parking lot of Ariel's apartment complex.

"What did you see?" Keith asked.

Right on cue, an explosion rocked the area. Smoke billowed up as flames consumed the building to our right.

Ariel's building.

Another explosion, then another and another. The rest of the buildings went up in flames too, one by one.

"This," I whispered. "I saw this."

Before I could even consider the idea that Ariel might have been inside, four figures emerged from the flames of her building. For a second, I thought that perhaps she and a few others had escaped just in time.

But then my breath caught in my throat, because they all had horns protruding from their skulls.

CHAPTER 19
RILEY THOMAS: DEVIL SLAYER

A S I MENTIONED BEFORE, SOME OF MY PROTAG'D moments presented themselves in the form of objects—items that wound up in my possession for whatever reason. I usually tried to get rid of them on SellBay, and most of them went quickly.

There were, however, a handful of items that never sold, and I'd set them aside in case that ever changed. Some were in a box under my bed. One was in my closet, and I rarely ever looked at, let alone touched it.

It was (apparently) a legendary and magical sword, and it was stuck in a chunk of stone. It had found its way to me a couple of years ago when a car crash happened on my street. A truck involved in the accident had been transporting valuables to a museum a few towns over. One item in said truck was a blade known as "Faithkeeper." I'm not entirely sure of Faithkeeper's history, but as far as I know, it's basically a lesser-known Excalibur.

Like any other well-meaning pedestrian, I'd hurried from my home to help pick up the mess of artifacts scattered across my lawn. I'd picked up Faithkeeper by the handle, intending on standing it upright, but the sword had slipped out of its stone with ease. It was as if the slab were nothing more than a sheathe.

The truck driver had been astounded at the fact that I'd successfully removed the sword. I guess he and some of the others he worked with often tried to jokingly remove it, but it never budged. I would have thought that the crash had simply loosened the blade, but this was not the case.

A moment or two after I accidentally removed it, a cloud of blue mist settled on my driveway, and a small army of dead medieval knights and soldiers appeared all around me. They looked well and alive—not ghastly or corpse-like, as you would have expected. They were just men glowing with ghostly light.

The truck driver was so taken aback when they appeared that he spun around and fled down the street.

Every one of the knights knelt in my presence, and the apparent ringleader of the bunch walked up to me. He was tall and handsome, his face clean-shaven, a crop of messy ginger hair atop his head. He had a helmet in one hand, and he rested the other on the sword at his belt. "Sire," he said, bowing his head. "We have waited so long to return to your side."

"Hello," I said with an awkward wave. "Who are you guys, exactly?"

"We are the Most Holy Men, sire." The man motioned at his peers. "Even in death, we are loyal and brave, as we always have been."

"Okay."

"Thou must not remember." He gestured to himself. "I am Tyrus of Eldengard."

"Hello, Tyrus of Eldengard. Sorry to say, but I actually don't think I'm your king."

Tyrus laughed. "Thou pulled the blade free, did thou not?"

"Well, yes, but—"

"Only the righteous king, the successor and ancestor of the great King Nicholas Ironheart, has the power to wield the legendary Faithkeeper."

"Ohh," I said slowly.

"Indeed." Tyrus glanced around at the neighborhood. "I must say, the land looks a great deal different than it did while we were alive. What kingdom shall we conquer in your name first, sire?"

"We don't really do the 'conquering' thing anymore."

"Ah," he said with a hint of disappointment. "I see. Well, perhaps we shall find a small village to raid? Preferably one in the land of your enemies? We are not animals, after all."

"We don't really do that anymore, either."

Tyrus made a face. "Well, what *do* we do now?"

"I dunno." I shrugged. "You guys could come inside and watch *Jeopardy!* or something."

"Are there no kingdoms? No empires?"

"At least around here, there isn't anything like that. But there's—there's neighborhoods. Towns, cities, countries. That sort of thing."

"What of fabled heroes? Of legendary battles?"

I paused, trying to think of the next closest thing. "I mean, we have *Survivor*?"

Tyrus took a step back, his eyes wide, his jaw practically on the ground. The other warriors looked at each other in confusion. "What hath become of the realm? When did men become so . . . subdued?"

"Well, we made it to space at some point, and that was definitely a big deal."

"We have climbed to the heavens?"

"Well, we didn't *climb* there. We built spaceships and flew there. There's a lot of science and math involved in it, which I don't understand any more than you guys would, but yeah."

Mentioning science probably wasn't the best move. At the mere mention of it, the warriors drew their swords. "You speak of the devil's magic!" Tyrus shouted. "Men alone cannot achieve such a feat!"

"False king!" another knight bellowed. "He will only lead us to temptation and sin!"

"He stole the sword!"

"He seeks to rob us of our kingdom's riches!"

Tyrus pointed his blade at me. "Perhaps there is another way to prove whether you are truly our kingdom's heir."

I started to slip Faithkeeper back into the hunk of rock I'd pulled it from. "I already told you I'm not, dude. I'll just put the sword back."

Tyrus lunged toward me. "No, wait—"

But it was too late.

The moment I finished sliding the blade back into the stone, Tyrus and the others disappeared.

I looked around at where they'd been standing. "Huh," I said, then walked back into my house.

I figured that would have been the end of it, but when authorities and even some of the museum staff arrived to collect the scattered artifacts, *none* of them took the sword.

It was as if they'd completely forgotten about it, or they couldn't see it at the end of my yard. None of them asked about it. Hell, nobody on my street even seemed to notice it.

Keith saw it, and he tried removing it from the stone a couple of times, but the blade was stuck. I let it be an eyesore in my yard for about a month, but then I decided to move it inside and get rid of it myself. With Keith's help, I carried it into my house and tossed it in the closet.

I listed it on SellBay on three different occasions, but no one showed any interest in it. After a while, I stopped listing it. I considered taking it to the dump, or maybe driving it to whatever museum it belonged to and telling them they forgot it at my place.

But by then, I couldn't be bothered with it. I could hardly remember it was in my house half the time, unless I happened to spot it in the corner of my closet.

And so there it was that Faithkeeper stayed.

But why is that relevant? Let me get back to where I left off.

After Ariel's apartment building exploded, four horned figures casually walked out of the building, as if the fire weren't even there. They spotted Keith's car within seconds and began bad-guy walking straight for us.

"Keith," I started, "I think we should leave."

"What the fuck are *those*?" Tasha cried, her voice raising an octave with each word.

"They ain't Grocery Hut customers." Keith hit the gas

and spun the wheel around, swerving the car out of its parking spot.

Suddenly one of the horned figures combusted, vanishing in a flash of flames and embers. A second later, there was a similar explosion on the hood of Keith's car, and the figure—a man—*reappeared* there.

He was familiar, but I knew we hadn't met. I just felt as though I'd encountered someone almost identical to him. He had short, messy blond hair, and he wore torn jeans and a shirt with ripped-off sleeves. Minus the horns, he looked mostly normal—except his eyes were inhuman, lizard-like, and when he grinned at me, I saw he had sharp fangs rather than regular human teeth.

As soon as the horned man appeared on the hood of the car, Tasha screamed, and Reggie hissed. Keith yelled as though he'd just seen his parents naked, then switched on the window wipers.

The horned man reminded me of the man in the bar, Adra. This man—or demon, I guess—watched the wipers go back and forth a few times before seizing them with his bare hands. Sparks crackled around his hands, and fire consumed the wipers, melting them in his grasp. The smell of burning metal invaded my nostrils.

Keith's eyes went big. "Oh shit!"

The demon's grin widened as he stared at me through the glass. "Look who decided to play ball." His voice was high-pitched, reminding me of a weasel. "I guess we get to have a final showdown after all."

Keith jerked the car to the right, but instead of getting us out of there, the vehicle began to slow, then stopped altogether.

Tasha screamed again, leaping from one end of the back seat to the other. Heat seared the right side of my body, and I turned to see a demon-woman standing beside my door. She had the same horns, eyes, and fangs as the demon-man. Her shoulder-length black hair was buzzed on one side, and she wore a cropped, short-sleeved leather jacket.

The metal of my door turned red-hot and began to melt. The demon-woman roared, yanking the door from the jeep.

Before I could react, she reached inside, seized my arm, and wrenched me out of my seat, my seat belt snapping as she pulled me free. Then she chucked me to the ground as if I were a piece of garbage.

I hit the pavement hard, and pain dragged across my bare skin like sandpaper as I somersaulted and hit the back wheel of a parked van.

Two pairs of combat boots stopped next to me. It was another demon-man and demon-woman, each possessing the same horns and eyes and fangs as the first two. The demon-man wore a crimson hoodie and had shaggy brown hair that almost covered his eyes. He pulled a butterfly knife from his pocket and twirled the blade around. "Man of the hour," he said, his voice that of a stereotypical stoner's.

The demon-woman next to him grabbed me by the shirt and rammed me up against the van. She had long straight black hair and a T-shirt that held the design of some metal band I'd never heard of. Dark leather pants covered her slim legs, her combat boots supported by tall, chunky heels. I imagined it wasn't the most practical footwear for the apocalypse, but it seemed to work for her, so what did I know?

She leaned in close, opened her mouth wide. Her breath was hot on my neck, and my heart nearly stopped. Was she about to *eat* me?

"Easy, Jozz," the stoner-demon said. "Boss says she wants him alive and unharmed."

Jozz let out a disappointed grunt but ceased her drooling. For now.

Shrieks sounded from the jeep—Tasha and Keith. In my peripheral, I saw them get yanked out of the vehicle and tossed to the ground.

Stoner-demon turned around, still casually flipping his butterfly knife every which way. "Thox, Gelv. Bring 'em here."

The blond demon and the demon with the side shave grasped Keith and Tasha by the shoulders and dragged them toward me. The blond one—Thox, I think—looked Tasha up and down as she struggled against Gelv. "We can do whatever we want with these two, right?" He licked his lips, leaning in closer to Tasha. "This one looks totally—"

Tasha booted him in the face. "In your fuckin' dreams, you creep!"

Thox rushed to cover his nose with a hand. When he lowered it again, I spotted blood trickling from his nostrils. He growled at Tasha. "Bitch."

"Chill out, Gelv," stoner-demon said.

I guess I was wrong on the names. Whoops.

Gelv wiped the blood from his face, glaring at Tasha. "Keep that attitude, Hot Topic. We'll see where it gets you."

The demon with the side shave—the *actual* Thox—finally spoke. "Are we just taking them back, Viga?"

Stoner-demon—Viga—stopped his constant blade spinning and caught the knife in a closed position. "That was the order for *him*, at least," he said, gesturing at me. "I dunno about the other two, but I say we play it safe and take them with. Don't wanna assume we're in the clear and start flaying too early."

Jozz jerked her head at something to my left. "Who's the geezer?"

I looked that way. Rivers sauntered toward us, both of his zombie-goons following close behind him. He'd parked his vehicle only a few yards away from where Keith's jeep broke down.

Rivers smiled at the demons. "Ladies, gentlemen. Fancy meeting you here."

"Don't I know you from somewhere?" Viga asked, stepping toward Rivers.

Rivers shrugged. "Maybe I just have that kind of face."

"Yeah. Maybe, dude."

My heart was beating so fast, I thought it might break my ribs; they were working overtime to contain it. I glanced at Keith and Tasha, and they appeared to be as shaken up as I felt. Thankfully, they also appeared to be unharmed.

Wait, I thought, *what about Reggie?* I looked at the jeep. It seemed Reggie was still inside the bag in the back seat, moving around but not making any noise.

Had the demons simply not seen him? If so, I hoped it stayed that way.

"At any rate, we gotta get going," Viga said.

"By all means," Rivers began in the kindest tone I'd ever heard him speak in, "leave them with me and be on your way."

Viga flipped out his blade and whirled it around again. "Actually, my man, we gotta take 'em with us."

Rivers grimaced, as if the conversation had just become very awkward. "Actually, no. I'm afraid they're staying with me." He pointed at me. "Especially *that* one. He's rather important."

"Yeah, dude. I know." Viga was starting to show the slightest hint of irritation. "That's why he's coming with *us*."

Gelv handed off Keith to Thox and stomped up toward Rivers. "Seriously, pal. There is no 'you' in this equation. We're taking him, like it or not. Word?"

"Word," Rivers replied sarcastically, and snapped his fingers. "Abe. Clint. Clean house, please."

In the blink of an eye, Rivers's zombies lunged forward. They each seized one of Gelv's arms and easily tore him in half, as though he were made of wet clay. He howled in pain, but it only lasted for a second before turning into a weak squeal, then a gurgle, then silence.

Blood spewed forth, and the goons dropped Gelv's remains. The pulled-apart corpse tumbled to the ground, and I saw dark purple embers glowing among its bones and innards.

"Holy fuck!" Thox shouted, letting go of Keith and Tasha.

Jozz released me as well, and after that, the zombies jumped the remaining demons, the fight essentially becoming a cartoon dust cloud with flashes of the demons' orange fire.

I hurried away from the scuffle, rounded the van toward Rivers and my friends. "Well," Rivers said, "this was certainly fulfilling. But it was also an absolute waste of time."

Stomach clenching, I faced Ariel's building. I thought about running inside, to see if she was in there, if I could save her. But the fire was so intense, so hot, that anyone or anything inside had surely been reduced to ashes.

As I stared at the inferno, horrible memories came flooding back to me. I now understood how all of this was connected, and a lump formed in my throat. I was experiencing the same loss all over again.

Ariel was gone. And even if she wasn't, everything she owned, all her paintings—her very heart and soul—had been in that apartment.

My stomach turned again. I thought I might vomit, but still, I couldn't look away from the fire. The dancing flames were almost as hypnotic as Reggie's eyes.

A hand rested on my shoulder, and I pulled myself out of my trance. It was Keith. "Maybe she wasn't in there," he said.

Tasha arrived on my other side. "Yeah, I bet she's fine."

"What if she's not?" I gazed at the building once more.

"That's the double-edged sword of love," Keith said. "On the one hand, it's love, and it's great. On the other hand, it's a scary leap of faith, and there's a chance you'll get hurt, you know? Either you grow old together, or one of you gets hit by a bus. Sometimes love just kinda . . . ends."

Nobody said anything for several moments. "That was surprisingly profound," Tasha suddenly said. "I think."

"Thank you," Keith replied.

"Profound" was certainly a way to describe it. "Inspirational" felt like a better fit, but not in the way you might think. As I mulled over Keith's words, I was reminded of a certain legendary sword stashed in my closet back home.

Could that be the "weapon of love" I was supposed to slay the She-Devil with? The blade called Faithkeeper?

It made too much sense. The thing had found its way to me all those years ago, and it had come equipped with its very own army of Holy Knights—ideal for battling the She-Devil's forces of Hell.

I actually kind of hated how perfect it was. If I'm being honest, it sounded contrived and lame, but now wasn't the time for critiques of my cosmic epiphany.

I raised my head to look at the sky.

The atmosphere was a deeper red than it had been this morning, and it was growing darker, slowly but surely. Not only that, but the sun had gradually changed from bright yellow to fiery orange, even though it was still early in the day.

For the first time in my life, I knew what I had to do. And it didn't involve stepping back out of danger's reach.

"I think I figured it out," I said.

"Figured what out?" Keith asked.

I turned to Rivers. The fight between his goons and the demons continued behind us. "Can you give us a ride to my house?"

Rivers snapped his fingers. "Abe."

One of the zombies—Abe, I assumed—leapt away from the brawl, and I noticed that out of the four demons, only Thox and Viga were still alive.

The other zombie—Clint—was horribly burnt but unfazed as he continued beating down the demons.

With his massive hands, he knocked Viga to the ground, then grabbed Thox and squeezed her skull between his hands.

Thox clawed at Clint's wrists, and fire crackled on his skin. He didn't react, simply squeezed her head until it caved in.

Viga leapt to his feet and charged toward my friends and me. Abe moved to stop him, but he was too quick.

A screech overhead, a shadow swooping into my line of vision, and Reggie landed on my shoulder. Viga stopped dead, staring hard at Reggie. The demon's pupils dilated to an unbelievable size.

Abe and Clint stepped up next to Viga, and the demon blinked a few times. "No way," he murmured. "No fuckin' way!"

As if in response to Viga's muttering, Abe and Clint each readied a fist to punch. They sent their fists flying, and their knuckles tore through Viga's chest. Blood and guts splattered into the air, all over my friends and me, and then the zombies finished the job by ripping the demon in two, just as they'd done to Gelv.

Tasha gazed down at her gore-covered clothes and gagged. "Oh. My. God."

"Yeah," Keith said. "I could've done without that."

The entrails smelled like a rotten egg that had survived both a washer and dryer cycle, only to be cracked open and made into a candle. Purple embers and flames sparked within them, but even as I tried wiping the gunk away, I wasn't getting burned.

Reggie shook himself off like a cat, spraying even more demon viscera on me, and I raised a hand to weakly wipe some of the greasy mess from my eyes. I should have been totally disgusted by all this, but I'd been covered in worse, so it wasn't too bad.

Rivers cleared his throat, and I pivoted to face him. Unlike the rest of us, he only had a drop of blood on his shoulder. He brushed it off with irritation. "Shall we go, then?"

The following drive to my house was silent. Like, seriously—for the entire twenty-minute trip, nobody said a word outside of me occasionally giving directions. Keith, Tasha, and I sat across from Rivers, our stares shifting between him and the chaos outside the vehicle's windows.

Well, "chaos" wasn't an entirely accurate term for it anymore. By this point, the initial destruction seemed to have moved past its early stages. Now all the cars were abandoned in the streets, and people wandered around mindlessly, buildings burning behind them.

Part of me wondered whether there would be a world left to save after this.

We arrived in front of my place, and I climbed out. "I'll be right back."

I ran up my drive. Out of habit, I glanced over at Carlos's house. Surprisingly, he appeared to be okay.

He sat on his porch, shovel in hand. Bruises covered his face, but other than that, he seemed to be unharmed. With his free hand, he offered me a wave. "Hey, neighbor. Lovely day, huh?"

"Is that sarcasm?" I asked, stopping in front of my door.

Carlos smiled. "Yes, it is."

"Well, don't worry. I'm gonna try to fix all this."

Carlos gave me a thumbs-up. "I believe in you, buddy."

I threw open my door and hurried inside. Molly sat in her usual spot on the couch, and the early warning system beeped loudly on the television. Static as the channel changed, but the EWS blared on that one too.

"Sorry, Molly," I said, dashing across the living room. "It might be like that for a bit."

I hastened down the hall. Between the bathroom and my room was the closet, where I stored the legendary sword.

I slid the door open. Faithkeeper rested against the far-right wall of the closet, still stuck in its chunk of stone. The blade gleamed under the dim light, as if it had just been discovered in a dark cave by its destined wielder. I could feel it almost willing me to remove it, as though it somehow knew its time had finally come.

I grasped the hilt and took a deep breath. "Okay Riley," I said quietly to myself. "This is gonna be mega awkward, but you got this. Just talk to the ghost knights. It's only the fate of the world. No pressure."

I pulled the blade out of the stone.

Right on cue, a light-blue mist settled throughout my hallway, and Tyrus of Eldengard manifested before me, just as he had years ago. "We are once again reunited with you, si— Oh." Tyrus's smile dropped. "It is *you*."

I gave him an awkward wave. "Hello."

Tyrus crossed his arms. "What do you want?"

I gave him the stink eye. "Is that any way to talk to your king?"

He raised a brow at me.

"Okay, listen," I went on with a sigh, "I know that when we first met a couple of years ago, we got off on the wrong foot, but—"

"It has been *years*?"

"*Yes!*" I cried, exasperated. "And I need your guys' help to—"

"I thought it had only been a few *knights* ago," he interrupted again, this time with a sly smile.

I glared at him. "Do you guys wanna fight a bunch of demons and save the world or not?"

"This doth intrigue me." His expression grew serious. "And what would we receive in return?"

"I dunno." I shrugged. "Honor and glory?"

"Very well," he answered with almost zero hesitation. He turned around. "Lads!" The mist grew thicker, and more armored knights and battle-ready soldiers of ye olden times came into view, cramped together in the tiny space. "Tonight, we shall battle all of Hell!"

The militia of ghostly warriors jam-packed into my hallway raised their swords and spears, axes and shields, and let out a deafening chorus of cries.

Tyrus held out a hand to me. In his palm, the presumed scabbard of Faithkeeper appeared from the mist. "With this sheathe, we shall always be by your side. Loyal and true, even in death."

I took the scabbard from him and slid Faithkeeper into it, and he and the rest of the army faded away. "Cool," I said, hastening back toward the front door.

As I entered the living room, Rivers sauntered in through my still-open front door, his hands in his pockets. He spied the sword, and his eyes went wide. "Is that what I think it is?"

I held up the weapon. "I'm pretty sure this thing will kill her."

"The mighty Faithkeeper." Rivers bit his lip. "Weapon of God's 'unconditional' love." He tilted his head, carefully stepping closer. "I suppose it fits the bill."

"So, let's go find the She-Devil and end this, then."

Rivers took a hand from his pocket and pointed at me. "You've got the right idea." He made a face as though somebody had suggested his least favorite restaurant for dinner. "But what if . . ." With a smirk, he pounced forward, swatted the sword from my hand, and shoved me aside. I stumbled, caught my balance. But he had Faithkeeper in his possession before I could even try making a dive for it.

I lunged toward him. He punched me in the face, sent me hurtling into a wall. I slipped and landed hard on my butt. Pain arced through my jaw.

Twirling the sheathed sword, Rivers returned his free hand to his pants pocket. ". . . *I* deal the killing blow?"

"Seriously?" I rubbed my aching cheek. "What happened to helping out?"

Rivers looked at me as if I'd made him nauseous. "Please. I was waiting for one of you to—hopefully—discover what the kill-move was. Mason didn't know; can't say I'm surprised. He's a barbarian, not a bookworm." He nodded at me. "And you? I wasn't expecting much of anything from you, but would you look at that." He removed his hand from his pocket and tossed Faithkeeper into the air. Caught the sword, his teeth bared in an excited grin. "As I said before, Mr. Thomas. Five-star service." He knelt beside me and punched me again. My cheek felt stiff, and it hurt to move my jaw. I pressed a palm to my face as Rivers stood up once more. "Now all that's left is to kill you, and then I'm off to slay the She-Bitch."

A loud thumping noise in the wall behind me. The thumping turned into scratches, slowly trailed up toward the ceiling. It sounded as if Freddy Krueger were dragging his finger-knives through the inside of my wall.

Rivers paused and glanced down at me. "Sounds like you've got some mighty nasty pests."

Another strange sound. This one came from my couch, and it was like hollow glass cracking. The house suddenly felt several degrees colder. Goose bumps prickled on my skin as I craned my neck to gaze past Rivers.

Molly sat there, her head turning toward us, the porcelain of her neck and head squealing, fracturing.

Cracks began to form on her face and the other visible parts of her body. Within seconds she was completely crazed with them. And then, suddenly, her usually expressionless face contorted in a vicious sneer.

Her mouth opened, gaping like a viper's, and a chilling, maddening scream of rage erupted from her, echoing all around me, reverberating so violently I could feel it in my bones.

An invisible force launched Rivers into the air. The sword flew from his hands and clattered to the floor next to me. He struggled as he floated up, up, up.

Molly's scream faded, replaced with the sound of bones breaking, and Rivers's head swiveled round and round, round and round on his neck.

More cracks as his limbs were forced to do the same as his head. It was as though he were a ragdoll, as though his owner were twisting his head and limbs until they snapped free.

Finally, the invisible force pitched Rivers sideways, and he struck the wall opposite of me with a sickeningly wet splat. Swallowing hard, I grabbed the sword and climbed to my feet. My breath escaped my lips in a cloud, the temperature of the room continuing its descent.

I turned to leave, but Rivers had already started recovering. There was popping and other disgusting noises as his broken limbs began to repair themselves. He blinked as if awakening from a deep sleep, glared at me with more wrath than ever before.

He reached for me with one arm. However, the invisible force was back again, hurling him into the air and mutilating him just as before. This time it even mangled his fingers.

He slammed down onto the floor with a *crunch*. Then he returned to the air, and the cycle repeated itself.

I dashed to the door and shot Molly a thumbs-up. "Thanks, roomie!" Once outside, the front door slammed shut behind me.

I thought that would have been the end of my problems—at least until I faced off with the She-Devil—but I discovered an entirely new issue waiting for me at the end of my drive.

Rivers's vehicle was up in flames. Abe and Clint had been shredded to pieces and set on fire, their remains scattered across the pavement.

Worst of all, Keith, Tasha, and Reggie were nowhere to be seen, and three new demons stood before me.

The demons chuckled and walked toward me.

Before I could pull Faithkeeper free, there were hands on my shoulders, and fire in my eyes.

Everything went dark. For a moment, I felt as if I were midair, bouncing on a trampoline.

Light returned. I blinked, immediately concluded that I was dead.

A demon had caught me from behind, had killed me. It was probably the same demon who'd killed my friends. Had to have been. Because otherwise, I couldn't be here.

And otherwise, *she* couldn't be here.

Ariel Quinn stood in front of me, in the center of the carnival we'd attended for our date. She was as beautiful as always—almost ethereally so. Her long red hair was down, just as it had been that day, and she wore the same white-and-scarlet sundress and black leggings too.

Hands behind her back, she stared off at the nearby rides, which were in motion. She turned to face me and smiled. "I was wondering when you'd show up."

I couldn't form words. I could only stare at her in shock.

Then I realized the sky was still red.

Wait, how could that be? Why would Heaven and Earth have the same sky?

I managed to tear my eyes away from Ariel, saw that the active rides didn't have anybody on them, and that the damaged attractions and other equipment hadn't been repaired since Rob the Eliminator's rampage.

I looked down at my hands. I was still clutching Faithkeeper.

What?

"Riley?" Keith said from behind me.

I spun around. Keith and Tasha were on their knees, two demons grasping them by the shoulders. A third demon had been assigned to Reggie-duty; he confined Reggie with a bear hug that both held the infant cryptid and covered his large red eyes. Muffled screams sounded from underneath Reggie's pinned-down wings, but he couldn't wiggle free. Mason—covered in blood and bruises—sat on his knees on the ground several feet from the demon holding Reggie, and three more demons had to work together to keep him secure on the ground.

No.

Multiple flashes of fire, and more demons materialized behind me, smiling wickedly. A bunch that I didn't know and the ones that had just been at my house appeared behind my friends.

Then I saw the mound of bodies. Some strangers, but also some people I knew. At the very top of the pile lay Detective Kardoza.

This isn't right. This can't be what I think it is.

I faced Ariel. Her smile was sad now. She brushed a strand of hair behind her ear and offered me a hand. "Wanna take one more ride on the Ferris wheel before the world ends?"

CHAPTER 20
TIGER STRIPES

AT LEAST I COULD SAY THAT I'D BEEN CORRECT IN one assumption: Ariel Quinn was *definitely* too much woman for Riley Thomas.

In my attempts to avoid any and all cosmic responsibility, I'd somehow stumbled into a supernatural romance novel. That fact alone was enough to infuriate me, but the grief and confusion overcoming me at the realization that Ariel was the She-Devil easily drowned out all other emotions.

"Th-this is a trick, right?" I stuttered. "Y-you're the She-Devil, but you're—you're just using Ariel's likeness to, like, torture me or something." Clearly my mouth hadn't caught up to my brain, or maybe a part of me was in denial. Deep down, I already knew the truth.

"Sorry, lover boy," Ariel said. "It's definitely just me."

My hands tightened around the sword. I held it close to my chest. "Was it you the whole time?"

She nodded solemnly. "The whole time."

A demon circled me, laughing sadistically. His hair was buzzed short, a silver ring hanging from his left horn, piercings riddling his face. He stuck out his forked tongue at me. "You were so clueless. You didn't even know!"

Before I could respond, Ariel snapped her fingers, and the demon burst into a cloud of ash and cinder.

I waved the debris away from my face. Ariel's expression was sterner than I'd ever seen it.

I chanced a glance back at my friends, noticed that the other demons had gone quiet and still. There wasn't a single whisper or snicker to be heard. Keith and Tasha were also silent, staring at me in horror.

I returned my attention to Ariel.

She fidgeted with her hands, as if she was nervous. We briefly made eye contact before she let out a frustrated breath. "Okay, look. Ideally, I didn't want you to have to find out like this." She stepped closer, the heels of her black boots clunking against the concrete. "I was hoping that maybe, once we had our second date, I could ease you into things, but everything happened so fast. Next thing I knew, it was D-Day, so . . ." She gave me a half-hearted shrug. "I'm sorry, Riley. I really am."

I looked down at Faithkeeper. "Does this mean we have to fight or something?"

She tilted her head, her sad smile returning. "I think we both know that's not going to happen."

"Well, I mean, I came prepared."

"Yeah, I see that. Cool sword."

"Thank you."

We didn't say anything for a bit, probably because despite the situation we were in, the interaction (somehow) felt genuine and normal.

I didn't know what to do next, so I pulled Faithkeeper free of the scabbard. Light reflected off the blade, giving the weapon a heavenly glow. Ariel furrowed her brow as Tyrus and the other knights of the Most Holy Men materialized around me.

Tyrus bowed to me and drew his sword. "If hell is what they want, then hell is what they shall have!"

The other warriors released furious battle cries and charged toward the crowd of demons. Tyrus, however, charged at Ariel.

I figured that going after Ariel was what I was meant to do, so I followed his lead. I held the sword at the ready, sprinting toward her. But she didn't even move. She just stood there, watched us come for her.

When we arrived at melee range, Tyrus and I swung our swords together. In that moment, I felt as if all the powers of Heaven were behind me. As if they were in my sword.

Faithkeeper hit Ariel's shoulder—and the blade promptly shattered into thousands of pieces. It was as though it were made of nothing more than glass.

Tyrus's eyes went big as his own blade passed through her without effect. "Th-this cannot b—"

Before he could finish his sentence, he aged at a breakneck pace. He went from young, to old, to dust within about a second and a half, then faded away once and for all. I stared at the hilt in my hand, completely dumbfounded.

Gathering my wits, I swung around, saw the other knights had suffered the same fate before striking a single demon.

Awkwardly, I turned back to Ariel. She crossed her arms. "I don't think that worked."

"Yeah." I dropped what remained of Faithkeeper. "I was wrong about it, I guess."

"Was it supposed to hurt me?"

"I thought it might be my Chekhov's gun."

"Ah." She looked down at the blade's broken pieces. "Shame, too. It was a cool-looking sword."

A long pause—long enough for me to tally across the board just how screwed I was. "I guess that's it then, huh?"

She snorted. "Just about." She reached out. Took my hand in hers. "But I thought we could have one last carnival run before the timer hits zero."

I chuckled in defeat. "I guess that's as nice a way to go out as any."

She led me to the Ferris wheel. As we neared it, I saw that in the seat waiting for us was a tub of blue cotton candy, as well as Ariel's tiger plushie.

So that's where we left it.

We climbed into the seat and pulled the rail down in front of us, and the ride went into motion as if of its own accord.

Ariel picked up the tiger plush and set it in her lap, then took a piece of cotton candy and popped it into her mouth. Her face lit up the same way it had during our date. "Man, I'm gonna miss this stuff."

I leaned on the safety bar and stared out at the horizon. At the pile of bodies below, at the demons surrounding Keith, Tasha, Reggie, and Mason. "What's going to happen to them?"

Ariel leaned on the safety bar as well. "I'll make sure they go quick and painless. You know, before any of the *really* horrible stuff starts."

I didn't have a response for that.

We sat for two entire rotations before we shared any more words. During those two rotations, I thought about the past several months since I'd met Ariel—the day she'd first started at Grocery Hut. How she'd always been nice to me, how I'd always liked her.

Love at first sight sounds cheesy, but I don't have another way to explain how I felt. The world was just more colorful with her around.

Between her paintings and what little she'd told me of her hometown . . . Well, now I knew there was no hometown. If anything, it was some bottomless pit halfway across the world.

Then again, she'd said it was pretty boring, so perhaps she hadn't lied about *everything*.

Puzzle pieces started fitting together, and details started returning to me. All of them made the reveal much more obvious, and I didn't have any excuses. In love or not, I simply hadn't seen it.

I decided to break the silence. "Were you always planning on ending the world? Ever since we met?"

Ariel didn't face me, but she smiled, warm and genuine this time. "At first, yeah. When I rose, all I could think about was my mission. Grow stronger, end the world. Crush all who oppose me." She held up a hand, and a ball of red flames appeared in her palm. "I was so weak compared to now." She waved her hand, and the flames vanished. "But I wasn't *that* weak. There were these guys who found me fairly quickly. The 'Fathers of Free Will,' or something like that. Bunch of warrior priests who were preparing to face me."

Her smile faltered. She turned to me, and we locked eyes.

"It took me less than ten seconds to wipe all twenty of them off the face of the earth." If it weren't for the genuine remorse that she seemed to feel for her actions, the chill that ran down my back would have been far more intense. She curled her hand into a fist. "It felt good at first, you know? I had my purpose. I was winning the day . . ." She unfurled the fist. "But something was missing. There was no . . . excitement. No race to the finish line, no obstacles."

"Nobody standing in your way," I murmured.

"Exactly," she said. "Then, I found out about you. How your name was on my tablet. Turned out *you* were supposed to be my obstacle, so I came here to start the Harvest."

I blinked a few times. "Start your what now?"

She paused. Rolled her eyes with a bashful grin. "God, I forgot to explain that too." She gave the side of her head a gentle rap with her knuckles. "To reach my full potential, I had to devour sixty-six souls. So, I harvested people here in town." She sounded much more indifferent about these murders than she had the others. "It started with rude customers that I had to deal with in the bakery. Then it became any customer in the store. Now, I'm picking outside of the usual spot, but it doesn't really matter at this point."

I closed my eyes, realization washing over me. "The fifty-six missing people."

"Yeah, I couldn't destroy the bodies at first. Not until the fifth or sixth soul, I think. After that, I just disintegrated them whenever I finished."

Well, that explained a number of things. Mainly how the missing people's bodies were never found. Also, if her first several victims *had* been discovered, Kardoza would have naturally assumed it to be the work of a spree killer of some kind.

That reminded me.

"What about Kardoza?" I asked, motioning at the mound of bodies.

Ariel gazed that way. "I told you he'd realize you were innocent. And he did. Right after I had my demons bring him to me."

"I feel like he was just doing his job," I countered as gently as I could.

"Yeah, well, he treated you like shit, and I wanted him to leave you alone."

"What about gun-hand guy?"

Ariel let out a tired sigh, her attention falling to the crowd of demons below.

"Some of my demons thought it would be a good idea to torture one of my souls while they waited for me to get off work. They melted an Abyss Crystal to his hand. Something Adra used to do to people, I guess. Anyway, they sped up his Follower transition and accidentally let him escape."

"Oh."

"Yup," she replied with a hint of embarrassment. "He probably recognized you as the Chosen One, and since he was somewhere between being normal and being murderous, he must have decided to kill you." She leaned back in the seat and stared up at the sky. I did the same. "Originally, I was going to kill you too, just to secure the win."

I found that quite strange, and also a bit scary. Mostly strange, though. I looked over at her. "Wait, really?"

She laughed. "Uh-huh. Then I decided to toy with you a bit. I figured you'd step up to the hero-plate and try to stop me." She met my eyes. "But you never did."

I felt as though I should say something, as though I wasn't saying enough. But by this point, what even was there to say?

Ariel focused on the sky again. "I got so bored just doing the same old things. Bored of waiting for my life to get exciting. So, I started doing new things." With one hand, she lifted the tiger plush. "I learned about tigers and other animals on TV. I saw beauty in the big blue sky."

She waved her free hand as she talked about the sky, and the red tint in the atmosphere changed to blue for a fleeting moment, then rippled back to red.

"I saw the sunsets, how gorgeous they were for a short time every day. I discovered painting, and before I knew it, I fell in love with the world as it was. The world I was about to burn down." She looked at me, a tear trickling down her cheek. "And then I fell in love with *you*."

Her words made me smile. She mirrored my expression as she wiped away her tear.

"I started dragging my heels," she continued, "because I wanted to slow down and enjoy things for a while. I didn't want to be the She-Devil anymore. I wanted to be Ariel Quinn." She let out a shaky breath, her composure crumbling.

She wiped her face again. "But, now we're here. At the end of the story." Staring at the tiger plush, her lips quivered.

I looked out across the town, bathed evermore in fire. "What if this doesn't have to be the end of the story?" She jerked her head to face me. Watched me curiously. "You don't have to keep being the She-Devil. You don't have to destroy the world. I was supposed to be your 'Chosen One.' I was supposed to stop you, but I didn't. If I had that choice, then maybe you do too."

Ariel mulled that over before responding quietly. "Don't live your life for me, or anyone else. Live it for you."

"Exactly." I took her hands in mine. "We can set everything right. Start over. Be regular old Riley and Ariel instead of a failed hero and a She-Devil."

Ariel laughed and squeezed my hands. "That sounds amazing." She shook her head. "But . . . I can't."

"Why not?"

"I have to do this. It's the balance of the universe, Riley. Good and evil. Light and dark. I have to play my part just like you had to play yours."

"But I didn't play my part," I insisted. "Not really."

She giggled. "Dude, you showed up here with a *sword*. You tried to find me and save me the moment things went sideways. If that's not heroism, I don't know what is."

"But I didn't save anybody! Not a single person here."

She let go of one of my hands and lifted her own to caress my cheek. "You don't have to save the world to be a hero, lover boy. You just need to try."

Instantly, any anger I might have felt was washed away.

"Besides"—she pulled my face closer to hers—"you did save somebody."

She kissed me then, and for a short time at least, we were just regular old Riley and Ariel.

Eventually, however, the kiss had to end, and when it did, she finished her thought. "You saved *me*."

It was incredibly corny, but I wasn't going to tell her that. She meant it entirely, whether she knew it sounded bad or not.

She tightened her grip on my hand. "No, I have to do this. No matter how much I don't want to."

"Are you sure I can't change your mind?" I asked, placing my hand over hers on my cheek.

"Tigers can't change their stripes, Riley. Even if I stopped everything now, I'd still be the She-Devil. I'd still have world-ending power. I'd still hunger for human souls. Reckoning would still come."

I could tell from the tone of her voice that there was no changing her mind. So, I bit the inside of my cheek and nodded. "How much time do we have left, then?"

"Once I devour soul sixty-six, the reckoning will begin."

"And how many souls have you devoured so far?"

"Sixty-five."

"Oh . . ."

Another squeeze. "I want it to be you," she said. "I want the world to end with you and me."

"You want me to be the last one?"

"I do. I really wouldn't want you to see what happens next. Besides, if I take your soul, I'll always have a piece of you with me."

I smiled a little.

She giggled. "I know that probably sounds just as lame as what I said before."

"No." I shook my head. "Actually, it's kind of sweet."

"Well, good," she said with faux pride. "That was the intention."

An idea struck me suddenly. I let go of her hands. "If we're shooting for sweet, then I have one last thing."

"Oh?"

"You know, before you suck out my soul and turn me to dust."

"Of course."

I took off my necklace and lifted it for her to see. "This old coin means a lot to me. It's kind of my good luck charm." I held it out to her. "I got it from my sister before she died. I want you to have it."

Ariel clutched her heart. "Are you sure?"

"I can't exactly take it with me," I said with a shrug. "Besides, consider it one more piece of me to keep with you always."

Her smile returned. Gently, she took the necklace from me and looked it over in her palm. When she turned to me again, there were fresh tears in her eyes. "How dare you one-up me," she said.

Now we were both laughing. And crying.

She held it to her chest. "I'll treasure it forever."

I nodded. She undid the chain and put it around her neck.

The clasp clicked shut, and she pulled her hair free and struck a pose. "How do I look?"

"As amazing as . . ." I trailed off. The coin was . . . glowing? And it was red-hot, as if it had come straight from the Earth's core.

Ariel let out a sharp yipe and looked down. "What the hell is going on?"

"Are you allergic to silver or something?"

She tried to remove the necklace, but the chain glowed and heated just as the coin had. The skin on Ariel's hand sizzled as she touched it.

She yanked her fingers away with a hiss of pain. "I'm not doing this!" she cried.

"It's literally just an old coin," I said. "I have no idea what's going on either!"

Ariel screamed in agony. Floated up out of her seat, into the air.

Her body ignited with intense light and heat, as if the energy from my necklace was pouring into her. She screamed again as she tried to pull it off.

All the while, I couldn't move. I was paralyzed with fear. I watched helplessly as Ariel glowed brighter, hotter. As she screamed louder.

And then she exploded in a shower of cinder and ash.

Embers rained down on me, and I shielded my eyes with one hand, clutching the safety bar with the other, as the shock wave from the blast rocked the Ferris wheel back and forth.

The wheel groaned but continued spinning. It sped up until I was close to the bottom, then slowed to a stop and died completely.

I raised the bar, exited the ride. Stopped at the base to glance back up.

Ariel was gone, embers floating down from where she'd exploded. The hellish red hue of the sky was quickly fading, replaced once more by blue.

I heard shouts of anger, surprise, joy, all coming from behind me. I swung around. Keith, Tasha, Mason, and the demons watched the sky. They seemed just as shocked as I was.

One of the demons caught me staring at them and screamed in fright. "Holy shit! He actually did it!" One by one, the demons started to vanish, fleeing from the scene in puffs of fire and smoke.

Within the span of a few minutes, the apocalypse had ended, and Ariel Quinn—the She-Devil—was *dead*.

CHAPTER 21
ALL'S HELL THAT ENDS HELL

A GENTLE BREEZE SWEPT THROUGH THE AIR. THE shower of ember and ash had ceased for the moment, and I still stood underneath the Ferris wheel, trying to wrap my head around what had just happened.

My necklace was gone. Ariel was gone. But at least the world was saved, right? So why did I feel so bittersweet about the whole thing?

I supposed that this time I hadn't expected the situation to work out in my favor. Or maybe I hadn't wanted it to.

Mason stepped up next to me and looked around. "Well, I hate to say I was wrong, but you really did step up at the end there."

"You think?"

"I don't know. Maybe." He walked past me to inspect the area. All the while, Reggie landed on my shoulder, and Keith and Tasha arrived beside me.

Keith gave me a gentle pat on the back. "You okay, bro?"

I had to think before answering. "I don't know."

"Well, I'm pretty sure you just saved the entire world," Tasha chimed in.

"Yeah dude," Keith agreed. "That's worth celebrating. Wouldn't you say?"

"Yeah," I agreed. "I guess it is." Reggie chirped in my ear, settling into a little ball and tucking in his wings.

Keith removed his cap and held it over his heart. "You will be missed, Ariel. Not so much the She-Devil stuff, but yeah. You were nice, and funny, and you really took care of Riley. Game recognizes game. Rest in Pepto, sweet girl."

I blinked a few times, unsure of what exactly I'd just heard. But after a moment of deliberation, I decided to let it slide. "Rest in Pepto," I repeated.

Silence hung in the air, until finally Tasha waved her arms a bit. "I need, like, four showers after today."

I'd forgotten all about the demon blood and other fluids and substances we were covered in. I glanced down at myself to find I didn't look much better than Tasha.

Ariel had been nice enough to kiss me anyway. Now *that* was true love.

The realization hit me like a bus. "Oh my God!"

Keith and Tasha jolted to face me. "What?" they cried in unison.

"It was *love*!" I shouted, burying my face in my hands. "I'm so stupid! It wasn't a weapon at all, it was weaponized love. Giving her that necklace is what killed her."

"Don't get ahead of yourself," Mason said coldly. He picked up something small from the ground and brushed soot off it, revealing the silver of my necklace. As he walked back toward me, he let the coin hang for everyone to see. "This yours?"

"Yeah," I said, reaching for it.

Mason yanked it back and motioned at it with his free hand. "That's a shekel. Real deal Jewish shekel. Christ himself probably touched this way back when." He dropped it into my open palm. "You lucked out. All there is to it. Now, I'm not gonna take away the win, considering that your stupidity *saved* the entire fuckin' world, but I'm also not gonna forget that it almost *destroyed* the entire fuckin' world."

I stared down at the coin, unsure of whether Mason's reasoning made me feel better or worse. Either love killed Ariel, or Jesus did.

Mason pointed at me. "You stay fuckin' clean and out of my goddamn way from now on, understand?"

I nodded furiously. "I'm officially retired from the hero-business. I've had the world-ending prophecy of a lifetime."

Mason scowled and let out a sharp, "Ha!" Then he pushed past me and walked off, mumbling as he did so. "Hero-business, yeah right . . ."

Glaring at Mason, Tasha threw her hands in the air. "You're welcome, you fucking creep!"

"Welp," Keith said, and Reggie hopped from my shoulder to his. "I say we leg it back to my place, hit up the snacks, and play some video games."

"I'm going *home*," Tasha said sternly. "I need this shit *off* me. Then I'm building a bunker in my apartment and never going outside again."

The two of them started walking off ahead of me. I gazed down at the necklace once more before stuffing it into my pocket and following them away from the carnival.

They began talking, discussing everything from work to Reggie, and Keith recounted my story to catch Tasha up on how we got here. Well, he recounted most of it, anyway. I had to fill him in on a couple of things.

But for the most part, I wasn't present. Keith and Tasha faded into the background of my mind. At the forefront was Ariel, and every single conversation we'd ever shared. I needed to memorize them, because I wasn't going to be getting any more of them. I had to hold onto the ones I could.

Soon some of her advice came back to me, and I pulled my phone out of my pocket and went into my photos. Listed under my favorites was the selfie she'd snapped of us on our date. *"If old pictures are hard to look at, we'll have to start taking new ones."*

Tears sprang into my eyes, a sad smile slowly curling up my lips.

I put my phone away and caught up with my friends.

I knew what I had to do, and I didn't need to slay any more devils to do it.

We all returned home that afternoon. Granted, Keith and I *did* wind up seeing one another later.

I was expecting there to still be chaos at my house, but it was suspiciously peaceful. As I wandered up the driveway, I saw Carlos tending to his flowers as if nothing had happened.

He waved at me. "Hey, neighbor. Rough day?"

"Yeah." I stopped halfway up the drive. "I mean, there was a literal apocalypse."

He cocked his head at me. "An apocalypse?"

"Uh, yes? Didn't you see the red sky, the chaos?"

"What are you talking about?"

I paused. "You don't remember it, do you?"

"Remember what?"

I gestured at our wrecked neighborhood, at the totaled vehicles. "Everybody went crazy. There were demons, and I came home to get a sword. We said hi." I pointed at him. "You have bruises on your face! You got attacked or something."

Carlos chuckled. "No, buddy. I fell down my porch stairs carrying a bag of fertilizer this morning. Banged my head on the step." He waved a hand dismissively. "All I've done since we, uh . . . 'hung out' last night . . . is watch TV, sit on the porch, and work on the garden."

I was dumbfounded. Even though the world had nearly ended, Carlos didn't seem to remember anything about it.

A bell jingled from behind me, and I turned around. A boy pedaled past on a bicycle. Not only that, but cars drove by at respectable speeds. People seemed to be getting back on their metaphorical horses and riding off into the distance, as though they hadn't all just been beating each other to death a few hours ago.

Carlos and I said our goodbyes, and I approached my front door. I had to mentally prepare myself for whatever evil I was about to find inside. Molly, or Rivers.

Or both.

I pushed my door open and peeked in. I'm not going to lie—the place was trashed. All my furniture had been tipped over. Blood stained my floors, cracks riddling the wall in the farthest corner of my living room.

Curiously, neither Rivers nor Molly was in sight. After searching the home to survey the damage and collect clues, I found that they weren't even in the house. All they'd left behind was the damage from their scuffle.

It was as if they'd simply vanished.

Thankfully, my shower was still functional, so I started my recovery with a hot shower and a fresh change of clothes.

Once I was clean and dressed, I picked up my necklace and tried to decide whether I should continue wearing it. But before I could figure out what to do with it, Keith arrived for yet another boys' night, this time with Reggie in tow.

For the rest of the day, Keith and I played video games and ate snacks while Reggie napped on the couch, and every now and then, I'd catch a hint of red out of the corner of my eye, as if the heavens had reverted to their previously apocalyptic hue.

But then I'd look over and see that the sky was still blue.

It really was over, wasn't it?

HELLO I AM... RiLeY

epilogue
HAPPiLY eVER AFTER...?

IT WAS AN UNEVENTFUL TUESDAY NIGHT AT GROCERY Hut, the store empty and silent. Not that I was complaining. I had an entire backstock cart of markdowns that still needed to be worked onto the shelves.

As I organized can after can of yet another shipment of the vegan cat food that we still had no marked shelf space for, a weight settled on my shoulder. Reggie purred in my ear, curling his wings around himself and staring at the cans in my possession.

"What?" I asked. "Are you hungry? Did Keith forget to feed you again?"

Reggie continued to purr, so I rose from my kneeling position. I set the cart aside so it wouldn't be in any potential customers' way, then started toward the front of the store.

"All right, let's get you food," I said, putting my hands in my pockets.

Keith was wandering around somewhere, probably doing "Keith" things, such as stashing candy and recreational drugs in the various hiding places he'd selected throughout the store. The only other employee on shift until closing was Tasha. Surprisingly, she hadn't quit after the whole She-Devil debacle. In fact, she'd started showing up to work more often, and she'd even begun working overtime.

She told me it was mostly to build up a reliable savings fund so she could get as far away as possible from this place.

I reached the break room and walked to the fridge, then opened it and pulled out a half-eaten package of mashed tuna in a tube. Normally these were cat treats, but Keith had discovered that Reggie loved them even more than he did Bottle Caps. At first, I thought it was a tad concerning that the Mothman species ate meat, but then I decided that so long as it was just fish, it wasn't a problem.

I ripped off the top of the tube and handed it to Reggie. He took it in his little hands and began feasting.

With my side quest complete, I turned to make my way back to my cart. Tasha rounded the corner, and we almost collided in the break room doorway. "Oh shit," she said. "Sorry, Riley."

I moved out of her way. "No worries. Just had to get Reggie some food."

"Again? Keith fed him, like, twenty minutes ago."

As if on cue, Reggie leapt off my shoulder, spread his wings, and flew out of the room.

I rested my hands on my hips as I watched him fly off into the store. Tasha grinned, walking toward the punch clock. "Dude, you got *so* fuckin' hustled by that little guy."

"I guess I did," I said quietly. Tasha inserted her punch card into the timer. There was a loud mechanical snapping sound, and she pulled the card free and slotted it into place. "Are you leaving?" I asked.

"Duh," she replied. "It's closing time."

I checked my watch. It was two hours to close. "No, it's not."

Tasha pointed at the punch clock. It was two hours ahead of my watch, and it was never wrong, as it had to be manually changed by someone with key access. And only Henry had key access.

I sighed in defeat. "Time really does fly when you're two hours behind."

"Do you want me to stay and help you close up?"

I waved her off. "Nah, go home. I just need to move some carts to the back and shut the registers down."

Tasha shrugged. "Suit yourself." She grabbed her jacket off the coatrack and put it on. "See you tomorrow, loser." Then she walked out the door and left.

I spent the next half hour getting the store ready for closing. Keith was still on to close with me, so the two of us managed to finish everything rather quickly. While Keith locked the doors, put away the remaining backstock carts, and rounded up a certain tuna-loving mothball, I returned to the front to shut down the registers.

We had gone from a single functional register to a fully operational front end again. That was good for business and rushes, but bad for closing shifters such as myself. With over three times the number of registers than before, it took forever to count their contents and prepare them for the next day.

Tonight, I spent that time reflecting on how the past two months had unfolded.

I'm surprised to say that after Ariel's death, my life became relatively normal. I hadn't had a single Protag'd moment since the day the world almost ended. The people in town had also had their minds wiped of the ordeal—folks who'd died during the chaos were buried and mourned as usual, society rebuilt as though the apocalypse had just been the wind knocking stuff over.

The only people who seemed to know what had really happened were Keith, Tasha, and me. Henry was back to business as usual, and if he did remember the events of that fateful day, he was an expert at hiding it.

Interestingly enough, a new hire for the bakery had popped up almost immediately. Henry didn't seem to remember Ariel at all, and what little he could recall was as insignificant as "she was good at her job."

The owner cashed out some insurance, and he used it not only to repair the registers, but also to overhaul the store. We now had two more aisles, as well as a slight expansion of the back room. He even added a second picnic table for employees behind the store.

Best of all, though, was when he bought a brand-new coffee pot for the break room. The coffee at work was now halfway decent, when before it had been a suicidal concoction for only the most desperate on shift.

I finished the last register and hit the power button, then took the money to the safe, turned off the lights, and locked down the room. After that, I just had to turn off the lights behind the service counter.

Keith rounded the corner, Reggie on his shoulder. The

baby Mothman—or "Gynnidosapien," which Keith claims is the more scientific term for them—was finishing his extra tube of food that I'd been scammed into giving him. "Okay, bro," Keith said. "Floors swept, doors locked, Reggie *extra* fed. I think we're good to jet."

"I think so too." I exited the service-counter booth, and we made our way to the break room and clocked out. I grabbed my jacket off the coatrack before making my way to my locker on the wall of employee lockers—another addition to the building, thanks to the insurance collection—and grabbed my backpack and camera from inside.

"Come *on*, Reggie," Keith whined from behind me. I turned around to see that he was trying to cover Reggie with a little black-and-red sweater-vest. "Curl up. We do this every time." Reggie chirped in response, still clutching the empty tuna tube in his small hands. Keith held the vest higher. "It's getting colder, little man. This is for your own good." He took the tube from Reggie and tossed it into the garbage. "Tuna's gone, let's go."

Reggie chirped again, much more sternly than before, and finally did as he was told, wrapping himself up in his wings. Keith slid the sweater-vest over Reggie, covering his body but leaving his eyes and antennae exposed.

"There, see? Was that so hard?" Keith asked. Another muffled chirp came from under the sweater.

"Say cheese," I said. I flipped on my camera and lifted it to line up a shot. Keith gave me a grin and a thumbs-up, and I snapped the photo. There was no flash; I'd learned almost immediately after starting up photography again that bright flashes were *not* something Reggie enjoyed.

I double-checked the picture quality and smiled. "Another good one. Real photogenic. Also, Keith, you look fine too, I guess."

Keith pointed at me. "Ha ha! Jokes on you, I know my boy is dashing as fuck."

I scrolled through some of my photos until I found one of a sunset that I'd taken the week prior. My chest grew tighter as I looked at it.

Every time I saw a perfect sunset with plenty of red and orange and purple in the mix, it was hard not to get sad. It made me think of Ariel.

I turned off the camera and slid it into a pocket on the side of my backpack. "Okay, ándale, let's get the hell outta here." I motioned at Keith as I stood by the door, and he exited the room. On my way out, I turned off the lights, and we headed through the back doors.

We climbed into Keith's new car, a quirky orange AMC Gremlin. He'd bought the used vehicle with the insurance money from his jeep's untimely demise. Compared to his previous car, its condition was questionable at best, but he didn't seem to have any complaints. He even planned to remodel the back seat into a more comfortable area for Reggie.

As we buckled up, Reggie hopped off Keith's shoulder and into the back. "You getting your new car soon?" Keith asked. "I don't mind giving you rides, you know. Just curious."

"I'm hoping so," I responded. Keith started the engine. "Even if it's something like this. So long as it can get me to work, maybe a little farther."

"Ah, I'm sure you'll find something nice."

"Car talk is for later, anyway," I said. "I need to figure out what I'm going to do with myself for the rest of the night. I could download some photos and work on them, but I'm also pretty deep into a new book. I'm not sure what I'd rather do."

"You could do both at the same time," Keith suggested.

"No, I don't think I could."

"Not with *that* attitude."

For the rest of the drive home, we went back and forth about our current hobbies. I gave Keith a Cliff's Notes version of the book I was currently reading, and he gave me some new information he'd learned while researching how to better care for an infant Mothman.

It didn't take long to reach my house. I waved goodbye to Keith and Reggie, and before heading in, I glanced at Carlos's yard. The man was nowhere in sight, but his flower bed was coming along nicely. He had the beginnings of a greenhouse constructed in his backyard too, positioned directly over where we'd buried Sal.

Really, I can't blame him for building it there. With that thought, I turned away from his yard, unlocked my front door, and stepped inside.

It was quiet and dark. Ever since the day of the almost-reckoning, Rivers and Molly hadn't returned. I wasn't too concerned about what had happened to Rivers, but I found myself missing Molly, especially when I was home alone. I'd gotten so used to her being around that, in her absence, I realized I'd come to expect her presence.

I flicked on the light, illuminating the living room. Everything was clean and organized, although my walls remained pink from Molly's previous return. Some of my furniture had been damaged in the fight between her and Rivers, so I'd had to use my spare funds to buy cheaper alternatives. Also, the hole in my wall was still present, but I was seriously close to being able to afford repairing it.

I dropped my backpack next to the couch and walked to the kitchen, then turned on the lights in there and headed toward the fridge.

On the top half of the fridge hung a medium-sized magnetized whiteboard along with three markers, also magnetized. On the lower half hung a mess of colorful magnetic letters. After the world had gone back to normal, I'd bought these things per Ariel's advice, but considering Molly had never returned, I was starting to wonder if the purchases were a waste.

There was just one more thing on the fridge, and I'm not ashamed to admit that I found myself stopping to look at it often.

It was the photo of Ariel and me at the top of the Ferris wheel.

Bittersweet warmth filled me as I stared at the picture. I couldn't help but smile before opening my fridge and setting to work.

Thankfully, my fridge was stocked for once. I got out some ingredients and made myself a sandwich, then took my plate to the living room, set it on the coffee table, and retrieved my camera from my backpack. My previously mentioned book sat on the opposite end of the table, a bookmark sticking out from the center of its pages; I had yet to decide what I'd be doing after dinner.

Removing my jacket and work vest and preparing to sit down, I realized that I hadn't grabbed anything to drink. I returned to the kitchen and took a can of soda from the bottom shelf of my fridge.

As I closed the fridge door, a soft thumping noise sounded in the ceiling above me. I looked up, waited.

Silence.

It didn't happen again.

Maybe I actually have rats this time.

Voices suddenly filled the room. Soft music, too. I swung around, peered through the doorway, and saw that my television was on.

Rats that like television.

Cautiously, I walked back to the living room and was met with one final surprise. One final reminder that normalcy would always be out of my grasp.

The whiteboard from my fridge now sat on the couch, perched atop the very same cushion a certain jester doll once loved to occupy.

In bright-red marker were two words and a smiley face.

Miss Me? :)

*If you would like to follow D. R. Mills's journey or the **MONSTERS** series specifically, check out the author's official Twitter and Instagram accounts:*

Instagram: @monsters_bookseries

X: @MonstersSeries

Facebook: @Monsters/100067554032850

TikTok: www.tiktok.com/@d.r..mills

If you enjoyed the story, dont forget to leave a review on your preferred platform! Reviews help authors find more readers, and if you'd like D. R. Mills to be able to release books faster, reviews are the best way to support him.

CHECK OUT D.R. MILLS

MONSTERS

SERIES

D. R. MILLS

is a young-adult horror author who is currently hard at work on his debut series, *MONSTERS*. He was born and raised in Wyoming, where he's still lurking around somewhere. When he isn't writing, he's playing video games a borderline unhealthy amount or spending time with his beautiful wife.

WWW.SEAOFINKPRESS.WORDPRESS.COM